DOCTOR WHO™

Short Trips: A Universe of Terrors

A Short-Story Collection
Edited by
John Binns

BIG FINISH

Published by Big Finish Productions Ltd,
PO Box 1127
Maidenhead SL6 3LW

www.bigfinish.com

Range Editors: Gary Russell & Ian Farrington
Managing Editor: Jason Haigh-Ellery
Consultant for BBC Worldwide: Jacqueline Rayner

ISBN 1-84435-008-8

First published June 2003

With thanks to Guy Wigmore, Paul Cornell and Alison Lawson

Printed and bound in Great Britain by Biddles Ltd
www.biddles.co.uk

CONTENTS

The Exiles

Lance Parkin

The light seemed reluctant to follow them as they hurried in.

Eyes sharper than human eyes struggled to see the structure in the centre of the room. Stumbling forwards, the two of them found it, grasped it. She managed to guide his hands to the controls.

He mumbled something.

'Grandfather?'

'I said don't touch anything, child. This is a delicate scientific instrument.'

'But we have to hurry - '

'I am very well aware of that.'

'Why is it so dark?'

'The circuits have no power. Very little power. Questions, questions. Here.'

He twisted a switch; the double doors whirred shut.

'Grandfather! Now there's no light at all.' She paused. 'Grandfather? Are we safe now?'

'Child, please be quiet.'

'But if those two saw us, then - '

'If we had been seen, we would already be... be.... we would not have made it here. I just need to find...'

A pause, in which the only sound was the beating in her chest, the sound of her breathing. Then a terrible roaring noise, one that seem to rise from impossibly deep below, to pass right through them and then soar up, before drifting back down. The sound rose and fell, and as it did, time and space seemed to fold around it.

They were moving, although it was impossible to say in which direction.

The floor seemed to lurch. It was so hard to tell in the darkness. It was as if they had been grabbed by some vast hand, as if the whole ship were just a toy.

'Grandfather!' Susan cried out. 'They've caught us.'

She could hear him crying out. While she'd managed to cling to the console, he'd been thrown to the far wall.

'Stay where you are, child.'

'They've found us!'

'No. Now observe and think. Look around you. Listen.'

She couldn't see anything at all, but Susan had some innate understanding of what was happening. The floor evened out, the noise was still there, but... somehow it wasn't. It was outside. The whole room was throbbing, now, a slight variation in the vibration making it seem almost alive.

'We're in flight.'

'We have left our home planet,' she heard her grandfather say quietly from the corner. 'We haven't been detected. We are underway, following our escape trajectory.'

'We're safe.'

There was a rasp, then a faint point of firelight.

Her grandfather's eyes twinkled at her. He'd appeared at her side, without her hearing him get up or move. 'I most certainly did not say that. Everlasting matches. An invention of mine.'

'Is there an oil lamp?'

'I'm sure there must be.'

'I mean did you bring one?'

No reply for a moment, then: 'My dear Susan, time was of the essence, and I only had one small bag. I could hardly have packed something for every eventuality.'

'It's obvious that we might need a torch!'

'By the same logic, you should have brought one. Hmm? Now, we don't have much time. Help me with this console. We need to take control of this vessel.'

'You're not in control?'

'I have launched the ship, but for the moment it remains at the mercy of the ebb and flow of time.'

'How do I help?'

'Hold the match so I can see,' he replied tetchily.

Susan kept the match just above the console, to give Grandfather a better view of the controls. The firelight made the wrinkles on the back of his hands stand out, made them look even older.

The hands moved around, a little hesitantly at first, then with more confidence. He knew what he was doing, she reassured herself. She wouldn't have the slightest idea how to set the machine moving; he'd managed it in total darkness. He'd closed the door, too. She trusted him.

'Yes,' Grandfather would say. Or 'I see.' At last he came up with: 'Of course!'

One hand reached down and almost yanked one of the dials off.

Nothing happened at first. Slowly, though, lights started to appear on the console, backlit buttons began fading up into view; displays, dials and meters began to illuminate. In the centre of the console, a large crystal tube full of twinkling mechanisms was lifting and drifting down, like a piston. Grandfather had brought the console to life. Susan moved round, eagerly, trying to work out for herself which controls operated which parts of the ship, which instruments could tell her about their journey.

'That's the main power supply to the console,' Grandfather told her. There was a little more light, now, and her eyes were getting used to the gloom. She could see Grandfather's silhouette. He was hunched over the controls, head cocked as if he were listening to the subtleties of the roaring, grinding noise outside.

Susan watched, not daring to break his concentration.

Finally, he reached over, brushed his hand over one lever, then another. The room seem to steady itself. Not just physically... Susan felt more calm, all of a sudden.

'You've done it, Grandfather!'

He shrugged. 'I've levelled it out, yes.'

'And no one saw us leave?'

'I should say it will be some considerable time before we are missed, what with - ' he hesitated. 'No one saw us leave,' he confirmed, finally.

'And where are we heading?'

A long pause.

'Where are we heading?'

'I heard you, child,' he snapped. 'That I don't know. Not yet.'

Susan shuddered. 'But we are moving. We must be going somewhere.'

'This is a time machine, Susan. It's not as simple as that.' He paused, and Susan expected him to elaborate, but all he came up with was a final 'Yes.'

'I suppose it's good that we don't know,' Susan said after a moment.

'How so?'

'If we don't know where we are, or where we are heading, then how could anyone follow us?'

Grandfather chuckled for a long time at that.

She had found the controls for the lights soon after that. Everything on the console had been locked down and switched off. The ship had been in long-term storage, after all. Grandfather preferred the term *hibernation*, and explained to her how some animals spent the winter curled up in their burrows, rather than braving the cold. The ship, he explained, was rousing itself from a long sleep, and would react best to gentle persuasion, a quiet word.

Susan worried what would happen if they startled it. She'd heard stories about bears that slept in caves all winter. If anyone disturbed them they became wild, chased whoever woke them, and tried to kill them.

Grandfather was scratching notes and diagrams into a little pocketbook he'd brought with him. The console was complicated, but whoever had designed it seemed sensible enough.

The light switch was a small button near a gauge that told them what the temperature of the interior of the ship was. Grandfather had pressed it, and the lights had slowly, ever so slowly, suffused the room with a soft glow.

Now there was light, Susan could see the control room properly for the first time. It was a small room, hexagonal. The walls and floors were bone-white. The floor was completely featureless, but the walls all had neat rows of circular indentations about as wide as the span of her hand. The light fell drowsily from them. Above the console hung a great machine, the purpose of which Susan couldn't begin to fathom.

There were four other features. The first was the double doors, the ones they'd passed through to enter. Susan pressed her ear to one of the doors, but couldn't hear anything outside, just the gentle thrum of the engines.

Susan had been the one to find the second feature, the alcove with the machine. Grandfather had identified it as a 'diagnostic subsystem', then, looking at Susan he'd explained that it was a 'fault locator'. He seemed satisfied that everything on the ship was working exactly as it should.

'It's only a question of getting everything working for us,' he chuckled.

Before Susan had found the alcove, Grandfather had been studying the third feature, a flat patch of wall with what looked like a hatch at head height.

'A scanner,' he concluded eventually, waving his hands vaguely at the console. 'Operated, I should say, from there. The switches in question must be on either the nearest panel... either the nearest panel, or the one opposite. Hmm... we don't need the scanner yet.'

The final feature was a door.

'It must lead to the rest of the ship,' Susan said excitedly.

Grandfather looked troubled. 'Again, child, we don't need to go there. Not yet.'

Grandfather had found three folding chairs in the fault locator alcove.

Susan set two of them up while he continued his investigation of the console. Susan sat in the chair and watched him. He wasn't touching the controls; he was making a careful note of them, moving around, regularly checking the read-outs and displays.

'Can you fly the ship?' Susan asked.

'Oh yes. This isn't the first time I've been in a time machine.'

Grandfather had been an ambassador for their people. Susan didn't really know any of the details of that part of his life - it had been long before she had been around.

'You flew ships like this when you visited other planets and times?'

Grandfather hesitated. 'Not exactly like this one,' he conceded. 'And much of the actual flying was done by technicians. But I made a very careful note of what they did.'

Susan found herself frowning. But Grandfather must know what he was doing, or he wouldn't be doing it.

'I think that's enough for now,' Grandfather said. 'The time path we are following is clear of any obstruction. The instruments are very firm on that point.'

'Where are we heading?'

Grandfather's face twitched. 'This instrument says something about the S-K System,' he said. 'Or maybe that instrument is the S-K system,' he said, his voice trailing off.

He came over to the other chair and sat down, settling into it a little ostentatiously.

'We have time for a little rest,' he told Susan.

'But the ship - '

'The ship will look after itself, and it will look after us. The very worst that can happen is that while we rest, the ship will come into land. The process is entirely governed by the computer, and it would be arrogance to suggest we could do any better. So, sleep we shall.'

Susan couldn't sleep.

Grandfather was resting alongside her. Was he asleep? His eyes were closed, his hands were clasped over the handle of his walking stick, and a smile kept flickering across his face. He looked like he did when he was listening to music. Or perhaps he was dreaming.

Susan stood, and Grandfather didn't so much as stir.

Mindful of her Grandfather's warning, Susan just stared at the mysterious door at first. She wanted to see the rest of the ship. Although she was used to the dim light by now, the control room was a little cold, and it was very austere. The folding chairs were metal, and their designer had clearly given no thought to comfort. She knew little about time travel, or interplanetary journeys, but she knew that people had to eat, to sleep, to have somewhere quiet to just think. All of that would be through the door, perhaps just beyond it.

You might find operating instructions there, too, she found herself thinking.

Susan frowned. She wasn't sure what that meant.

A book. A list of instructions and procedures. To fly the ship, to operate all its systems. To take control.

Susan moved towards the door. She knew her people - there would have to be at least one library on the ship, somewhere. She was right, of course - there must be operating instructions somewhere, too. She imagined it would be a large, fat, book, with very thin pages and very small writing.

She had a picture of it in her head. It would have metal covers, to protect it.

It was through that door.

Susan pushed the door open. It warm through there. She stepped through, found herself blinking in the light, even though it was only at the normal level. She'd got so used to the dark. It was just a bare corridor, one that led about twenty feet before turning left. The walls had the familiar round pattern on them. They were glowing softly, comfortingly. Behind some of them, Susan could see... things. Control switches, she thought, or things stowed safely away. She knew better than to touch them.

The floor was humming here, just as much as it was in the control room.

There were no shadows, which was a little unnerving. The light arranged itself in a way that prevented any shadows from forming.

Your Grandfather will be very angry.

Susan glanced back. When he woke, he'd see the open door, he'd know straight away that she'd disobeyed him.

She closed the door, heard it click shut. Now there was just her and the clean, bright corridor.

It was a novel feeling, being somewhere she'd never been before. It made her realise just how sheltered her life had been. She'd always seen herself as adventurous, as somehow more inquisitive and impulsive than those around her. But she'd never strayed too far, never been anywhere that was less than well-trodden. Who was the last person who'd been down this way? How long ago had they lived and died?

Liberation.

The word just popped into her head, but it was exactly the right one. She practically ran down the corridor, racing to see whatever was round the corner.

She saw herself.

It was a full-length mirror, just sitting in the corridor.

Susan studied herself. She barely came halfway up the mirror. Her brown robes had seemed perfectly normal before, now they looked flat and dowdy. She'd never really studied her face before. Everyone she knew, practically everyone, anyway, was an old man, hunched with wrinkled faces. She'd never realised quite how she must have stood out. Her face was sharp, her skin was smooth. While she was above such things as vanity, her hair was rich, thick, jet black, and she much preferred that to wispy white and grey.

She felt lonely, suddenly. There had always been chatter from the next room, she'd always been able to hear people talk or think or breathe. That had always been a bit stifling. No one she knew was like her, or interested in the same things. Now it was just her and Grandfather. And that scared her, a little. She wanted more people here. At least one other person.

There was a door here. Susan went through it.

Rails and rails and rails and rails and rails of clothing.

The room was cavernous, and dark, with only spots of light every so often (Susan couldn't see where the light was coming from, it just seemed to appear in pools on the floor). She'd been to this sort of place before - before all the ceremonies, she'd been to the robing room, her dresser had fitted whichever robe that particular occasion demanded. But the clothes here were so colourful, so *different*.

She pulled one off the rack. She didn't know the word for it - a sort of split tunic, in a green fabric. She just dropped it on the floor, and continued her exploration. There was a big coat, almost a cloak, something that would only fit the fattest man. And some clothes that were too small even for her. Susan decided to find something to wear, and she realised she would have to have some sort of system to complete her task. She'd have to have a rough idea of the colour and style of clothing, she'd have to find something in her size. She found a thick top, made from wool, with colourful patterns knitted in. A swirling red pattern, some sort of symbol, and jagged red lines. The right size for her, but surely not anything someone would really wear?

Susan had no idea how long it took. The shoes came first - stylish, smooth black boots, with a slightly raised heel. She tottered on them a little at first, but soon got used to them.

She assembled an outfit. A one piece dress, grey, barely below the knee. Thick socks, mainly to make the shoes (which were a little large) fit better. A wide belt.

Susan pulled off her robes quickly.

She hesitated.

'Who's there?' she asked. She was sure she...

It was cold in here. Colder than the rest of the ship. Which was silly, if people were going to get dressed in here. Surely it should be as warm. Warmer.

She pulled the dress on over her shift.

There was someone...

She whirled around.

No one.

She wriggled until the dress was on properly. She held the belt in her hand, unsure what to do.

The ship was empty. Wasn't it? It hadn't been used for centuries. It had sat in its berth, at least half-forgotten. Grandfather had explained all this. It wasn't stealing, was it, if no one would even notice it had gone?

Someone had noticed. Someone had followed them.

Susan's mouth had gone dry. They couldn't go back. That was what Grandfather had told her. He'd explained everything to her, as best he could, and told her that once he'd made his choice there would be no going back. No one had left. Ever. It wasn't that there were no records of people leaving. There was no concept of leaving. No one had ever thought to. Why would they? Grandfather had the idea, and it was dangerous, but it was the right thing to do.

Grandfather said he had good reason, and Susan trusted him. She was too young to know all the details.

Or so he said.

For the first time, doubt crossed Susan's mind. It had never occurred to her to doubt Grandfather before. But wasn't that another thing that was dangerous, but the right thing to do? What if Grandfather was wrong? Or lying?

Question marks.

Susan hurried back out into the corridor. The mirror was there.

She was frightened to look in it.

Now she was being silly. She wanted to see what she looked like in her new outfit. It felt comfortable - almost ridiculously light compared with her normal tunic and robes.

It made her feel more nimble, younger. She wanted to run and climb. And dance. She'd never danced.

She also felt smaller, somehow.

Why didn't she want to look in the mirror?

There was no rational reason. It was just a mirror. She could imagine what she looked like - more than that, she could look down, and see the clothes on her.

So why didn't she want to look in the mirror?

She plucked up courage, found herself closing her eyes until she knew she was in front of the mirror, ready to look.

He was only in the mirror, not in the room with her. She didn't even have to turn her head to check. She just knew. He dominated, so much so that Susan barely registered her own reflection, despite her new clothes. He loomed over her, filled the mirror. He was behind her, the top of her head barely level with his chest. He wore long, dark robes, and that only made his pale skin more pale. He was young. Not as young as she was, but not quite an adult.

He reached out.

His hand passed through the surface of the mirror, not even rippling it. Her own reflection had gone.

Susan held out her hand.

He took it, then bowed down low. Then he pressed his lips to the back of her hand.

He straightened up again, smiled, revealing fangs, not teeth. Susan had studied taxonomy. This was a carnivore, a predator.

She glanced down at her hand. He hadn't so much as grazed her skin when he kissed her.

'You are not the one. This is not the time,' he said, in a language she didn't recognise.

The mirror was empty.

Susan ran back to the control room.

Grandfather listened patiently to Susan's story, occasionally stopping her to clarify a detail or two. For Susan's part, she left nothing out, except the kiss. He wasn't angry that she had disobeyed him. He was pleased she was unharmed - but at the same time, Susan could sense that he gained some satisfaction that he had been right to warn her not to leave his side.

When she'd finished, he spent a moment or two thinking, then concluded. 'Time echoes.'

Susan waited for the explanation.

'We are travelling through time. In some ways, such words as "past", "present" and "future" have no meaning in here. So... what you saw was something from the past.'

'But what?'

'That must remain a mystery. The past of our people... it is not something to be revisited. Certainly not by you or me.'

'And that thing has been in here all along? All the years the ship was hibernating?'

'No child. You misunderstand me. What you saw was... a reflection, if you like. A glimpse of the past.'

'But I felt it touch me.'

Grandfather smiled. 'The mind plays tricks, Susan. Whatever it was, it's gone now.'

Susan nodded. She couldn't feel it, and she knew she would be able to were it here.

Grandfather shuddered.

'What is it?'

'The past is behind us, child. It need not scare you. From now on, let's concentrate on the future.'

'And there won't be things like that in the future?' Susan realised she was almost disappointed at the announcement.

Grandfather gave a mischievous smile.

'Oh... I never said that.'

Mire and Clay

Gareth Wigmore

'You are tired, Chesterton *buzoor*?'

It was a voice in the darkness, and not a kind one. It woke Ian with a start, and he had to gulp down a startled cry of panic. He didn't want his captors to hear his fear. Doubtless they could see it on his face though, lit by the flaming torches they held close to it. The heat was searing after the steady cool of the cellar in which he had been kept for a time that he couldn't even guess at.

'Yes, I'm tired,' Ian said, finding his tongue stumbling over the words in his dry mouth. 'What do you care? What do you want with me?' His voice had a raspy quality that made him sound utterly unlike himself, and he could feel the hairs from his unkempt beard brushing his lips. 'Give me some water, why don't you,' he added before he began to cough.

Gul Zaheer's teeth glinted yellow and red in the torchlight as he bared them in a grin. 'Oh, soon, soon,' he hissed. 'Soon Chesterton will have all the water he could wish for.' His fellow gaolers began to laugh that high-pitched Afghan giggle that Ian had grown to know over the past months, and he began to sense that some grim task or torment lay ahead.

'I won't play any more of your games, Zaheer,' Ian said, trying to sound defiant, though he knew he didn't feel it.

The face of Ian's torturer came close to his, bringing the smell of raw onion with it. 'You will do as I say, Chesterton *buzoor* or - ' At the moment Ian heard that local word - it meant 'sir' or 'lord', and Zaheer always used it with an ironic sneer - he felt cold steel against his throat, just under his ear. He instinctively jerked his hands to brush it away, but they moved barely an inch from the wall to which he was manacled. 'Or I will slit you open like a pig and let the blood out of you so slowly that it will be a week before you are dead.' And Gul Zaheer began to trace a line down Ian's throat with his knife-point, taking care to just break the skin in one or two places.

As if he doubted it, one look into the Gilzai's face made Ian sure that this was no joke. Gul Zaheer had the wild, staring eyes of a madman, black and bottomless wells of cruelty set in a skeletal head, the skin taut over prominent cheekbones. There was no beard, unlike most of the Afghans, just a thin and drooping moustache that merely emphasised Zaheer's long skull. His few teeth were sharp as knives.

'This will be our final game, Chesterton,' he whispered into Ian's left ear, with his blade still pressed close underneath it. 'I will make you pay for the dishonour you have brought to this land. You will not return to this room.'

When he looked back on it, it was only then that Ian's stomach began to growl and his bowels began to churn, a feeling he'd had time and again since he'd begun to travel with the Doctor. He'd seen the most marvellous things, no doubt, been to incredible places and experienced wonders that no human before him had been lucky enough to experience. He'd also been shot at, poisoned, tortured and terrified more times than he could count. But the face of Gul Zaheer leering at him with a long knife at his throat, as he sat manacled in a dungeon in 1840s Afghanistan, ranked as utterly frightening as anything thrown at him by any distant corner of the universe.

Zaheer moved backwards and sheathed his knife. One of the gaolers stepped forward and roughly loosed Ian's hands, leaving him shaking and rubbing them in the darkness. 'Get up, *feringhee*,' the gaoler said. The word meant 'European', with connotations of 'infidel', and was accompanied by a hefty push or two. The other gaoler laughed his little Afghan giggle. Ian calculated the chances of escape. He could push the first man over into the second, grab a knife from one of their belts, and try to slash at them both before Gul Zaheer was on him. Or he could go for the torch in the second gaoler's hand, dash it in Zaheer's face, and make for the stairs. *And with one bound he was free*, he thought with a grim smile.

But then the second gaoler moved forward with another giggle, and bound a rope around Ian's wrists in a flash. That was it: all chance of escape seemingly gone. Without a weapon, he'd never make it far.

'Up! Get up!' the first gaoler shouted, and Ian lurched up unsteadily, suddenly longing to stay in the dungeon he'd been desperate to leave for so long. As the gaolers led him up the stairs, with Gul Zaheer bringing up the rear, Ian thought that if he could see the Doctor now, he'd throttle the old man. He'd give the world to see him and the possibility of escape and normality - normality! - that he offered, but he'd happily throttle him too. This was all his fault, as usual. It was he who had gone exploring unprepared when the TARDIS had landed. It was he who'd dropped the key to the Ship when they needed it most. It was he who had merrily conversed with the Gilzai tribesmen who had captured them, and sent Ian and Barbara off to the British in Kabul - into the middle of one of the biggest disasters in military history. And it was he who had stirred a lunatic like Gul Zaheer into such a fury, as a punishment for which Ian was now about to die.

If ever there was a time and place not to be, Afghanistan in 1842 was it. A few years earlier, Barbara had told him, the British had stormed out of India and occupied the treacherous land of mountains, sand and snow, to try to keep Russia from expanding its interests in the region. But they'd underestimated the Afghan hatred of their new rulers and, when an opportunity came in Kabul, the ordinary people rose up against them and against the puppet regime that they had put in place. Bad planning and worse leadership dogged the British forces, who found themselves trapped in their cantonments outside the city, rapidly running out of food.

It was in the middle of that siege that Ian and Barbara had found themselves, but worse was to come. Akbar Khan, the son of the deposed ruler of Afghanistan, had negotiated what for the British was an ignominious surrender, and offered them safe passage to Jalalabad ninety miles away. Some sixteen thousand people marched from the cantonments - five thousand of them British and Indian soldiers, the rest their hangers-on, servants and family members. But Akbar Khan's safe passage was a lie, and the weary column of marchers was attacked relentlessly by snipers, horsemen and looters as it shuffled through the snowy hills. Thousands died in the freezing Afghan nights, and bullets rained down in the days. It was the closest thing Ian had ever experienced to hell.

Barbara had told him that only one man of the entire sixteen thousand would make it to Jalalabad. A few others - maybe fifty, including the British families - survived by allowing themselves to be taken hostage by Akbar Khan. At least that meant that Barbara was safe, Ian consoled himself, as they shuffled out of the cellar and along a miserable stone corridor lit by torches. He'd seen the Doctor and Susan welcome her and the other British women and children into Akbar Khan's custody, even as a dozen knives had pressed into his back and stopped him in his tracks. She'd tried to come back, as had Susan, but the Doctor hadn't let them. Ian frowned as he thought about it: he was glad they were safe, but he felt desperately alone now. They wouldn't know how or why he'd died. He wondered if they were even still in nineteenth-century Afghanistan, or whether they'd given him up for lost long ago and were off on the other side of the universe somewhere. He half-hoped one, and half the other.

It occurred to Ian that even if the Doctor was to burst through the door at that moment, the old man might not recognise him. Ian hadn't seen a mirror for weeks. The blue-black cavalry uniform he'd adopted was dark with filth from the cellar, and the cavalry whiskers he'd grown - partly to amuse Barbara, and partly to fit in - had long been lost in a ugly, sprouting beard. Likewise, his hair was wildly out of control. A few minutes with one of the TARDIS's shaving machines would soon see him right, but for the moment he probably looked like Robinson Crusoe. The Doctor would almost certainly stroll right up to him and say, 'Young man, have you seen my friend Chesterton? And perhaps you ought to think about cleaning yourself up a little, sir.'

Ian spluttered out a laugh as he thought of it, and was rewarded with a dig in the ribs from one of his gaolers. 'You must not laugh, Chesterton. You go to meet your god now,' the Gilzai said almost kindly, spitting against the wall as he did so.

They led him into a wide room, brightly lit. There were windows here, high in the walls. Watching the sunlight stream in somehow made Ian feel worse. It wasn't even the middle of the night, but a time at which people were going about their business, carrying on regardless, while he was probably about to be executed. Even if anyone had known, they would probably join the fun and see the *feringhee* die, rather than lift a finger to help.

The room was of that dull rock from which most of the Afghan buildings seemed to be made, but it was bigger than any Ian had previously seen. What was odd about it was that there were wooden platforms covering the entire middle section of the floor. The look of those platforms made him nervous, though he didn't know why. His stomach growled and his insides shifted uncomfortably. Around the walls every few yards were clumps of Gilzais in twos and threes, so that there were about twenty men in the room in total, who fell silent gradually at Gul Zaheer's arrival. They were all dressed in that traditional Afghan fashion like Zaheer and the gaolers: leather boots, pyjama trousers covered by long sheepskin coats, and then ugly, spiked helmets on their heads.

He jumped at a noise from the corridor from which he'd just come, and then out of it came some more Gilzais, their long knives and blades clinking as they brought out an enormous man, well over six foot and broadly built, with huge shoulders. Ian instantly recognised him. It was Lieutenant Symonds.

When Ian and Barbara had turned up at the cantonments outside Kabul, most of the occupying British forces and their hangers-on had accepted them without any problem. After all, Ian had been dressed in the uniform of a cavalry captain, taken from the body of one of the horsemen they'd seen killed within minutes of arriving in Afghanistan.

The British had suspected a few reinforcements might be on the way from Jalalabad to bolster Kabul's defences, and the only peculiarity was Barbara's being there. Even claiming that she was Mrs Chesterton was a little strange. Bringing wives to the cantonments when the country had been peaceful, as many officers had done, was one thing, but everything was different when the threat of Afghan violence was so strong. Still, Barbara claimed to have just discovered that she was pregnant, and refused to leave her 'husband's' side. Some of the wives went along with that, although others had sniffed and implied without too much hanging about that she was an idiot.

Apart from the strangeness of Barbara's presence, their story seemed to pass muster. Ian had taken documents from the body, too - letters to be delivered, orders and so on - and, ultimately, why else would two British subjects be in Afghanistan? Nonetheless, one man had been suspicious of them all that long time they were under siege in the cantonments, and that was Symonds. Whether he was just suspiciously minded, or whether he was somehow better at spotting a liar, he was always hovering around waiting for one of them to make a mistake, as they inevitably did from time to time. But he had uncovered nothing too incriminating - or at least, he hadn't acted on it. What would have been the point? The British were fighting a desperate siege action, and Ian hadn't shirked from being fully involved in the fighting at every turn. Throughout, though, Symonds had made a point of trying to argue with Ian's orders, challenge his knowledge of military matters, and generally embarrass him in front of the men. There had even been one or two times when Ian had fervently wished in the middle of battle that a bullet from one of the Afghans' long *juzails* would find Symonds and get him off his back. And here he was, as large as life, his red uniform coat stained brown from his captivity, his face hidden behind his beard.

'Chesterton, you remember Symonds *huzoor*?' Gul Zaheer hissed in Ian's face, grinning widely as he pushed him down on to his knees.

'Good God! Are you all right, Symonds?' Ian called out to him.

'Just about, sir,' the Englishman replied, as the Gilzais manipulated him round to the other side of the wooden platforms that split the room. 'You?' But that was enough for Ian to know that Symonds must have been in a pretty bad way - he'd always made a point of refusing to call Ian 'sir'. Symonds's voice was hoarse and thin, as though his throat were dry, which it probably was.

'Ah, a happy reunion!' Zaheer said, looking away from the prisoners and appealing to the Afghan men clustered around the room. 'I wouldn't worry - you have a long journey to make together, to wherever it is that you *feringhees* go when you die. Mind you, one of you will be making it shortly before the other.' He laughed, and some of the men began to laugh too, that characteristic, almost feminine, almost feral giggle. Ian's eyes were drawn back to the men around the room, and it struck him that this was an arena. It was what he imagined dog-fighting rings underneath east end pubs would be like.

'What's he saying? You speak the lingo, Chesterton,' Symonds said, his voice low but not concealing his fear. Ian wondered whether his was as he replied, 'What? Oh, just threats, Symonds, you know the sort of thing. How long have you been here?'

'Lord knows. Too long. A month?'

'About the same as me, then, I'd reckon,' Ian replied. 'I went as a hostage with the women and children just before we reached Khoord-Kabul. I got Barbara - my wife - to Akbar Khan, but Gul Zaheer found me at the last minute.'

'She's not really your wife, is she?' Symonds asked.

Ian shook his head, grinning. 'No. But I care for her, and it doesn't matter what they do to me much as long as she's safe.' He hadn't quite thought about it in that way before, but as he said it, he felt some of the fear in his stomach draining away. He had protected Barbara, got her back to the Doctor and safety, and that was the important thing.

'I knew all along,' Symonds said in a tired voice, shaking his head. 'What are you, Ruskie spies?'

'No, no. Just travellers in the wrong place at the wrong time.'

'You're not a Russian?' Symonds sounded crestfallen. 'I was sure that you were.'

'No, I'm as English as you are.' Ian found himself laughing, and Symonds soon enough joined in.

After a moment's pause, Symonds said, 'Then thank you for helping us out. Sorry if I made things tricky for you with the men, in the field.'

'Forget it. Let's just think how we're going to get out of here.'

Symonds waved his hands in front of him, bound with rope. 'Don't know about you, old man - '

'But you're a bit tied up at the moment? Yes, I know how you feel.' Then Ian felt a kick in his ribs from Gul Zaheer, and the conversation was over.

'Oh, talk away in your *feringhee* prattle, Chesterton, by all means,' the Gilzai chief said, strutting angrily between the two Englishmen. 'We're not here. We're not important. Just use us whenever you like. That's what you English do, isn't it?' He punctuated the diatribe with a swift kick to Symonds's ribcage as well and, just to make the point, spat a gobbet of yellowish phlegm in Symonds's face. 'You come to our country and take it with your pathetic puppet king, this Shah Shujah not fit to wipe the excrement from my horse's arse. We have never done you wrong, we have never come to England and taken your land. We have not even courted the favour of the Tsar as you say we have.' Zaheer was working himself up into a fury. 'But we shall teach you, oh yes. There is nothing left of your army now, they are all gone, all of them, and your general's head lies in the snow outside Jalalabad as a warning to all.'

'A new army will come, Zaheer,' Ian said, 'and they will be without mercy as they retake this country from Akbar Khan and his father.' His voice was calm and measured; he knew it was true. Barbara had told him as much of the history as she knew. She claimed it wasn't much, but it had saved their lives a couple of times already. Ian probably knew it wouldn't do so now, but there was no harm in a bit of heroic bluster.

'Bring your infidels on, Chesterton!' Zaheer shouted, appealing to the crowd. 'Bring them all! Drain England dry of its men-folk and let us take on them all! My Gilzais have a ball in every *juzail* for their guts! They have a knife for every throat!' There were whoops of delight from the Afghans, some of whom drew their scimitars and waved them aloft.

'I don't think so,' Ian said, shaking his head and imagining reading a history book on the first Afghan war and the retreat from Kabul in the TARDIS's library if he ever got out of this. Would it mention him or Zaheer, he wondered? Or Symonds?

Zaheer snarled. 'Enough of this, Chesterton. It is time for you to die.' He clapped his hands and turned to the rest of the room. 'Open it! Hey, come on, open it!' And that was when Ian's bowels began to churn inside him once again. If he was going to die, he'd like it to be quick. A bullet or a knife-thrust would be fine; he was rather less enthusiastic about whatever Zaheer had in store for him. As he watched, some of the Gilzais around the room moved into the centre and began to take up the boards from the floor.

What raised a surge of panic in Ian's chest was that they did so incredibly carefully. The Gilzais did almost everything with a swagger and flair that seemed to say that they feared nothing. But when something was important, they behaved gingerly and with great caution. They were unbelievably good marksmen partly because their bullets were their own, and they didn't pull the triggers of their *juzails* until they knew they'd not have to expend a second bullet on the target. And they lifted up the boards from the centre of the room with the same calculated care.

'What's this, Chesterton?' Symonds said. 'What was he saying?' It suddenly occurred to Ian that the fact that he could still understand the Afghans' speech might mean that the TARDIS was still here. He knew nothing of their language – he could only speak and understand it because the Doctor's ship worked its magic and translated things for him. If it were gone, then surely he'd be left as unable to cope as Symonds was.

'Nothing good for us, that's for sure,' he replied, and that was when he was pushed and pulled on to his feet again, with Symonds being dragged up as well. Ahead of them, the Gilzais had begun to chatter among themselves excitedly, as they stepped back from the space where the wooden panels had been.

'Are they going to kill us?' Symonds asked, his voice cracking.

Ian's teeth were gritted and his eyes were desperately darting around for an escape route. 'Can you see any way out of this?'

'All the exits are blocked.' Symonds was beginning to sound frantic. 'There's too many of them and we're in no shape to fight.'

'Then, yes, they're going to kill us.'

As he moved through the room towards the centre, Ian saw in the clear brightness of the sunlight, reflected off the room's rough rock walls, that the panels had been covering a pit about ten or twelve feet deep. Now that it was uncovered, it entirely split the room in two, a trench running right through the middle of it. Pushed, pulled and cajoled to the edge by the gaolers, he looked down and could see water below.

There were things moving in the water, small, darting shapes that wriggled like the nerves in the pit of Ian's stomach.

He couldn't help it. Involuntarily, he looked at how he was going to die and said, 'My God.'

'Yes, where is your god, *feringhee*?' Gul Zaheer shouted across the room at him. 'Is he in this room to watch you die? No. Just as he deserted your army as they left Kabul, he will not save you now. He will not save the next of your armies when it comes to claim what is ours again. But our God will guide our bullets and our knives, and the sand will be stained with English blood.'

Facing Ian about ten feet away, the other gaolers brought Symonds up to the opposite edge of the pit. On looking down into it, he slumped to his knees and began to pray. The Gilzais around the walls began to giggle again at the sight of it, and one of the gaolers gave him a wallop on the back that sent him reeling a couple of inches closer to the edge, and to the water, and to whatever was down there.

'The rope! Come on!' Zaheer instructed his men, with what Ian thought was an edge of hysteria in his voice. He turned to look at the chief, and he was practically frothing at the mouth with anticipated pleasure.

One of the Gilzais nearest to him said to another, 'Five on the big *feringhee*. Look at his arms!' The one he'd spoken to looked from Ian to Symonds, deliberating carefully. 'I like the look of the little one. He is not on his knees and soiling himself like a pig before the butcher. I'll give you ten on him.' Little exchanges like this started taking place all around them; there was the clinking of money as it was put down on to the rock floor. He even heard one Gilzai saying he didn't have any money, but he'd put his goat on the big infidel winning.

In fact, most of the bets Ian heard were on Symonds and not on him. He could see why, though: compared to the big lieutenant, Ian looked like an afterthought. He was hardly a small man himself, reasonably well built, moderately wide shoulders and, it had to be said, his time with the Doctor had made him physically stronger than he'd been at any time in his life, even national service. It was running away from countless aliens and Afghan hordes that did it. But Symonds was a brute of a man: he looked like he could have gone several rounds in the ring with Hercules Cortez. If whatever Zaheer made them do involved sheer strength, Ian knew he was in trouble.

'You English have a game, do you not?' Zaheer announced as the gaolers began to undo Ian's and Symonds's hands. 'I have seen you at it in Kabul, when you are not busy with your cricket and play-acting.' Before Ian had a chance to act in the second he was untied, the end of a long rope was bound round his wrists, bunching them together. Then his gaoler tossed the rope over to the other side of the pit, where the other end of it was tied around Symonds's wrists. 'It is called the tug of war,' Zaheer continued, his few teeth bared, his eyes flashing like a madman's. 'I do not understand your cricket or your play-acting, but the tug of war is the best thing you *feringhees* have brought here. I like it so much, I decided that this place would be ideal for it.'

'What's down there?' Ian was impressed that his voice sounded relatively level, though his heart had begun to pound like a drum.

'What does it matter, Chesterton? They are hungry. What's down there will eat you alive, and their young will grow up swimming around your bones.'

Ian looked across to Symonds. Horror was writ large on his face, his eyes panicked and wide, his mouth hanging open. 'But what's in it for us, Zaheer?' Ian found himself saying. 'We fight each other, one of us goes into the pit. What happens to the other one? You're not going to set us free.'

'There is always a chance, *huzoor*,' Gul Zaheer replied, his voice taking on an ironically soothing tone. 'True, I may toss the stronger of you down into the pit to follow his friend. Or I may take him back to the dungeon and have him there as my champion, to tug with the next prisoner who comes along.'

'What are you saying, you Afghan bastard!' Symonds screamed across the pit. 'What is he saying?'

'There's no guarantee whichever of us wins won't go straight down after the loser,' Ian called back to him, beginning to sit down. 'I won't fight if you won't fight.' The image of the dog-fighting ring came into his head again. 'They can do what they like to us, but why should we give them the satisfaction of reducing us to animals?' Something in Symonds's face made Ian think that the big man wasn't going to go for the reasoned approach. 'Damn it, man. We're Englishmen! Let's die with some dignity,' he added, trying to appeal to his Victorian sentiments.

That did the trick, it seemed. 'Yes,' Symonds stammered, the tears beginning to stream down his face. 'Yes, Chesterton, you're right.' He hadn't risen from his kneeling position, and just sat there as the Gilzais around them began to giggle and point at this last act of defiance by the *feringhees*.

Gul Zaheer smiled in a patronising way underneath his drooping moustache, and moved round to Ian. Panic began to rise up in Ian's chest again; Zaheer had tortured him often in the past month, and he recognised the swagger with which he approached as a cue for suffering. 'You are a stubborn man, Chesterton *huzoor*,' he said quite pleasantly, like a man who knows he will get his fun eventually. 'But the lieutenant is not. He is a coward, and I can make him fight.' He pointed over to one of the Gilzais on Symonds's side of the room. 'Pretend to take away his balls.'

The Gilzais roared with laughter and one of them stepped forward to Symonds with a long knife. 'He's going to threaten your vitals, Symonds,' Ian shouted across the gulf between them, 'but it's just a show. It's just a show! They want to get us to fight for them!' The knife was out and the Gilzai had laid it flat against Symonds's thigh, poking the point up towards his genitals and shaking his head sadly. What with that and

Ian's warning, Symonds panicked, giving a shriek that was nothing short of girlish. He leapt to his feet, pushing the Gilzai away and began to tug desperately on the rope that stretched from him to Ian.

Sitting cross-legged on the floor, Ian was jerked forward by the sudden jolt until he was lying on his front, being dragged toward the pit. He shouted in pain as his wrists took the strain and then his shoulders felt as though they were being wrenched from their sockets. He scrabbled desperately for a foothold or anything by which he could lever himself up, but there was nothing. When he looked across the trench, Symonds was frenziedly tugging on the rope for all he was worth, a manic expression on his face as though he'd just been pushed too far. 'Symonds, stop it! Let go!' Ian called out stupidly, but then felt the pain diminishing a little as a pair of strong arms came round his body and pulled him to his feet.

'Not all you English fight fair, eh, Chesterton?' the Gilzai chief said with a giggle, letting go of him and retreating away from the trench. 'Symonds *huzoor* might have taken away our fun. What's the point of a contest if it only takes a minute or two? We want a show.'

Ian didn't have a chance to look at him while he said this. For a second while Zaheer had been pulling with him, Symonds had been off-balance. But now he was righted again, hauling away on the other side of the trench, roaring like a wounded bull, the rope taut between his bound hands. Around the room the Gilzais nudged each other, pointing out this and that, calling across the trench and putting more money down.

As he tried to bring his arms up and edge his feet backwards, Ian knew that he was in a life-and-death struggle now. Symonds seemed to have lost all reason and had given in to the madness of the situation. There was only one way this was going to end, and that was with one of them in the water.

Symonds seemed to be bracing himself for a renewed assault, wrapping the rope once or twice around his wrists, and Ian could sense that a great pull was going to come. He dug his heels into the floor and waited for it, offering little resistance when it came. As he hoped, the bigger man tottered backwards, nearly overbalancing, his shouts breaking off uncertainly. Ian jerked forward a little with it, but his foothold was pretty good and he managed to capitalise on Symonds's surprise, reeling him in a little and jumping backwards a little with a groan of agony as he did so. His wrists burned as the rope began to wear through the skin, and his teeth broke the skin of his lower lip, filling his mouth with blood.

Symonds didn't take long to recover his poise. He found a little indentation in the floor that he could plant his feet behind, and heaved on the rope with enormous power once again, sending waves of pain through Ian's arms and shooting down his back. He felt like he was being ripped apart, and he couldn't help but scream. Next to him, Gul Zaheer clapped his hands with glee. But Ian had found another decent foothold and was getting every possible bit of purchase out of it. He wasn't going to win on strength, though, that was certain. Symonds seemed even stronger than usual in his madness, and Ian could only hope that he could out-think the bigger man. He wasn't just going to give up - his time with the Doctor had taught him that more than anything - but he barely believed that there would be any prize for victory in this contest beyond a minute or two's extra life. Around them, the Gilzais were whooping and giggling and chattering, and he could hear splashes from the water below, as though whatever was down there knew that a meal was on the way.

'Come on, Symonds! We don't have to do this, man!' Ian shouted across the pit at him again, but appealing to his better nature was obviously going to do no good. Symonds gathered himself for another great pull, and before Ian could try to put the same trick into action that had nearly swept his opponent off his feet, he was rushing forward towards the pit, unable to check himself. Pain seared along his arms, and he could hear himself screaming. His fingertips grazed the ground and ripped open as he instinctively searched for a handhold. From a position of four or five feet from the edge, Ian was suddenly lying on his face again and moving closer to the end all the time. In a second or two the floor was gone in front of him, and there he was peering over the edge, looking at the drop to the water below. His stomach leapt into his mouth. He thought of Barbara, and Susan, and the Doctor, and of everything he'd never see or do. His heart pumped so quickly he felt it was about to burst out of him.

Then he realised that he was stopped on the edge - that for some reason he hadn't fallen. The stench of onion was strong; he glanced to his left and Zaheer was at his shoulder waiting to watch the fall and the carnage once he reached the water. Then he looked over at Symonds, who was panting on the other side of the pit. The fury had left his big, sweating face, and he looked shocked, as though he'd suddenly woken up and found himself in a situation he couldn't remember.

'Symonds!' Ian shouted.

'Sorry, Chesterton,' Symonds panted between gulps of breath. 'I lost control there. I should know better. We can die like Englishmen.'

Ian scrambled to his feet and stepped a relieved foot or so back from the edge as the Gilzais began to shout angrily all around them. Zaheer snarled at his side and made a slashing gesture with his right arm. 'Get rid of him,' he said, disgust apparent in his voice. Two of the men behind Symonds moved forward and took him by one arm each. 'No!' he had time to shriek, as they flung him over the edge of the pit and down into the water.

Ian jerked forward as the rope grew taut, and was so busy making sure that he wasn't pulled down too, as Symonds flailed about, that he barely saw what was going on down there. But he could hear the frantic thrashing in the water, the screaming, and a few half-articulated cries in English, almost drowned out by the cheering of the Gilzais crowding round the edge of the pit. Terrified, he made himself glance over the edge and saw that the water was frothing as surely as if someone were heating it from underneath. Symonds was trying to climb the walls, but kept falling back into the heaving mass. It was as though a hundred tiny mouths were each taking a piece of him every time he hit the water. In less than a minute, the water was crimson with his blood and he had stopped screaming and struggling. Ian looked away, wanting to retch but somehow not doing. His head felt light, and he wondered if he was going to pass out.

'You like what you see, Chesterton?' Zaheer turned to him and gave him a wolfish smile. 'That is how *feringhees* die. Prepare yourself to join Symonds *huzoor* in the next world. Do you follow?'

That was when there were shouts from outside and a large door on the other side of the room burst in, flooding the room with extra light. Another group of Afghans came sweeping in, barking orders at the Gilzais to stay where they were. Their swords whirled in their hands and scythed down the one or two Gilzais who resisted. And then through the door came an old man with notably lighter skin than his companions, wearing a grand colourful coat and ornate silken trousers tucked into long leather boots. On the top of his head he wore a green turban. He was slightly built, but had a commanding presence. His eyes darted round the room quickly before settling on Ian. 'Yes – that's Chesterton, there!' the Doctor said.

Ian noticed that Gul Zaheer was still standing next to him at the edge of the pit, seemingly frozen to the spot by the suddenness of the interruption. Ian blinked a couple of times and saw darkness gaining on him, about to smother him. He looked up at the Gilzai chief who had tortured him this last month. 'No,' he said, almost under his breath.

'You follow.' With that, he brought both his hands, still tied together with the flailing rope attached, crashing down on the back of Zaheer's left knee. It was a good blow, taking his leg from under him and sending him sprawling to the floor. Without thinking, Ian leant down and put his shoulder down into Zaheer's body, like a rugby player joining a maul. 'No, Chesterton!' the chief cried, but by then Ian had bundled him over and down into the pit. As he heard the thrashing of the water begin again, he slumped down to his knees, and then on to his face, and remembered nothing more.

When Ian woke up, Susan's hand was stroking his face. He grabbed it instinctively, pushing it away with a yell and making her gasp. 'Susan?' he asked, and then let it go.

'Oh, Ian!' she said, smothering him in a huge hug. 'Oh, Ian, we were so worried!'

He put his arm around the girl's slim shoulders. 'It's good to see you too, Susan.' He felt like crying. 'It's very good to see you.'

Susan jumped back from him as though a sudden thought had struck her. 'But I should fetch Barbara!' she said, with a childish laugh at the back of her throat. 'Stay there!' she instructed him, already halfway through the door.

'Oh, I will,' he called after her, knowing he could barely move if he tried. He was in a soft double bed, in crisp white sheets. It felt like heaven. He hadn't been in a bed for months, not since before the retreat from Kabul. What was more important was that he was in the TARDIS, for the first time in at least three months. There was the gentle, reassuring hum of power that Ian could almost feel as much as hear, and the stark lines and the whiteness of the room left him in no doubt. Afghanistan was long behind them, at the other end of the cosmos. He was safe.

What was more, he was clean. He'd been shaved and washed, his hair had been cut into its familiar simple shape, and he was dressed in clean white pyjamas. His wounds had been lovingly tended and dressed. Breathing a sigh of utter relief, Ian nestled himself under the covers and rested his head back on the luxurious pillows until Susan came back, Barbara with her.

They didn't really say a lot for a while. Barbara just came right up to the bedside and kissed him, embraced him and didn't let go. He felt her tears, warm and wet against his cheek. After a moment or two, Susan decided to make herself scarce, coming up with some excuse about going to tell her grandfather. When Barbara pulled away from him, Ian thought she looked beautiful. Her long, sharp features were taut with worry and there were bags under her eyes; Afghanistan had not been kind to her either. But there was a smile on her face, and it was so good to see her with her long dark hair in its usual style and her everyday clothes, a simple white blouse and black culottes. She was the normal life that had almost seemed an illusion to him back in Gul Zaheer's dungeon. They sat together for a long time, sometimes talking, sometimes just touching each other to make sure they were really there.

Third in the procession of visitors was the Doctor. Gone was the extravagant Afghan garb that Ian could only just remember; he was back in his familiar Edwardian frock coat and check trousers, his long white hair flowing down to his neck.

'Where are we, Doctor?' Ian asked as the old man sat on the bed, the two of them alone.

'We're not there, Chesterton, that's what matters, hmm?' he replied. 'We're on our way to somewhere new, far away from that terrible place.'

'Somewhere safe, please, Doctor. I could do with a rest.'

'You don't leave this bed, or this ship until you're ready, my boy.' The Doctor's voice was mock-stern. 'You take your time. My goodness, you saw some dreadful things back there. The cruelty! The barbarism! The place where we found you - oh! It makes me shudder.'

Ian breathed out through his nose carefully, and frowned. 'I did some dreadful things too, Doctor, don't forget.'

The Doctor waved the comment away. 'A man does what he must. You did nothing you didn't have to do.'

'That's not true. Oh, I know that once I was in the battle, pretending to be a soldier, I had to fight or die.'

'Quite right,' the Doctor interjected. 'Quite right.'

'But,' Ian said carefully, 'I pushed a man to his death down that pit, Doctor. I didn't have to. I wanted to.'

'The scoundrel who'd kept you locked up? Tortured you?' The Doctor stared off into space momentarily, before returning to look at Ian. 'Well, I wouldn't lose sleep over him, Chesterton. The British wouldn't have left him alive once the new army had moved in. He only had months to live in any case.'

Ian shook his head. 'It's not so cut and dried. I was scared. I'd been scared for a long time. I watched Symonds die and I wanted to kill Zaheer. I could kill him, so I did kill him.'

'Perhaps before he killed others, eh?' the Doctor added after a pause.

'Perhaps you did a great favour to some other poor man. There were enough in his dungeon who would have thanked you, I know.'

Shrugging, Ian sank his head back on to his pillows and looked up at the TARDIS's featureless ceiling. 'I don't know, Doctor. Before I wandered into this ship, the most I'd done was squash a fly or set a mousetrap. Now I'm beginning to lose count of the number of things and people I've killed, directly or indirectly. I've seen more death than I ever thought I would.'

'I don't envy you that march from Kabul, Chesterton - the piles of the dead, the frostbite... Barbara's still having nightmares, you know.'

'I'm just tired of wondering whether I'll live another day. And of wondering what I'll have to do - who I'll have to hurt - to make sure that I live through it.' Ian sat up a little, so that he could look at the Doctor again. 'I think Gul Zaheer is the first person I've killed in cold blood, Doctor - the first person I killed even though I didn't have to. What kind of a man does that make me?'

The Doctor put a hand out and patted Ian's arm affectionately. 'Only you can answer that, by your actions in future. But I know you as a good man, someone who can be relied on to do what's right. I know that I've brought you to places you might rather not have seen, places that have made you take actions you might rather not have taken, and for that I'm sorry. You were in mortal terror, pushed to the limit, and you acted to survive. Who's to say that Zaheer wouldn't have thrown you down there before we'd got to you, if you hadn't done what you did, eh?'

'That's an excuse.'

'Perhaps it is, but perhaps not.' The old man smiled and looked into Ian's face earnestly. 'That one action doesn't make you evil, Ian. Why, it was pure instinct.'

'But I have to live with it. With thinking what I might have done differently.'

The Doctor shook his head, stood up and headed for the door. 'You should rest. We'll talk again, hmm?' he said before he shut it behind him, leaving Ian alone with his thoughts. His heart thumped as he replayed the deaths of Symonds and Gul Zaheer in his mind. His wrists and shoulders began to throb with the memory of the pain. What was done was done, and couldn't be changed. But *he* had changed. In a flash, he understood that nothing could terrify him more than knowing what he was capable of when pushed. It was a thought he didn't like at all, and he settled down with it into uncomfortable sleep.

Ash

Trevor Baxendale

Steven couldn't sleep. Wouldn't sleep. His mind was humming like a hyperdrive, and his body refused to relax. He twisted and turned for a while and then let out an impatient sigh. Eventually he rolled out of bed, sweating.

For a few seconds he stood there and tried to collect his thoughts. He hadn't been sleeping well recently, not since leaving the planet Kembel. Helping to foil the Daleks' mad scheme to conquer the galaxy, he had seen two friends die horribly and he couldn't shake the depression that followed. He felt tense and truculent and scared.

Steven ran a hand roughly down his face, trying to rub some feeling and expression back into the clammy skin. He took one look at the tangle of sheets on his bed and decided against sleep altogether. He pulled on a Chinese silk dressing gown and went to find the Doctor.

The Doctor never strayed far from the controls of his ship, even at night. Steven fully expected to find the old man still bent over the wide hexagonal console, feverishly working at the brightly lit array of switches and dials in his constant attempts to direct the path of the TARDIS through time and space.

But the lights were dimmed when Steven reached the spacious, slightly clinical chamber. The only source of illumination came from the glass column at the centre of the console, its delicate glow shimmering up and down the walls as the thing pulsed slowly in its great socket. Even the distant hum of the ship's engines seemed muted, as if trying quietly to propel the vessel across the dimensions without disturbing its master.

The Doctor was sitting in a tall wing-backed chair, away from the console, apparently asleep. This was unusual enough for Steven to find it perturbing: he was not used to seeing the Doctor so obviously vulnerable. In fact the old man was so still as to appear lifeless.

In profile, the Doctor's hawk-like face looked drawn and brittle, the skin almost as white as the hair that, brushed severely back over his skull, reached easily down to his collar. His dark blue silk cravat was tied at his throat with customary precision, the winged collar of his shirt brutally stiff and stark against the funereal jacket. The hands that were clasped over his waistcoat were thin and bony. But there was no movement. He didn't even seem to be breathing.

Steven reached out fearfully, but before his fingers touched the Doctor's sleeve, the old man's eyes snapped open and caught him in a bright, alert stare.

'Steven, my boy! What d'you think you're doing, creeping around like that, hmm? You could have frightened me half to death!'

Despite feeling a little foolish, Steven gave a heartfelt sigh of relief and sank back into the armchair opposite the Doctor. The old man sat upright and steepled his long fingers, the big blue gemstone in his ring glittering in the light from the console. He continued to fix his companion with his most imperious gaze.

'I couldn't sleep,' Steven told him. It felt like a confession.

'My dear boy, you don't want to waste your life away snoring!'

'I mean I couldn't settle.'

'Ah. Well, of course not. You're thinking about Katarina, and Sara Kingdom.'

Steven smiled weakly. 'I'm not normally so morbid.'

The Doctor made a noise midway between a tut and a hush. 'Don't apologise. They were good friends to us, Steven, and their deaths shouldn't pass unnoticed. It is most distressing, most distressing indeed.'

The Doctor waved his fingers agitatedly as he spoke, almost as if, despite what he said, he wanted to be free of the subject. Steven supposed that the Doctor, too, must have been dwelling on the aftermath of their last adventure. For a long moment the two men sat in silence, listening to the clicks and whirrs of the TARDIS controls.

Eventually the Doctor climbed stiffly to his feet and checked the various settings and gauges arrayed around the console. He peered confidently at a particular dial and rapped sharply on its glass face with his knuckle, apparently satisfied. Steven often suspected that much of this was showmanship, that the old man really held only the most basic understanding of the workings of his ship, relying on intuition and even blind luck to operate it. Steven was always careful to keep these suspicions to himself.

The Doctor turned and sank back into his armchair and the leather upholstery, or perhaps his bones, creaked audibly. He looked at Steven, who suddenly found himself trapped in the brilliant glare of those damnably clear eyes. Sometimes it felt like that stare could see right inside his head.

'Something on your mind?' Steven asked bluntly, prompted into some kind of response.

'I was thinking,' began the Doctor, 'of something that happened a long time ago. Yes, a long time ago indeed. Before I met you, Steven my boy. Before I had even left the planet Earth.'

The Doctor seldom talked about himself, or even reminisced, and Steven was instantly fascinated. He chose to say nothing, not wishing to spoil or distract from this rare moment of introspection.

The Doctor's attention had turned inward, to his memories. 'You never met my granddaughter, did you, my boy? No.'

'You've mentioned her in the past. Susan, wasn't it?'

The Doctor flashed one of his sudden smiles, gratified by his companion's recall. 'Yes, yes. Susan, a dear child. We lived together on your planet for a while, you know... a long time before you were born, I might add. The twentieth century, in fact.'

Steven quickly struggled to remember what he could of that period, some three hundred years before his own time. He vividly recalled from his childhood that the learning pill for the twentieth century had been difficult to swallow. It had been the time of mankind's first feeble steps towards space exploration, when global communications were limited to primitive radio waves and even complex networks of wires. When weapons of mass destruction had seemed like the only answer to international rivalry.

'Must have seemed pretty barbaric, back then,' Steven ventured.

'Sometimes,' conceded the Doctor, but his eyes narrowed slightly. 'In some ways it was quite charming. Yes, quite charming.'

It wasn't a word Steven would have used. He could imagine the smog-thick streets, crammed with buildings made of stone and wood and glass, layered with the grime of two hundred years' worth of industrialisation. How would people have travelled in those days? Horse and cart? No, simple metal cars powered by internal combustion engines - messy, loud, kicking out toxic pollutants like tomorrow didn't matter.

But the Doctor's face, in contrast to his companion's ruminations, had taken on a look of cosy reminiscence. 'The city Susan and I lived in - London - was still recovering from a terrible global conflict, which had taken place some twenty years previously. Things like that always take a long time to sort out, but on the whole people were doing their best to forget it.'

War was something Steven was very familiar with. He sat back, unconsciously making himself more comfortable, to listen to the Doctor's tale.

'We had some interesting times on Earth, my granddaughter and I,' he continued. 'Once, when I had been forced to accompany her to the theatre - Susan could be very wilful...' (Here Steven suppressed a smile; *I wonder where she could have got that from?*) '... but I wouldn't have let her venture out alone at night, not then... Well, to cut a long story, er, short, we found ourselves in an unfamiliar part of the city.'

'You were lost,' clarified Steven.

'Now now, don't be so presumptuous! London may not have been all that big a place, but it had been built over many hundreds of years, lane upon lane, road upon road, and building after building. It could be a very confusing place to be, and it's not at all surprising that Susan became so easily befuddled.'

'*You* weren't lost, then,' Steven pointed out mischievously. 'Only Susan.'

'Quite! I had a good idea where we were: somewhere around Shoreditch at any rate, not that that will mean anything to you. It was a part of London that had been badly damaged by enemy bombs during the war. Most major cities had been on the receiving end of something they called the *Blitz*: a massive and sustained aerial bombardment of civilian areas, night after night. The destruction was horrendous! There were still condemned buildings around in some parts. Susan insisted on taking a wrong turning and before I knew it we were, erm, lost. I remember that it was very cold, and to my shame I became rather cross with the poor girl. We had words. I tried to lead her back to the proper route, towards the more well-lit areas, but we could not find our way out of the back alleys into which we had stumbled.'

The Doctor shivered, as if remembering the chill of that night. 'It had been a clear night when we left the theatre. I recall looking up at the stars - those few visible through the glare of the city lights - and looking for... well, not home. Our home was here, in the TARDIS. But once we were lost, a fog started to build up. Nothing serious - London could produce fearsome fogs - but enough to make our task of finding the correct way back to the Ship even more difficult.

'We stopped and tried to listen for the kind of sounds that might guide us: motor cars, people and the like. We could hear them all right. But every time we moved towards the source of the noise it would disappear. We distinctly heard a bus stopping around a corner, but when we got there - nothing. No bus, no cars, no traffic at all. Just another empty back street smeared in fog.'

Steven shifted uncomfortably. Forcing a laugh, he said, 'You really were lost!'

The Doctor did not smile. 'We were worse than lost, my boy. Much worse. The more we advanced, the more distant the sounds of the city became. Doubling back, we tried to find an alley that would lead us back to a major thoroughfare, but we never found one. Gradually, we stopped hearing the engines of the cars and taxis that are the constant backdrop to city life. We stopped again and strained to listen for anything. We might have been all alone in the world at that moment, my boy... all alone. We could hear nothing, *nothing* but the sound of our own breathing!'

The Doctor had sat suddenly forward, eyes glaring at Steven, his old fingers rubbing worriedly together against his chest. He quickly changed the nervous gesture into an absent-minded pat of his jacket lapels and sat back in his chair. 'Poor Susan was beside herself. She was starting to panic. She was sometimes prone to hysteria, it has to be said. I did my best to calm her down... '

Steven could picture the scene: the Doctor in his cloak and scarf, huddled over his granddaughter, offering up soothing words: *There now, child, stop fretting! We'll find our way back in a moment, you'll see. Try not to let your imagination run away with you, for goodness' sake. You're letting yourself get upset. Here, dry your eyes. I'll find our way home, Susan my dear. Of course I will! Oh yes...*

'In truth,' continued the Doctor, 'I had no idea which way to go. I tried to examine my surroundings more carefully. We were in a long lane between two tall, brick-built buildings. The only windows I could see were high up, the glass black and lifeless. There were narrow pavements on either side of the roadway, which was roughly cobbled. There were thin streams of dirty water in the gutters. There was a smell in the air that I recall very sharply: something beyond the simple stagnation of the water... something borne on the cold night vapours like a distant memory. It was a fleshy, organic scent: not quite the smell of cooked meat, but something less wholesome, less comforting. But it was cold and damp, and difficult to be sure.

'I made Susan walk on with me, asking her to link her arm through mine as if I needed the support of a younger body. I thought it would help if she thought she was being of some use, or at least had something to occupy her mind. We pressed on, exploring the narrow avenue. I talked, trying to keep her spirits up: I blamed the weather, blamed the city - even blamed the silly film we had been to see. I swore I'd never set foot outside the Ship again!

'We turned every corner we came to, and with every step I knew we were moving further and further from civilization. But now I refused to turn back; we were already hopelessly lost and to try and retrace our steps would only suggest to Susan that I was at a complete loss.'

Intrigued, Steven watched the Doctor's fingers twitching in agitation, stirred by the cold memory of that dark, bitter night.

'Eventually I heard something,' he went on. 'It was totally unexpected: the sound of a voice, singing. Most remarkable. It was some way off, but quite discernable. Susan and I looked at one another quickly: who was it? Where were they? Instinctively, we called out: "Help! Where are you? We're lost!" But there was no response. We listened again, still full of excitement: we could hear the singing, too faint to pick out an actual tune or any words, but definitely a finely tuned voice. A young girl, I imagined. It sounded a rather gay tune, and it lifted our spirits immediately. We hurried towards it, our footsteps echoing along the empty streets.

'Suddenly we emerged into a wider avenue, full of shops closed for the night. Our relief was profound. There was no one about, and the girl, wherever she was, seemed to have stopped singing, but at last here was somewhere that represented life!

'It was Susan, bless her, who first noticed the broken glass. The windows in the shop fronts were all smashed. Perhaps we had wandered into one of the rougher parts of the city. There was glass everywhere, all over the pavement. We crunched across it to inspect the shop fronts more closely, and I became aware of another sound - occasional cracks and bangs as more debris settled inside the buildings.

'Immediately I thought that these shops appeared to have suffered bomb damage, and I felt the first touch of cold dread. I gripped Susan's arm and tried to pull her away, worried that the buildings could collapse at any moment. We slipped and stumbled on the broken glass and when we steadied ourselves, something else caught my attention: in the jagged remains of the ironmonger's window before us I could plainly see our reflections. I was standing behind Susan, holding her tightly by the shoulders. I could see her face in the glass - only horribly distorted... her eyes looked sharp and narrow, screwed up beneath a terrible frown. Whereas normally Susan's eyes were large and full of intelligence, now they looked wicked and cunning. Her lips were drawn back in a snarl. I could see her teeth - sharp and pointed as needles.

'I confess that I was startled, Steven my boy. With a cry I spun her around in my arms and looked at her face directly. "Grandfather!" she said. "What's the matter?"

'At first I did not reply. There was nothing wrong with her face.

Susan stared back up at me, as beautiful and innocent as ever. I checked the window again, but there was nothing untoward there either. Susan looked back at the glass as well, and we stared at our own reflections. "My child," I said, "we must get away from here. Immediately!"

'Then we heard the song again, right behind us. We turned to see a young lady on the opposite side of the street, watching us. She was smiling, but I was too shaken to be relieved. "Great Heavens, young woman!" I cried. "You've just given us the fright of our lives."

'She apologised quickly enough and asked if we were lost. Well, you can imagine how we felt about that! Even with my nerves aggravated, I couldn't help but be grateful for any help. She said her name was Joan and she offered to take us to her home, because we were obviously very cold and needed something hot to drink. Now the offer of a pot of fresh tea at this juncture was most welcome, my boy. Most welcome. I readily agreed and we followed Joan to her parents' house. It wasn't far. Joan was about Susan's age, and they chatted easily as we walked. Susan was so relieved to have found another soul! For my part I was looking forward to a warm welcome and a cup of tea as well, but I was still rattled by my experience with the reflection. I wanted to put as much distance between us and that shop as soon as possible!

'Joan hurried us along, bright and cheerful but, I sensed, a little nervous. It was late at night, and foggy, but there was something else worrying her, I could tell. She looked pale in the weak moonlight, and her large grey eyes held an almost haunted look, I thought, as if she expected disaster to strike at any moment. She glanced up at the sky at frequent intervals, although all I could see were the wet, dark clouds, which at that point were swiftly drawing over the moon.

'I told Joan that I did not recognize any of our surroundings. Were we anywhere near Coal Hill? She shook her head and gave a strange little laugh - sounding almost guilty, in my opinion. But, apart from this aggravating nervousness of hers, she seemed a capable young lady. She wore practical shoes and a good raincoat and hat. Slightly old-fashioned, I suppose, by Susan's standards, but who am I to pass judgement!

'Presently we came to her home - a small house at the end of a long row of rather dilapidated back-to-backs. Indeed, some of the adjacent properties appeared abandoned and in a terrible state of neglect. My enthusiasm for a cosy fireside and a warm brew began to wane; I could smell that strange, unsettling odour again - something old and mildewed. Very distracting!

'Joan fumbled for her door key in the gloom of the porch. There were no street lamps nearby, in fact none were working along the entire length of the avenue, and so I lit a match to help her see. But she jumped at the sudden light and stared at it fearfully. "Don't be so frightened, my dear," I told her, perhaps a little more sternly than I intended. "It's only a match, for goodness' sake. Now use your key and open the door, there's a good girl!"

'She quickly unlocked the door and we followed her inside. It wasn't that much warmer than outside. We shivered in the hallway and I blew out the match – I can remember very clearly the smell of the smoke as it was extinguished. Susan clutched my arm as the darkness closed around us. It was cold in here, and the aroma of the spent match lingered in the air.

'We followed Joan into the living room, a tiny little space filled with a couple of empty armchairs, a dining table and ironing board. There was a woman at the ironing board – Joan's mother. She was a small, but healthy-looking lady, in that she was not overly thin but stood as straight as a boxwood ruler. Her eyes, I recall, burned with a gentle determination. She looked at Susan and me and sniffed loudly, tipping her head back by way of inquiry. The thin light made her eyes shine.

'I removed my hat and introduced ourselves, thanking her for her daughter's hospitality. Although by now all thoughts of tea and warmth had deserted me: there was no fire burning in the tiny grate and the entire house was gripped in a damp, uncomfortable chill. Susan had been out for long enough; I didn't want her catching cold!

'Joan told her mother that she had found us wandering outside. The lady of the house sniffed again and returned to her ironing. "You're a good lass, Joan Calder," I heard her say, although I thought her words were heavy with a rather resigned sadness. There was a great melancholy hanging in the air. I cleared my throat and told the lady of the house that we had lost our way in the fog coming home from the theatre and required only directions: the nearest route to Totters Lane would be most appreciated.

'Mrs Calder turned her attention fully to me now. I could see her eyes clearly, red-rimmed and dry as marbles – the result, I postulated, of a surfeit of emotion. The poor creature had cried herself out, that much was obvious. I glanced at young Joan Calder, seeking some kind of confirmation, but the girl wouldn't look at me. She sat on the arm of the sofa, her hands in her lap and her face downcast. Most peculiar!

'"You won't find your way back from here," announced Mrs Calder abruptly. She offered no explanation, and I confess that the clammy atmosphere of the place got to me then and I shivered. Susan clung to me. She could sense the wrongness here as well. We were intruding. We were not welcome. Not welcome at all!

'"Please forgive us our intrusion," I said. "We will not detain you a moment longer. Come, Susan." I turned to leave, but Mrs Calder wouldn't have it. "No, you can stay," she said sharply, as if suddenly struck by a change of mind. "Joan, fetch us a pot of tea, be quick about it."

'You will already know, my boy, that I can extract the most information from the slightest of sources. I had taken this brief opportunity to make a study of our surroundings. There was something not quite right about the place, beyond the grim atmosphere I have already described. There was no television set in evidence, which was not unusual in 1963, and no telephone either, which was equally acceptable. There was, however, a wireless on the sideboard, a large wooden-cased affair of very primitive design and capability. There was a radio programme being broadcast at the time, and the set was tuned in to the relevant wavelength and switched on. But Mrs Calder quickly switched the wireless off. It seemed to me there was a furtive, cunning speed to the gesture. She looked across at me and this time I met her gaze.

'"Wouldn't be without the thing," she told me. "For the news. They say the whole of the East End will be flattened at this rate."

'I didn't say anything in reply. Joan came in with a tray and a pot of tea and some cups. She poured five cups. She asked if we took milk and I said that we did. She offered us sugar, and I accepted this too. You might think, my boy, that I am becoming obsessed with trivia in the telling of my tale, but this minor English tea ritual was so very important! I watched Joan pour in the milk and spoon in the sugar.

'I took my cup and stared down into the murky grey contents, lost in thought. Then Susan said, "Why five cups?"

'"There's one for Grandpa, too," replied Joan. She indicated an elderly gent sitting in the armchair in the corner of the room. Incredibly, I had completely failed to notice him on entering. At the time I put it down to my attention being drawn towards the rather austere lady of the house. If I had thought Mrs Calder to be a picture of health and vitality, then the old fossil in the corner was something else entirely!

'He sat slumped in the seat, almost moulded to the fabric of the chair like a long, elongated cushion flattened by years of use. He was frail-looking and thin to the point of emaciation. There was not a scrap of flesh on his old bones. His clothes appeared to be musty and frayed, his skin as brown and dry as winter leaves. He looked neglected and forlorn, his head hanging on his chest so that all we could see was the paper-thin skin stretched over the skull and mottled with liver-spots. Well, I wasn't sure whether he was even awake or not but I never forget my manners, so I bade him good evening. His brittle head tipped up to look at us with eyes screwed up like little berries, and his mouth opened in a soundless laugh revealing teeth like old twigs.

'It was an image to chill the blood, my boy. Dear Susan was quite alarmed. But what really shook me was my certain knowledge that, on my brief but detailed examination of the room only minutes earlier, Mr Calder *had not been there*.

'Mrs Calder said, "Dad was in the last war, weren't you, Dad?" She spoke loudly. Old Man Calder was clearly very hard of hearing. Probably shell-damage I shouldn't wonder, if he'd seen action in the trenches during the First World War. That had been some forty-five years previously. Human beings never learn!

'Old Calder was nodding ponderously, as if his scrawny neck might break if he moved his head too vigorously. "He could tell a few stories, mind," Mrs Calder added. I wasn't sure if she meant that he could but chose not to, or could if he had been able. I didn't like to look too closely; there was something about those tiny little eyes - something he shared with both his daughter and his granddaughter - a kind of withered, screwed-up intelligence that wasn't natural.

'"It was proper fighting then, mind," continued Mrs Calder as she ironed. "Man to man. None of this bombing innocent people. Nothing like the Blitz. Just the other night the whole of Fountain Street was hit. Nothing there but rubble now. We were lucky to keep our windows."

'Susan and I looked at one another. Could it be? Travelling through time was nothing new to us, but this was extraordinary. How could we have lost our way from 1963 without the TARDIS? How could we have walked back twenty years?

'Mrs Calder, I noticed, was watching us very carefully with her bird-like eyes. Waiting for some sort of reaction. I deliberately kept my face impassive, hushing Susan when she turned to speak to me, to voice her own fears. I returned Mrs Calder's look in equal measure. I made a comment about it being a very difficult time for everyone, and she nodded. "It's an awful time for sure," she admitted quietly. "Dad knows all about it, don't you Dad? Poor devil. He's not spoken a single word since he come home from the Great War. Something happened to him over there, something awful."

'At this point, although I had been careful not to taste my cup of tea, I asked Joan if I may have another spoonful of sugar. She happily obliged - but this time, there was no mistaking the sharp, warning glance from her mother! An error had been made, a grave error, and I knew precisely what it was.

'I moved to the mantelpiece and set down my cup and saucer. There was barely a sound in the room, except for the ticking of the carriage clock and the hiss of Mrs Calder's iron. In the mirror that hung on the wall above the fireplace I could see the entire room reflected. There was no sign of Mrs Calder by her ironing board, nor of Joan perched on the arm of her chair. Neither could I see Susan. All I could see was - ashes. The smouldering remains of the living room, reduced to dust.

'And behind me, facing the mirror, was Old Mr Calder. I could see his reflection. He looked up at me from his armchair, his venomous little eyes glittering blackly in their dry sockets, an insane grin on his rotten lips. Instantly he reminded me of something I had seen earlier that evening - the vile, twisted reflection of my dear Susan in the shattered window of the ironmonger's.

'I knew then that it was him - he was the source of this corruption!

'I swung around, full of anger. Susan was watching me fearfully from the doorway. She was sensitive to the unnatural currents of time and space that flowed through this house. She was ready to run. My anger, my fear, was born of a disgust that I might have so easily betrayed the sacred trust put in me by her parents, that I might have brought her into such terrible danger.

'"You cannot leave," declared Mrs Calder, sensing our intention. Joan had got to her feet, and Susan quailed. "Not until you've finished your tea."

'We hesitated. Joan spoke up; "Please don't go. I've only just found you! We don't have company very often."

'"What year is this?" I demanded, undeterred. "Tell me!"

'With an eerie calm, Mrs Calder said that it was 1943.

'"No, madam," I replied solemnly. "It is not. And you know it is not." Yet she continued to insist that it was 1943. I told her with equal conviction that this simply could not be. "You have a plentiful supply of fresh milk, and enough sugar to fill a bowl to the brim," I pointed out. "That would be impossible in 1943. War shortages and rationing would see to that. You have obtained these commodities in this time period, have you not? The year 1963."

'A moment of panic sparked in her eyes. She said, "I send Joan out for provisions. She gets them all now."

'We turned to look at the daughter. She was shaking her head sadly. An expression of complete misery settled on her young features and yet she did not cry. "It's been such a long time," she said. "A long time. We can't go on. Surely we can't go on... "

'It was then that I began to see. I began to comprehend, if not understand, how these people could still be here. Susan and I had not travelled back in time. The Calders had remained in their house, untouched by the passage of the years, unseen and unheard of, in this new, modern world without war. The Blitz had been left well behind, but these poor unfortunates were trapped, unable to break out of their pathetic half-existence or to even progress. Something held their lives in a paralysing grip. And I knew exactly what, or rather who, was responsible.

'Old Mr Calder still sat in his deep armchair, like a dried-up spider waiting for flies to roam too close. He still wore that mad grin, and now there was a dry, rasping noise coming from his shrunken throat: at first I thought it was laughter, or the first breath of life I had still to witness from his desiccated form, but then I recognised it for what it really was... the soft, crackling sound of flames.

'With it came the smell of burning, or rather, the smell of something that had *been* burned. At last, I could detect in full the faint aroma that I had noticed very early on, the pervading stench of something old and forgotten and dead - here in this very room!

'I will never forget the vision that followed: Old Man Calder's ghastly face screwing up like a ball of paper thrown on a fire. His skin blackening in a heartbeat, eyes crusted like over-cooked mushrooms. He opened his mouth to emit a gasp of foul smoke and then his clothes and flesh, eaten away in seconds in a long-forgotten blaze, turned grey and began to flake like cinders.

'Susan gave a cry of alarm. I turned to see Mrs Calder and Joan clasp each other in a last embrace as time caught up with them in an instant and they, too, ignited. A flame we never saw engulfed their brittle bodies and turned them into a fused mass of clinker.

'All around us the room, the house, began to disintegrate. The furniture crumbled, the china cracked and broke apart, and the wallpaper shredded from the walls, turning crisp and black. I grabbed Susan's hand and rushed to the door - only to come face to face with the dreadful, decaying Calder himself.

'He had somehow risen from his wretched armchair and pursued us, hands outstretched like claws and the same crazed expression visible on his ash-smeared skull. He wasn't going to let us go - at least, not while we still lived. There was no mistaking the murderous intent visible in his eye sockets - they were full of a wicked darkness. His rancid jaws gaped, the shrivelled tongue thirsty for blood.

'I reacted instinctively, lashing out with my stick. Puffs of smoke and ash burst from his head and neck as I tried to beat him back, but the man's cadaver fought with obsessive, demonic strength.

'"Susan," I cried out in desperation. "The mirror! Smash the mirror!"

'It was all I could think of; thank goodness the child never stopped to question me. She turned and grasped Mrs Calder's forgotten iron and hurled it at the mirror over the mantelpiece with all her strength. The glass shattered into a hundred daggers of fire, reflecting for an instant in its demise the fate of this cursed house - fire-bombed one dark night along with its neighbours in 1943.

'The effect on the remains of Mr Calder was instant. With a dry gasp of rage, his burnt corpse collapsed and scattered into nothing more than dust and ashes. The same dust and ashes that I had originally smelled on entering the house.

'We staggered through the ghostly smoke and out onto the street, running for our lives. We were very nearly run over by a bus! We had emerged without warning onto a busy London thoroughfare. It was cold and wet, a thin drizzle putting paid to any chance of fog now. All around us were bright lights and people going about their evenings, cars and taxis rushing to and fro. And behind us - nothing. No sign of the Calders' house, or even their street. It had long been bulldozed and flattened to make way for newer buildings. I hailed a taxi and we rode back to Totters Lane in silence. Neither Susan nor I wished to discuss the matter further.'

Steven sat forward in his chair, utterly captivated. A shiver passed through his shoulders as he thought he felt the damp, chilly London weather. 'But - what was it about that mirror? How did you know to break it?'

The Doctor looked up sharply. 'Hmm! Strange things, mirrors, very strange. You people only use them for looking at yourselves, or for toys: telescopes and microscopes and the like. A typically limited perception, if I may say so!'

Steven felt none the wiser, but he knew from experience how difficult it could be to nail down a full explanation from the Doctor. 'All right,' he said, a little peevishly. 'But Calder knew something, didn't he?'

'Did he?' The Doctor threw the question straight back. 'Did he? I suppose he might have found something in that mirror. *Or perhaps something in the mirror found him.*'

'But his family,' Steven protested. 'The woman and her daughter, Joan... weren't they innocent?'

The Doctor chuckled, watching his young companion with an expression of satisfied amusement. 'Steven, my boy, I have no more an idea than you. To this day I have never been able to understand the factors that must have been at work in that forgotten little dead-end of time. I don't believe I ever will.' The Doctor fell silent, contemplating the events of that horrid night afresh. 'But there was something about that mirror. They can be very odd, reflections. Sometimes they show us things we'd rather not see. I wonder if Old Man Calder discovered something during his experiences in the trenches... something that only he could see. Something about himself that was corrupt and atavistic.'

'But you saw the truth in the mirror, didn't you?'

'I don't know, my dear boy! I saw something - hideous. That is all I can say.'

'It's horrible,' Steven said at last, thinking about it. 'Those poor people... '

'Yes, those poor people. I like to think that Susan and I somehow freed Mrs Calder and her daughter from a nightmarish existence.' He paused, as if deep in thought. 'I'm not so sure about the old man, though. Not so sure at all.'

Face-Painter

Tara Samms

Thursday afternoon, and time to take the faceless kids on their weekly outing to Santa Monica Boulevard. First I tie their wrists all together with bright handkerchiefs, so they make a human chain. Then I lead them out into the street.

I used to feel self-conscious with them. I mean, they're OK from the neck down, I dress them in baggy white T-shirts and blue jeans and sneakers. But what can you do with the heads? Each one's just a big pink egg, smooth, blank, completely hairless. OK, I can put them in caps. Easy. But they don't got ears, or eyes, or a nose or nothing. It's like when you sometimes see a baby bird that's fallen out of its nest and left for dead. It's hairless and pink, sort of puckered skin. That's what my kids have got for faces.

Mostly I wrap big scarves round their chins, or dress them in balaclavas. They don't like it much 'cause it's July, and it's sooo hot out there, but it means less people notice the weird shit going on with their faces. Luckily in this part of West Hollywood, no one looks too hard at no one for long, unless they want trouble.

So my kids and me, every Thursday we go out to the Face-Painter off Santa Monica Boulevard. So many glitzy galleries and boutiques filled with avant-garde crap there that some people look at my boys and girl, and they think it's some kind of statement or something.

I should say, they're not really kids, and they sure ain't mine. They've got grown-up bodies – the girl's got tits under her T-shirt, and the boy's definitely a boy, even if I can't understand half of what he says with the accent and all. And the other guy, well – their heads all look the same but I think he's the oldest, though sometimes he can be more of a kid than either of his buddies. I'm paid to baby-sit them, look after them a little, and make sure they don't go running away. The boss don't want them running away no more – says they did that all the time when he kept them locked up by themselves.

I think maybe they like it better here with me, but none of them say much. Victoria's the worst for that. Real quiet. Not just because she don't have a mouth – they can all speak if they want, it just comes out kind of muffled, like I gagged them or something. Well, it weren't me that gagged them.

When they do talk it's freaky, 'cause their chin moves about like they're chewing. They can all see, too, though not so clearly, like they're looking through bandages. I don't know how that works, and I don't know how come they can breathe either. They even eat – though with the kind of crud I cook up, God knows they probably don't want to. If they try real hard then this little black slit opens up out of nowhere and lets stuff in. But I don't look too closely. That stuff still freaks me out a little, even after two months.

'Come on, kids,' I have to say, because they never seem to look forward to our trips to the Face-Painter, and they dawdle and drag like they're little kids and sulking. You'd think they'd like it 'cause they're kept shut away most of the rest of the time, and Face-Painter's not just a Face-Painter. Tattoos are his thing. I love to look at the different designs you can get. I got me one already on my butt, this little lamb. Least, I think it's a lamb. Real cute, anyway.

Face-Painter's got grey hair that used to be black. He keeps it slicked back in this big kick-ass ponytail thing so it looks wet and tight all the time, and like he's wrung half the colour out of it. He's a big guy. I mean, I'm pretty big myself, but with him it's all muscle. He wears one of those tight muscle-Ts that show them off. His arms are busy with all kinds of shit, eagles and knives and hearts and crossed-out lovers. He's kind of got this big doughy face and it's like his shades are glued to his nose or something, and he's got this pissed-off look there the whole time if he's not doing his thing, working with the needles – or painting the faces on my three kids. The second he starts doing the thing he loves, he's happy again. He lives for that stuff, I can see it, and when he gets started that's when I want to go right up and stick my tongue down his throat, *mmm*. Except I guess that would kind of distract him, and I don't want him mad at me. Or hurling all over his shop.

'Hey, Rachel,' he says as I drag my three inside. He likes us 'cause we make appointments, every week, and he writes them down. He likes having appointments, I can tell.

My three kids stand there. The paint always wears off within a week so their faces are just blank sheets each time we come to call on Face-Painter. 'So what's it gonna be?' he asks. He always asks me instead of them.

'Victoria?' I ask.

She pulls out the same well-folded piece of paper she does every week. It has this little sketch she did with some pencils I gave her. It's a girl with brown hair, blue eyes, a straight nose, full lips. There's something kind of old-fashioned about the picture, like the way she talks. Face-Painter sighs, he knows this picture off by heart. But he takes it from me: this paper that's been folded so many times it might crumble in his hands, and for once he looks at Victoria and he says,

'You want it just like this? *Just* like this?'
'Yes,' she says softly.
'You're sure?'
'Yes... please.'
Sometimes he paints in a brown fringe over her forehead, has it curl in round the edges. It's a nice touch. She likes it when he does that.
'How about you, Jimmy?'
He grunts. 'Jamie.'
'The bionic woman's name is Jaime, honey,' I say, 'it's a girl's name,' and Face-Painter cracks up. Makes my smile grow wider.
'Och, I dinnae care what you paint there. No one sees it in any case.'
'Temper,' I tell him. 'C'mon, who d'you wanna be this week?' He don't say nothing. 'Make him Brad Pitt,' I tell Face-Painter. 'A girl can dream, right?'
He laughs again, looks me up and down as he does it. And I guess he don't much like what he sees, 'cause suddenly he's nodding to the third little freak in my outing.
'Well, Doc?' I ask him. He thinks he's a doctor.
The Doc doesn't answer, just fiddles with his hands. I ask again, and one last time, but it's no good with him. He won't crack. He gets like this sometimes, and though he ain't got no eyes to show you, you look at him too long and you get to thinking maybe *you're* the freak.
'Give him something special,' I suggest. And, real obliging, he goes to the back of his little shop and gets out the board with all his personal designs pinned to it, just for me - the ones he made up himself that you can't get nowhere else. And I see there's this wicked sunflower thing there, and I point it out and say, 'Go for it. Let's see how it looks.'
And so the Doctor sits himself down nice and easy and Face-Painter goes to work with his airbrush, and within an hour there's a beautiful bright sunflower sitting on that wide, blank empty face.
'That *is* fine,' I say. 'Could you do me one of those round about here?' And I pull down the strap of my top a little, show him the part where my breast just starts to get a little fleshy. He looks, and his expression don't change.
'Uh-huh,' he says. 'Maybe. But these ones cost.'
'I'll make an appointment,' I say.
'Maybe so, but they cost. You can't get 'em nowhere else.'
I pull up on my strap again.
'Maybe just look at the one I done here,' he says, and waves his big hand over at the Doctor.
'Oh, I will.' I put his Dodgers cap on the Doctor's head and it's like,

a cap on a sunflower and it looks crazy and we both laugh, me and Face-Painter, while the other two just sit there hand in hand, silent, waiting to be next.

And Face-Painter does Jimmy just like Brad Pitt, it's hilarious. But Victoria he's wicked to – he paints the face on the paper exactly like he told her he would, only he's painted all those deep folds in the paper on her face too, and she looks like she's been in some real bad accident. And she starts making this sobbing sound though no tears can come out 'cause she ain't got no eyes, but she can see what he's done in the cracked mirror he holds up to her, and he's looking at me and saying, 'What the hell! Next week I'll paint her a new face and leave out the folds, what's her problem?'

'You're so boring,' I tell them, once we're back home. It was too hot to go outside, everything's sticking to me. 'You're just never happy, are you?' And I sound like I'm pissed at them for showing me up down Face-Painter's, but really I'm just pissed with the whole deal. This damn apartment with its dark chocolate walls and cracked windows, full of all my old shit I ain't got round to cleaning up yet, and this damn neighbourhood that's all chain-link fences and tied-up dogs that bark all night, and redneck junkies who crank up the TV real high then zone out in front of the NBA so it sounds like I got a stadium next door. And you go out just to get the kids some pizza or buy some groceries or something and on every corner you get these damn Ruskie immigrants hanging round, checking your ass and speaking Slav to their buddies and sniggering. *There goes the girl with the fat ass*, they say. I just bet. I bet they wouldn't even notice Victoria got no face, they'd just check the ass and bang! Pick her over me. And I get mad at my kids, just thinking about what those Ruskies must be saying, and I yell and shoo all three of them down to the basement, which is kind of where they live and where they spend most days.

It's not so bad down there. Got three little bunks side by side so they can sleep all together – not like *that*, I don't hear no noises or nothing. They're not like that, just friends. They care about each other, you know? It's sweet.

I got a little bathroom down there for them too. And they're real neat. Well house-trained, and no bother most of the time, unless Victoria throws one of her conniption fits. She makes me laugh 'cause she gets madder and madder and her voice gets louder and louder but her words, they're always clean. A good girl is Miss Prissy-ass Victoria.

But they know I look after them, so why should they want to piss me off? I give them stuff to read. Paper and pens so they can write and draw and stuff. If they get me mad, I could stop giving them that shit. I could do that, easy - and the Doctor, he's a real one for writing, he would just hate it if I cut off his supply. He draws all these weird diagrams and shit; math stuff, mostly. Anyway, they're not much trouble and the boss pays me just fine.

I get them little treats sometimes. A flower for Victoria. A real bright bulb they can screw into the single socket when the Doctor wants to do some of his mad professor scribbles. And Jimmy loves Big Macs. I get him one on Sundays. I used to get it for the others but Victoria went all hissy over the grease and shit and the Doctor, well, he hardly eats a damn thing anyway. But then, Jimmy works out, he needs the red meat. He runs round that little basement, and does press-ups and sit-ups and squat thrusts until the whole little hole stinks of his sweat. But the others don't say nothing. Jimmy says he wants to be ready for the day he gets out of here, for the day he steals back his face from wherever it's hidden. And I hear him plot and plan and it makes me kind of sad, but man, I love to stand at the top of those little steps and breathe in his sweat.

I turn out the light at 7.30 - the switch is on my floor, at the top of the stairs - and I lock the door. But first I make them say 'Goodnight and thank you for looking after me', because that is what I would've said each night to my mom and dad if they had stuck around. That is what my little Aylisha would say to me each night, if those prim city bitches had believed I was clean, and let me keep her.

I hear the kids talking after the light's off, even over the noise from next door and the deaf-aid lady clomping about in the place above. They don't know I listen, but the sound carries real well. There's this hole in the flue leading up from down there, see, where the last tenant must've punched right through the wall or something.

'How many weeks has it been now, Doctor?' I hear Victoria whisper. Jimmy's told her off before for asking that question so often, and she's tried staying quiet, but I guess she always finds it worse being trapped away underground when she's had her weekly trip outside.

'Well, we've had eight faces painted, now,' murmurs the Doctor. 'So that's eight weeks.'

'It feels like forever,' she says. 'At least when we were locked up before we were normal. We were *us*.'

'We're still us, Victoria,' says the Doctor, but it don't even sound like *he* believes it.

'Have you seen those jars yon big lass keeps in her room?' Jamie sounds thoughtful. 'I reckon we might find our faces in one of those.'

He cracks me up, and I take another swig of vodka. He's talking about a couple of bell jars I got stowed behind the couch, you can just see them from the hallway. I keep pennies and quarters in one and rubber bands, hair grips, all kinds of crap in the other. No faces, kid.

The Doctor's got this kind of flat note to his voice, like he can't believe he has to say this out loud. 'Jamie, I've told you before, I'm sure our faces haven't really been taken. It's a trick of some kind.'

'Well, have you no' got the trick to get us them back again?'

I hold my breath, stop crunching chips, while I wait for his reply.

'Not yet,' he says defensively. 'But I'm sure I shall.'

'You've been sure for a long time,' says Victoria softly, 'but we're still like this.'

I take another swig. 'You and me both, honey,' I mutter.

'The facial nerve is unaffected,' says the Doc, and then he's spouting off at them: 'We can still control the muscles in our faces, the glands in our palates still function effectively, taste-buds in the anterior two-thirds of the –'

'*We have no faces, Doctor*,' Victoria hisses, and from her breathing it's like she's building up to a conniption. 'And I can't bear it. Stuck down here out of the light, out of the sun... These dreadful, shapeless clothes, greasy, sickly food, smelly paint all over my face...'

'I know it's very difficult, but you must save your strength, Victoria,' says the Doctor firmly. 'Whoever's done this to us wants to diminish us, to wear us down, to make us despair.'

'The way it hurts to breathe, like you're breathing through a pillow,' Victoria carries on like he's not spoken. And he doesn't butt in again, just lets her speak about how hard her life is now.

I sit there listening and crunching my chips and gulping my drink and getting real mad, and I feel like going down there and kicking Victoria's skinny white ass and telling her to shut her mouth with all her complaining, 'cept she don't have one. Then I get to feeling kind of sorry for them all again.

And I get to wishing I could tell Face-Painter the whole story about them, next time I see him. Tell him how the big man pays me and all, for taking care of them, and how he chose me 'cause he knows I don't use, and he knows I used to take care of my girl real good till they took her away, and how he thinks that helping my little faceless kids will help me too. And it's true, I do feel better about myself. Still down, but better than I have in a long, long time.

I hear the guys next door screaming at their TV. I wonder if they've ever looked at my place and noticed anyone's alive in it.

And I get up and flick on the basement light and shout down to the boy, 'Hey, Jimmy. I want to see you up here. Just you. Let's go.'

And I wait till I hear him coming up the stairs. 'You try any tricks on me,' I warn him, 'and something real bad's gonna happen to your friends. *He'll* see to that.' He stays quiet. 'So promise me, no tricks.'

He promises, and so I turn the key and let him out.

He stands there, still dressed in his faded jeans and loose white T-shirt and if I'd drunk any more tonight I might really think I was looking at Brad Pitt. Face-Painter is good, and Jimmy's looking fine.

'What do you want?' he asks, suspicious-like.

'I want to show you something,' I say. And I take his hand and lead him in a passable straight line over to the jars behind the couch.

He sees them and his shoulders slump.

'I don't have your faces stowed away here, Jimmy boy.'

'Aye, well. Mebbe you keep them in another jar.'

I shake my head. 'What is it with you and the jar thing, huh?'

'All I know is, I went to sleep two months ago with a face and when I woke up it was gone.' He thumps his fist into his hand. 'And how can that be? And why are we being kept here with you, week after week?'

It's amazing, I'm hearing all this anger but Brad's face is placid and pure, smiling at me. It makes me want to smile back at him. 'Maybe someone wanted to borrow your faces,' I say. 'Maybe someone's running round pretending to be you, having such a ball they don't want to give you your face back.' I place my hand on his chest. Been so long since I touched a man. 'Was it good being you, honey? I bet it was real sweet, huh?'

He angles his bald head down to my carpet. I know he's sad. 'Someone else might have my face, you say?'

'Maybe. But what do I know?'

He turns around, away from me, and for a second I press my hand against his back. I guess I don't know what I'm doing. I'm feeling sorry for him, or for myself, but I'm thinking maybe my kids deserve better than this. Better than what's been given to them. Better than what I can give to them. And I know then I've had too much to drink because I'm feeling kind of warm and thinking maybe I can change and start that diet or save for the surgeon, and get myself straight and maybe get Aylisha back... All that crap.

And I'm thinking next week I might ask Face-Painter to put his own face on Jimmy's empty slate. Or tomorrow. Maybe I could go back tomorrow, who says I should wait for a week? He was mean to do that to Victoria's face, she would maybe lighten up if I took her back and got him to do it fresh. We would all feel better.

He turns back round and I take my hand away. He reaches for it, holds it softly in his.

'You lonely?' I whisper. 'Only I know what that's like, feeling lonely even when you got people there in your face, all around.' I could put my arms around him and shut my eyes and pretend he was someone real. I want to put out the lights and hold him and we could just -

He twists my hand. 'Give us back our faces!' he yells. 'Where have you put them?'

'You promised!' I yell at him.

'Where, woman!'

I swear and shout, though no one will hear me. They'll hear the game and those damn dogs, but they won't hear me. I struggle against him but he's reaching in to my pocket and groping for the key, and he's squeezing his hand there against my gut and I feel ashamed of what he must think when he feels all that flab, and then he's got the key and I'm hard on my knees on the floor, crying my eyes out, and I'm too drunk to get back up. There's a confused babble of voices from the basement, it carries right up to me. Then the three of them are suddenly free and skipping about my living room, and it's about the only real living been done there in years.

'Don't go,' I say, snot-nosed and dribbling, wiping my eyes. I liked looking after them. Been feeling happier. A better person.

'Doctor, what are you waiting for?' Victoria says, high and hysterical, hovering by the front door. 'Come on!'

'But she's right.' The Doctor's hopping from foot to foot like he just wet his blue jeans or something. That crazy sunflower face moves from side to side. 'Something bad might happen to us if we do this.'

'You're not wanting to go back down there!' Jimmy shouts.

'Each time we escape we're punished!' he yells. 'Something's taken away from us!' His hands hover round his pockets like he wants to stick them inside, but the pants are too tight. 'What will we lose next? Our voices? Our sight? Our freedom even to *think*?'

'What'll happen if we just stay here?' Jimmy insists. 'Nothing! Nothing ever! We have to get away!'

'We won't find our faces in any jar outside!' the Doctor storms, the centre of the sunflower one big eye staring out from the bald face. 'We won't find them hanging on a peg somewhere, ready for us to slip back on.' He holds out his hands to his friends. 'I've told you, we're suffering from some kind of illusion, a spell that's been placed on us somehow. That's all. We'll find a way out of this, I promise you. But if we try to leave now...'

Victoria and Jimmy stand there, all crumpled in their jeans and T-shirts. Brad looks calm and assured. The girl painted on Victoria's face has lines in all the wrong places. She looks terrible, small and frail in the oversized clothes I picked out for her. And the TV noise goes on outside, the tethered-up dogs bark same as every night.

'Listen to that dreadful din,' says Victoria quietly. 'Where could we run to, Jamie?'

She comes over and stands in front of me, where I'm still kneeling and snorting and crying and stuff. And she does this little curtsey and says, 'Thank you for looking after me. Goodnight.'

And down she goes to the basement.

The Doctor holds out his hand to Jimmy, who turns and faces the door. The Doctor stands there with his arm out for a full minute till Brad Pitt turns round and takes it, and they go down the steps holding hands.

The door swings quietly shut behind them. The key is still in the lock.

I turn that key.

'You promised,' I bellow down at the things shut behind the basement door. And I scream and I fling open my front door and I march out and hurl the key away into the noisy night, and then I follow it.

Next morning I pitch up at Face-Painter's, with all the cash I got – money that was meant for the kids, but screw them. They want to screw with me? No way.

He opens at 9.30. I hear bolts sliding and then the door opens up. He sees me. He's wearing his shades and I can't blame him; the sunlight's too bright and too yellow. I only wish I could find mine in all the crap back home.

'Hey,' says Face-Painter, and puts his sign out on the sidewalk. His biceps bulge under his shirt, and his tight gut spills over his waistband. I can see the little hairs standing up there. 'You all alone today?'

I don't want to talk about it. 'That sunflower you did yesterday? I want it.'

'Tattoo?' he asks. 'You sure?'

'Sure. I know I don't got an appointment, but...'

'Only, you know, a tattoo's for life.'

'I want it.'

'And they cost. Those designs.'

'I want it, Face-Painter. For life.'

'That's a real long time.'

But he beckons me and then I'm walking into his cool, sweat-stinking shop, right to the back, and I'm sitting on the leather, and thinking of Jimmy last night and how it felt to be touching his back and feel the warm skin beneath his shirt.

'Why d'you come to me, Rachel?' he asks, as he sorts through his inks.

'You're the best in the west,' I tell him, but he's looking at my eyes like he can see they're blotchy and red from all the tears last night.

'No. You come to me because it's the rules,' he says, flicking on the TV for reruns of some old black and white show. 'Thursday afternoons, time to take the faceless kids down to get painted. You don't come here any other time. So why'd you break the rules?'

'What you talking about?'

'Those three freaks of yours. You were getting good money taking care of them. So why'd you blow it?' He sounds like he's pissed at me, like he knows all about last night. 'You had to go and break the rules. You had to go and spoil things for yourself. You told the boss man you were through spoiling things for yourself.' He comes up close and he places one big hand on my face, holds it real tight, squeezes.

And I'm crying out in his quiet little shop, 'I just wanted to do something for me. This damn city's so loud you never get heard.' His fingers are digging in hard. 'Listen, I want the sunflower, that's all.' My voice is coming out all slurred and muffled through his thick fingers. 'I want to be looked at. I want to be *seen*.'

Face-Painter shakes his head. 'In this part of town,' he says, reaching for his needles, 'no one looks too hard at no one for long unless they want trouble.'

And behind his shades I see he ain't got no eyes. It's just bare skin. And I know he's gonna take something from me, and it might be my stupid mouth or my stupid cry-baby eyes but I reckon maybe he'll leave my ears because he knows I hate this damn town being so noisy all the God-damn time, and he knows I ain't never getting out, I guess just like my three kids are never getting out now and who'll take us down here on a Thursday? And my ears are full of the sound of screams and they're all mine as his smile falls away, and that big empty space where Face-Painter's mouth was is pressing up to me.

Losing Track of Time

Juliet E McKenna

'Have you ever been to Oxford, Jo?' The Doctor smiled down at her as he pushed open the TARDIS's exterior door.

'No, never.' Jo stepped cautiously out and found herself standing on grass, in front of an imposing building of golden stone. 'Ever.'

'I always find it very civilised.' The Doctor turned to lock the door. 'Not inclined to change much either, which makes it unusually restful for people like ourselves.'

'Doctor,' said Jo uncertainly. 'What's that?'

The Doctor glanced over at the other blue police box sitting in front of the Natural History Museum, casts of dinosaur footprints marching past. 'It's an exhibit, I believe. There's a great deal more to art in this decade than paint on canvas. Still, it makes this a very convenient place to leave the TARDIS. Come along, my dear.'

Pocketing the key, he led the way down the broad, tree-lined street in high good humour. There was little traffic, the autumn morning sun shone on Oxford's celebrated spires ahead, and a slight breeze ruffled the Doctor's shock of silver hair. On the far side of the road, a limestone wall dark with lichen hid ornate gardens and immaculate lawns, glimpsed briefly through the black curves of a pair of wrought iron gates. The Doctor paused to let a bicycle skid past him, and stepped past a harassed rider fumbling for a chain and lock. More students were hurrying in and out of the main gate of a college, burdened with books and bags.

'That's the other thing about Oxford,' the Doctor said softly. 'Everyone's so wrapped up in their own affairs and so used to visitors wandering around, newcomers rarely warrant a second glance.'

'I'd have thought the clothes would be a bit more different,' Jo commented, smoothing the jacket of her black trouser suit as she studied a laughing gaggle of girls disappearing into the college, flared jeans flapping above chunky soled boots and shoes.

'Fads and fancies come and go.' The Doctor adjusted the cuffs of his navy velvet jacket with a flourish as they skirted a clutter of cycles and passed a pub. 'Style never really goes out of fashion.'

'I didn't imagine the future would smell so strongly of coffee.' They reached a cross roads and Jo glanced up the broad street towards a bustling crowd of shoppers. 'And when did buses stop being red?'

'My dear,' the Doctor said with affectionate amusement as they halted at the kerb. 'I realise you're very new to time travel, but this is only a brief visit. Can the questions wait?'

'Yes, of course.' Jo gazed at the array of statues adorning a striking classical building in the form of a triumphal arch. More stone heads, Roman-nosed and crowned with laurel wreaths, punctuated a row of iron railings to the right, the elaborate confection of a theatre behind them crowned with a frivolous cupola. Beyond, a plain square building rose past three rows of blankly shrouded windows to a rampart-like roofline. 'Where are we going?'

'The Bodleian library,' The Doctor reminded her as they crossed the empty road and climbed a flight of broad stone steps. They passed through the arch of the triumphant building to emerge onto a square of gravel cut by flagstone walkways, one leading to another arch piercing the forbidding square building. Jo looked around, open mouthed as people passed in and out of the shadowed entrance. The Doctor gestured up towards one of the windows. 'You recall that strange piece of metal the Brigadier was sent from that dig on Salisbury Plain? I knew there was something familiar about it, and I remembered last night that I'd read an article in the *Journal of Roman Studies*, for the year 20-'

'Doctor!' Jo clutched his arm suddenly. 'That man, he just walked into that wall!'

'Where?' The Doctor's amiable manner turned instantly alert. 'Like a ghost? Or was there some sign of a dimensional portal?'

'No, I mean he walked into *the wall*,' said Jo urgently. 'That man there. He came out here and then he spun around and walked straight into the wall.' She pointed at a tweed-jacketed man in early middle age who was struggling to rise from his knees, hands scrabbling ineffectually at the ancient stone. 'Doctor, he's hurt himself, and broken his glasses, look!'

'So I see,' said the Doctor, concerned. They hurried over to help the man to his feet.

'My dear fellow, let's give you a hand. You've had something of a turn by the looks of it.' The Doctor's voice was calm and reassuring as he produced a fine linen handkerchief to wipe away the blood trickling down the man's cheek, the other hand encouraging him to lean against the wall. A swift glance took in the plastic-coated card clipped to the man's lapel identifying him as a librarian and the Doctor studied him more closely, eyes intense.

'I was in the stacks,' the librarian mumbled, bemused, his face cruelly scratched. He clutched at the broken frame of his glasses with nerveless fingers. 'Don't know what happened. Lost track of time.'

'Yes, you did, didn't you, old chap?' Deftly, the Doctor pinched the back of the man's curiously wrinkled hand and noted how slowly the fold of skin subsided. Jo looked at him, a question in her eyes.

'Let's get you back to your office, find you a cup of tea.' The Doctor passed the handkerchief to Jo and helped the man to his feet. 'Through there.' He nodded at an archway leading to the hollow quadrangle of the Bodleian, where the bronze statue on his marble plinth looked down at them with blank indifference. Jo hurried ahead and opened the door the Doctor was heading for, a blue and gold title above it in ageless Latin.

'Up there, it's the second door on the left, first floor.' The Doctor helped the librarian up the stairs, expertly supporting him with one hand around his back, the other beneath his elbow.

'This one, Doctor?' Jo knocked hesitantly and tried the handle. 'Hello, we need some help.'

The door opened to reveal a girl much Jo's age in sensible shoes, a plain brown sweater and a corduroy skirt. 'Yes?' Then she caught sight of the Doctor and his burden. 'Edmund!'

'We found him in the quad,' the Doctor explained as the three of them got the collapsing librarian into the office. 'Seems to have had some kind of faint.'

'Oh dear.' The junior librarian looked concerned. 'There's this 'flu going around, though he was fine this morning – '

'You saw him yourself?' asked the Doctor with just a hint of urgency.

'Yes.' The girl looked at Jo and the Doctor with the first stirrings of curiosity. 'I'm sorry, I didn't catch your name.'

'I think you should call an ambulance.' The Doctor made sure the librarian was safely resting in a low chair and walked briskly to the door. 'If you'll excuse us. Jo, we're going to be late.'

'Yes, Doctor.' She hurried after him, pulling the door closed behind her at his nod.

The Doctor lifted a finger to his lips and they listened for a moment. The junior librarian was already on the phone.

'In the office, yes. No, he was outside. Some visiting academic found him, a Doctor somebody, with his research assistant.'

The Doctor nodded with satisfaction. 'This way,' he mouthed to Jo and walked on light feet further down the corridor to another staircase.

'Where are we going?' Jo whispered as they made their way down the dusty oak-lined stairwell.

'The book stacks,' said the Doctor grimly. 'Our friend Edmund most certainly lost track of time down there, several days from the temporal shock in his eyes and the dehydration confusing him. We'd better find out what's going on.'

'Us?' Jo looked uncertainly at the door at the bottom of the stairs, where a stern sign forbade access to unauthorised personnel.

The Doctor knelt to apply his sonic screwdriver to the lock. 'I don't think there's anyone else qualified hereabouts, do you?' He glanced up at Jo.

'No, Doctor,' she replied with resolve. 'But how do we know we won't get all confused as well?'

'We're already out of our own time, so that's far less likely.' The Doctor stood and opened the door carefully. 'Stay close to me. These stores are enormous, reaching right underneath the library buildings in both directions.' He pointed to a yellow line painted on the floor. 'Even the people who work here sometimes need that to show them the way out.' He smiled.

'Right,' said Jo a trifle nervously.

The Doctor closed the door behind them, shutting out the sunshine from the stairwell's tall windows. The lights in the vast book store were dim strips running overhead amid a tangle of pipes and conduits. Ranks of tall metal shelves ran away on either side, disappearing into the gloom, packed tight with countless volumes in cracked and faded bindings. The air was dry, scented with papery dust, and utterly still.

'There's definitely something amiss here. That should be sending books up to the reading rooms for one thing.' The Doctor pointed at a motionless arrangement of conveyor belts. 'This way.'

He set off without hesitation, taking one turn then another through the ominous, looming shelves. Jo followed close behind, looking this way and that as they left the door to the stairs far behind. A pale crumpled shape down one dark turn caught her eye. 'Doctor!'

He whirled round and looked to see where she was pointing. Apprehensive, Jo followed the Doctor down a dead end. He knelt down, and Jo saw they had found a body.

'Is she dead?' Jo whispered fearfully.

'Yes.' Grim faced, the Doctor rolled the desiccated corpse over, a limp bundle of famished skin and bone in a stained and tattered dress that might once have been green.

Jo shuddered at the sight of the aged, shrunken face, bloodless lips drawn back in a soundless scream over discoloured teeth, half-open eyes sunken and dull in their sockets. The woman's long hair was a tangled mess, her fingernails chipped talons of ridged yellow, the skin of her withered hands like parchment.

'That's horrible,' Jo whispered.

'It is, Jo. And we really must put a stop to it.' The Doctor held up an ID tag and Jo saw a photograph of a friendly middle-aged woman with neatly cut short hair. He laid the dead woman's hands gently by her sides with a sigh. 'We can't be far from the heart of it now, if she was aged so rapidly.'

Footsteps silent, he led the way deeper into the labyrinth of shelves. Jo followed so close behind she was in danger of treading on his heels. When he stopped abruptly, she stifled a startled squeak. The Doctor took a stealthy pace backwards and moved slightly to one side. 'There,' he murmured.

Jo looked past his blue velvet shoulder to see a curious purplish light, shimmering in an open space where the conveyor belt rose upwards through a wire-caged shaft. There were two grey figures busy with a pile of books, more heaped high on trolleys to either side. These definitely weren't librarians. About as tall as Jo herself, the two creatures could barely claim to have a face, just a pair of many-faceted ruby eyes - shining eerily in the light from a large sphere, set in a triangular silver frame. Their lumpish heads joined stocky bodies without any suggestion of a neck and flowed straight to the ground like a pillar of clay. They had what passed for arms and hands, four apiece, fingerless yet deft, stretching and shrinking as they reached for more books, intent on feeding them into a squat box that glittered briefly as each volume vanished.

The Doctor signalled Jo to retreat and they crept back to the end of the shelves that hid them from the creatures.

'Tynakars,' whispered the Doctor curtly. 'I don't know how they managed to find their way here past the Time Lords' interdicts, but they'll steal as much of humanity's knowledge as they can, curse them.'

Jo spread helpless hands. 'Why?'

'To sell, my dear,' the Doctor replied with contempt. 'To sell without thought or scruple, in return for the minerals and salts they need to perpetuate their kind. They've destroyed whole civilisations, whole planets in their time, without a second thought. They live largely outside the usual timelines, so such things mean little to them.'

'How?' whispered Jo, incredulous. 'How do they destroy things by stealing books?'

'They steal knowledge.' The Doctor raised one finger. 'Then they'll sell the secrets of something like dynamite or machine guns to civilisations who've yet to invent anything more lethal than bows and arrows. That's easily enough done, for a quick profit. Better yet, for a higher price, they can fill crucial gaps in the knowledge of planets whose science has taken a different path. There are few things more valuable than information your rivals haven't got and have no means of discovering. Knowledge can change the fate of galaxies. The common cold wouldn't have stopped Wells's Martians if the Tynakars had sold them some basic bio-engineering.' He raised a second finger. 'Or if you're planning to invade another world, some more advanced culture, you can cripple your victim by stealing crucial knowledge from them, undermining the very basis of their learning.'

'You think Earth's going to be invaded?' gasped Jo.

'I doubt it.' The Doctor stole another glance at the featureless aliens. 'No, they're just here for whatever they can steal. But they're not just taking those books, Jo. They're stealing all the awareness of the learning within them, taking them right out of the Earth's timeline. Once those books are gone, from a library holding this much knowledge, mankind could lose half its awareness of physics or mathematics, the keys to understanding atomic power or space flight. Earth's technological development, mankind's understanding of the universe, they'll all be crippled. Scientists will have to go back to rediscovering first principles,' he concluded bleakly.

'Unless we stop them?' Jo looked anxiously back but there was no sign that the creatures realised they were discovered, just the continuous shuffle and thump of books fed into the deadly maw of the Tynakar box.

'That's the spirit.' The Doctor gave Jo a nod of encouragement, his eyes bright in the gloom. 'As long as they're still here, we've got a chance. That sphere, in the silver casing, that's their dimension penetration device. That's what's keeping them here. If we can shut that down, they'll be sucked back to their own planet.'

'How do we do that?' Jo looked round again.

'*I* do that.' The Doctor held her by the shoulders and looked intently at her. '*You* have to get that box, the one they're putting the books in. You have to get it as far away from the sphere as possible, or it'll just be sucked back to the Tynakar dimension as well. We have to keep it here, so the link is broken and all this malice is undone.'

'How do I do that?' Jo's voice quavered just a little.

'I'll distract them,' the Doctor promised. 'They'll recognise a Time

Lord and they'll know that means trouble for their whole pestilential race if I take word of this back to Gallifrey. As soon as I lure them away, you grab the box and run. Follow the yellow line on the floor to one of the exits.'

'Right.' Jo nodded determinedly.

'Good girl,' said the Doctor warmly. Squaring his shoulders, he strolled casually out into the open space by the book conveyor. 'You know,' he drawled, 'I really don't think you should be doing that, do you? Didn't you creatures learn your lesson on Kelak II?'

Jo crept to the end of the shelves. Both creatures had turned to face the Doctor, dull grey arms lengthening and growing talons that hardened to a diamond sheen. The closest opened a mouth to hiss and as Jo watched, the lipless orifice sprouted a myriad razor-sharp teeth. The other was growing taller, the amorphous mass of its body splitting into long legs with claw-tipped feet. It took a step towards the Doctor, putting itself between him and the dimension device.

The Doctor smiled and reached into his jacket for his sonic screwdriver. 'You don't think I came unprepared, do you?' Then, abruptly, he darted sideways and vanished behind a set of shelves. The first Tynakar pursued him while the second one shot upwards, almost snakelike as its head brushed the cluttered dusty pipes of the ceiling, strip lights striking rainbows from its faceted red eyes as it looked this way and that.

Jo watched as it showed no sign of moving away from the evil box on the table. As she wrung her hands in unconscious anguish, her rings dug painfully into her fingers. Inspiration struck. Twisting a heavy silver band free, she lobbed it high over the shelves to clink on the ground behind the Tynakar. The creature's head whipped round and it peered into the darkness. Lips tight with frustration, Jo threw a second ring, one of her favourites, set with a chunk of amber. It rattled down one of the metal fixtures and the second Tynakar immediately grew legs, creeping toward the noise with a wet slither on the tiled floor. Jo watched, tense as it disappeared behind a battered metal bookcase.

She darted out of her hiding place and grabbed the square box the creatures had been feeding books into. It was heavy and unwieldy, sharp corners digging painfully into her arms as she looked for the yellow line that the Doctor had told her to follow. There it was. Hugging the mysterious box tightly, Jo ran through the musty gloom. She had barely made a second turn when a chilling cry echoed around the endless maze of the underground store. Jo froze for an instant.

From somewhere behind her, she heard the slap of shapeless feet on the tiles and a faint malevolent hiss. Then everything went black. Jo bit her lip on a whimper of panic. The lights had gone out, that was all. She blinked and realised that dim red emergency lights had come on.

Jo ran, seeking out the yellow line on the floor in the half light. She turned, left, right, right again and came up hard against a wall of black tomes as tall as the Brigadier's biggest atlas. Faint light shone on the gilded titles on the spine.

Peterborough Echo, Jul-Dec, 1907

She looked down to see the yellow line disappear straight under the impenetrable shelving. Whirling round, she found more volumes of newspapers cutting off the path she'd just followed. Everything had been twisted around her.

What was it the Doctor had been saying about time? That it was all the same as space or something? A chill shook Jo, freezing the sweat trickling down her spine. If these Tynakar creatures couldn't confuse her perceptions of time, it certainly looked as if they could mess with the space around her. The sound of stealthy feet and a breathy hiss somewhere off to her left drove all such thoughts out of her mind. She looked fearfully into the ruddy gloom. The noise had stopped, if it had been there in the first place, if she hadn't just imagined it. There was nothing there. Or was there? She noticed a faint ruby sheen deep within a shadow. She blinked and looked again and this time saw the faceted roundel of a Tynakar eye just catching the light as the creature lurked, motionless, in wait.

Gritting her teeth and holding the box tight, Jo hurried away from the monstrous alien. She had no idea where she was going but the Doctor had just said to get the box away from the dimension device, hadn't he? She just prayed she didn't find herself heading back towards that eerie purple light.

Turning a corner, she choked back a scream as she tripped over the remains of the dead librarian. Time was still devouring the corpse, now barely more than a pile of rags and bones crumbling to anonymous dust as Jo's square toed boots inadvertently scattered them. Shuddering with revulsion, she fled, right, right again, left, left again. Rounding another identical, indistinguishable set of shelves, strong arms caught her. She drew breath for a scream of sheer terror.

'Hush!' The Doctor laid a firm yet gentle hand over her mouth.

Jo's shriek turned to a startled gasp. 'Doctor? Did you do it?'

'I'm afraid not,' he said grimly. 'There are more of them down here, not just the two we saw. I've been leading them all away from the dimension device as best I can.' He looked down at Jo, face unearthly in the faint light. 'I'm afraid I must ask you to be the decoy now, if we're to stand any chance of doing this. Can you do that?'

'I haven't got anything else on, not at the moment.' Jo gripped the heavy Tynakar box, her palms sweating even though her hands were cold. Her arms and back were aching and fear was a solid weight in the pit of her stomach. 'But which way do I go? They're shifting everything around somehow.' Try as she might to stay calm, her voice rose with a hint of panic.

'You noticed that? Good girl.' The Doctor approved warmly. 'Just keep bearing left, that should do it. I won't need long.' Turning her with inexorable hands, he sent her on her way before disappearing into the darkness.

Jo drew a deep, shaky breath and lugged the hateful box onwards. Left, always left, never mind the seductive lure of the yellow line catching her eye here and there with a promise of escape. She turned a corner and skidded to a halt as she saw the movement ahead. The blurred outline of a Tynakar resolved itself into a spidery figure, wiry arms already reaching out as it took long-legged strides towards her. She whirled round but another was coming up behind her, squat and toad-like as it scuttled along the floor, eyes gleaming a venomous red.

Jo saw her only escape; a narrow space between close packed shelves standing end on to the aisle. She forced herself into the gap, books sticking out from the shelves catching at her shoulders and elbows, knocking her painfully and covering her in ancient grime. A sneeze wracked her and then a second, her eyes stinging and the harsh dust tearing at her throat. She pressed on, twisting from side to side to drive the loathsome Tynakar box past the obstructive books. Finally pausing for breath, she tried to hear past the thudding of her own heart for any sound of the Tynakars pursuing her. What she heard was a steady clicking noise. Puzzled, Jo tried to work out where it was coming from. She looked down and saw grooves in the floor by her feet, chains just visible in the dimness. The clicking came again and she saw the chains slide with oily indifference.

It wasn't her imagination. These shelves were on some kind of roller mechanism and the Tynakars had found the handle, were using it to close the gap, trapping her. Dread threatened to choke her, but Jo tried to go on. It was no good. The merciless shelves pressed relentlessly inwards, books digging painfully into her thighs, crushing her arms against the alien box. She was stuck so tight it was a struggle to breathe. She screwed her eyes shut on tears of fear and anger. Paper rustled. Was that some Tynakar stretching out an impossibly long, thin arm to reach her even as she was caught between the shelves? Jo did her best to lift the box a bit higher. She could hit any questing tentacles with that, if nothing else.

Then the clicking noise came again and the iron grip holding her slackened, just a little at first then more quickly. Jo stood, frozen, fearful, looking this way and that. As the sliding shelves moved far enough apart for her to see, she saw the unmistakable outlines of Tynakars waiting at either end, white claws fringing their multiple hands and wide mouths lined with fangs.

With a book as long as his arm and almost as thick, the Doctor appeared and smashed the eyes of one with a nauseating soggy thump. The crimson orbs shattered like glass and the creature dissolved into a shapeless lump of grey ooze. 'Come on, Jo!' He made as if to throw aside the book then caught himself, carefully wiping slime from the cover and placing it carefully on a shelf. 'I beg your pardon, Sir Isaac.'

The Doctor held out a hand and Jo ran towards him, hearing the second creature hissing malevolently as it tried to catch her. The weight of the Tynakar box was almost unbearable by now, her arms numb as she clung to it, afraid she was going to drop it with every step. She threw herself out into the open space at the end of the shelving and the Doctor spun a wheel to close the gap on the pursuing Tynakar. 'Well done, my dear! Now, let me take that and let's get out of here'.

Relinquishing the box gladly, Jo looked at the fallen Tynakar. 'Is it dead?' The ooze was twitching, lumps rising and falling within it, globules sliding away and then flowing back.

'Not really.' The Doctor nodded towards a distant corner. 'Come on. I've wired their dimension device into the mains. It'll blow in a few minutes, and we really don't want to be too close.'

Her arms paradoxically aching even more now she'd given up the alien box, Jo hurried after him. The dim red of the emergency lights faded, to be replaced by the oily purple light of the dimension penetration sphere. Static electricity drove Jo's feathery hair into clinging, drifting madness. Her feet felt leaden and not just through tiredness. It was as if the air was thickening around them, slowing them more and more. She looked back and saw a Tynakar had reached its fallen comrade. The monster plucked one faceted eye from its own head and thrust it into the incoherent mess. The fallen Tynakar reared up at once, making a vicious, spitting noise.

'Here.' The Doctor's voice sounded as if it was coming from some unimaginable distance away, and the door he was pointing to looked even further away than that. They struggled towards it, the Doctor almost bent double by the burden of the Tynakar box. Jo grabbed the handle and shook it. Locked. She tried to snatch the alien box from the Doctor but the best she could manage was an endless slow fumble with numb hands. The Doctor reached for his sonic screwdriver with an agonising leisureliness and thrust it at the lock. The door sprang open and Jo fell through it, the crushing weight of the purple light suddenly lifted by the bright sunlight flooding through the windows beyond.

The Doctor reeled through the door and slammed it, leaning against the chipped and flaking varnish. A flash of purple radiance outlined him, and then it was all over. Jo prodded the Tynakar box that she'd been struggling with for what felt like half a lifetime. It fell over with a tinny, empty clang.

'Did we do it?' she wondered aloud.

'We did, my dear,' said the Doctor with a satisfied sigh.

As he spoke, the box began disgorging books. They cascaded across the floor, all shapes and sizes, from slim pamphlets to heavy bound copies of learned journals. Modern volumes in dour black bindings slipped across weightier tomes in fine Moroccan red or cracked brown leather, the gilt on their spines worn to illegibility. A few loose pages fluttered free, yellowed paper spotted with age, the print ornamented with curlicues and engraving. Jo found herself waist deep in the learning of centuries inside moments and began frantically stacking, to save them both from being crushed.

'You really did very well in there, my dear.' The Doctor fended off a tottering wall of books as he applied the sonic screwdriver to an outer door, humming under his breath as he did so. 'I really am most impressed. Thank you.'

Jo coloured slightly. 'So what do we do now?'

'I don't think we need wait around for some irate librarian to ask just why all these books need reshelving, do you?' The Doctor smiled with sudden impishness as he tidied the dishevelled ruffles of his shirt. 'You might like to dust yourself off a little, by the way.'

He moved on light feet up the stairs and deftly unlocked a door leading out into the imposing quadrangle of the library. Jo followed him out, brushing herself down as best she could.

'What about the Brigadier's bit of metal?' She looked up at the gleaming windows of the heedless reading rooms high above.

'That can wait,' the Doctor said firmly. He strode across the ancient flagstones and led the way through an iron-gated arch to the sunny splendour of a grassy square, medieval and renaissance buildings set cheek by jowl in companionable awe of the boastful dome of the central library building. Students and scholars hurried or sauntered about their business, depending on inclination and Jo shook her head, marvelling.

'They've no idea, have they, that all this nearly fell apart, right under their feet, to be lost for ever.'

'But it didn't, did it? There may be more things in heaven and earth, more terrors than most people dream of, but it really doesn't do to dwell on them, certainly not once the peril's passed,' the Doctor said easily. 'Come on, Jo: the Brigadier's book can wait; let's find a coffee bar. That's another thing about this decade: you're seldom more than a stone's throw from one, for some reason. I think we've earned a little time to ourselves.'

The Discourse of Flies

Jeremy Daw

'In the third year of the reign of the King of Clocks, Pyas the Goatherd lay down in the groves of his ancestors and dreamt... He touched the mind of the Machine.'

THE PROPHECY OF PYAS, CH. 2 V. 1, 4; THE FIRST BOOK OF THE MACHINE

The night breeze whispers gently through the sentinel trees. Their leafy branches sift the starlight. It drizzles languidly downwards, dappling the forest floor with spots of silver. In the short, springy grass, in the stumpy avaya *shrubs and the creeping, stringy growth of vines and flowering plants there is wondrous, joyous, glorious* life.

Aimarrh breathes in the tonic draft of the cool night air, thick with the delicate scent of corus *and* fij, *sharp with the tang of bark and earth. There is so much to be thankful for. So much moisture. So much greening. So much* life.

He raises his eyes to the night sky, to the stars glinting through the canopy like splinters of glass on a shady floor. He mouths the words of gratitude silently, not wishing to disturb the forest's quiet with vulgar speech.

The scent and serenity of the forest seem to call to him and his heart quickens as he begins to move further in. There is more than green life here. Small glossy rodents scurry nervously across his path. The shadows of night birds flutter gracefully at the edge of his vision. The soft grass cushions his feet as he walks. So much life.

The forest begins to thin and eventually Aimarrh reaches a clear space. The starlight paints the ground an ethereal silvery-green. Above him, the stars seem to burn brighter, colder, as if staring down at him with an implacable will. He shivers. For the first time the air around him seems cold, reproachful. The silence is thin and brittle. It sets his teeth on edge.

In the middle of the clearing, a squat humped shape sits. Moving towards it, the shape becomes more clearly defined and he realises that it is a solitary tree stump.

Aimarrh peers at it curiously. Something is obscuring its cleanly cut surface – something that makes small subtle movements, barely visible in the nocturnal light. There is sound, too – a rustling, soft susurration that builds in volume as he draws nearer.

Aimarrh takes another step. The stump casts a shadow across his path. As he moves into it, his feet seem to sink into the blackness. It flows over his toes and laps at his heel. Aimarrh frowns. This is wrong. He glances around him and gasps. The trees of the forest are transformed. No longer heavy with fleshy green leaves, they are stark and bare – twisted nightmare shapes, raising gnarled arthritic hands to the uncaring sky.

Where is the life?

The shadow at his feet moves. Aimarrh sees the strange surface of the tree stump bulge upwards. For a moment, his gaze is transfixed by a bulbous cancerous growth, twice the size of his own head, thrusting outwards from the severed wood. He sees his own face horribly distorted in the oily crimson skein stretched tight over a million quivering insect bodies.

With a soft wet ripping sound, a torrent of filthy black specks is disgorged into the night sky. Instinctively, Aimarrh flings his arms up in front of his face, but the stream of hissing blackness continues upwards, forming a thin column and then dispersing in a dark cloud above him. He tracks its movement across the sky. The light grows dim as the starlight fades. A cold wind whistles icily around him and he shivers involuntarily, wrapping his arms around his body, looking around him at the groaning nightmare trees that shudder as if in revulsion at the earth that holds them. His body is all that is left to him. The soft comfort of the grass, the peace of the trees, the stillness of the forest – it has all gone. He can find no solace in this place. He is alone.

The night sky hums with evil intent.

The stars flicker and go out.

The forest screams.

Plunged into darkness, Aimarrh resists the urge to run in panic, but he feels pain – wave upon wave of it crashing over him. The air is thick with it. The forest is dying. The forest fears…

Something is coming.

He hears a rumbling that seems to come from the earth itself. To his left, a series of loud cracks splits the air. They are followed by a mindless guttural roar. And then there is light. Harsh, searing light – cold and dispassionate. It blazes through the forest and Acharhh, squinting through agonised eyes, is astonished at how thin the tree trunks now seem as they thrust thin shadow fingers across the ground towards him.

The roaring grows and the bare trees snap into splinters and sawdust. Aimarrh can discern, pitched high above the bass rumble of shaking earth and juggernaut engine, the piercing insistent whine of lightning-fast axes and whirring saws. The words of the fourth catechism blossom incongruously in his mind.

We give our thanks to thee, O Lord, for in thy grasp we find shelter. In thy engine there is love. Receive from thy servants the detritus of the flesh that we may find comfort and safety in thy eternal perfection. Let it be so.

He stares. What is approaching him, in blinding light and crashing thunder, is far from perfection. It cannot be the Eternal Machine that has so occupied his thoughts these past few months. Yet it is a machine of sorts and, growling ferociously, pressing against his screwed tight eyes with an unwavering intensity of light, it bears down on him. He hears the harsh metallic snapping of vast steel pincers and whirring saws as it advances. He fancies he can hear the aggressive clanking of gears and the hungry gurgling of oil. Finally, his nerve breaks and he turns to run through the thrashing chaos of snapped tree limbs, churned-up earth and stinging whip-lashed dust.

The machine reaches out to him as he turns, impaling his left leg on the three glistening tines of a monstrous fork, and gracefully, with a smooth hydraulic motion, lifts him up to the boiling sky.

Pain courses through him. His blood streams down to the ground - below? Above? The world whirls around him - an impressionistic blur of the shattered forest, the roar of the machine that holds him, its foetid oily breath, the pressure of uncountable insect bodies colliding blindly against him...

He screams.

He sees, he hears, he feels a whirring metal blade precisely and efficiently sever his arm just below the shoulder. He watches it fall away and disappear in the darkness around him.

...we may find comfort and safety in thy eternal perfection...

He screams and the insects fill his mouth. Their dry, vibrating bodies clog his throat, his ears, his nostrils. They gnaw at the bloodied stump of his arm and cram themselves into the gashes and incisions in his flesh.

... the detritus of the flesh...

His body is broken like a twig by the implacable, unfathomable will of the infernal machine. As his shattered form is released by the pincers that hold him and he tumbles towards the tree-strewn ground, he sees only destruction and death.

... in thy grasp we find shelter, in thy engine there is love...

Where is the life?

All hail! All praise the machine!

Where is the life?

All praise the death machine!

'In the hearts of the poor and outcast, the Machine pours the oil of its mercy. In their dreams there is truth.'

THE MEDITATIONS OF GORUN, STANZA 7

Aimarrh awoke with a start of fear. The dream slid from his mind slowly. For a moment, he could still hear the whine of the torture blades and feel the coldness of the steel claw's grip against his skin. He blinked away the last vestiges of sleep and, with them, the dream faded like a desert mirage. He licked his dry lips cautiously.

The dawn sun had just risen, he saw. It was not quite high enough to appear over the compound walls, yet the clouds in the sky to the east were the colour of roses.

He shifted underneath the thin simple sheet. The sheet was damp, though whether it was with his own fear-tinged sweat or the dew dripping from the *curis* branches above him, he could not tell. It was tradition for believers like him to sleep in the compound's groves, he knew. Tradition, unfortunately, had little regard for stiff limbs and aching backs.

Aimarrh sighed. The dream had been... intense, troubling. Was it possible that..?

'Good morning, Initiate Aimarrh.'

Aimarrh sat up gingerly. Sitting cross-legged a few feet away from him was a middle-aged man in engineer's robes, his face a network of fine lines and creases. His eyes seemed to twinkle in the early morning light. Aimarrh had no idea how long he had been sitting there.

'Good morning, Engineer Fyan. May the eternal light at the heart of the machine illumine your mind and...'

'I thank you for your greeting, Aimarrh,' the engineer interrupted mildly, 'but I believe we can dispense with the formalities at the moment. There'll be a good number of them later on today.' A good-natured smile briefly rearranged the lines of his face and Aimarrh felt his heart contract sharply with excitement. 'The Council has decided. You were visited in your sleep last night. The Machine has reached out to you and touched your mind. You are the Chosen. This day is your day.'

With an extraordinarily fluid movement, the engineer prostrated himself before Aimarrh, arms outstretched towards the young initiate, palms pressed flat against the hard-packed earth. Even though his face was bent towards the ground, Aimarrh could still hear Fyan's joyful baritone echo around the compound walls. 'All hail! All praise the Machine!'

Aimarrh echoed his refrain.

'All praise the Eternal Machine!'

After a frugal breakfast of berries and bread, the rest of the morning was spent in careful and ritualised preparation. There were rites of purification and rites of consecration, all ultimately leading up to the final ceremony - the reason for his stay in the compound, the Rite of Passing. Aimarrh underwent them earnestly, giving his undivided attention to each section of the litanies, noting the cadences and rhythms of the familiar words. This was the last time he would hear them.

He tried not to think about that. As much as the prospect of Passing excited him, it also filled him with apprehension. In a sense, this was only to be expected. The Passing was a long journey - the longest imaginable - and the engineers and even the High Machinist had spoken at length to him about the doubts and fears that other initiates had encountered before their Passings.

The body fears what the heart embraces.

True enough, he thought. He found himself returning to that proverb, uttered by the First Ascendant himself over five hundred years ago, throughout the rest of the morning.

The sun was just approaching its zenith and the shadows of the buildings that sprawled within the compound walls were at their shortest, when Engineer Fyan came to his cell, followed by two fresh-faced acolytes. The acolytes were carrying bundles of cloth in their arms. Fyan smiled.

'Your robes, Aimarrh,' he said. 'It is time for the investiture.'

The acolytes quietly laid their bundles on his cot and, eyes averted respectfully, left the room.

'How do you feel?'

The question startled Aimarrh. He had heard so many words uttered from so many mouths this morning, many of them addressing how he was *supposed* to feel, but Fyan's question was the first time anyone had actually asked him outright.

Aimarrh swallowed. 'Proud. Blessed. Honoured.' He smiled awkwardly. 'A touch impatient, perhaps.' He fingered the soft black and gold silk of the robes on his bed. 'Afraid.'

Fyan nodded. 'I understand. The Passing is a mystery and, like all unknown things, it trails its fear behind it as an army leads a flock of vultures.' He paused. 'But the army may still win its battle, and the vultures may feast on its enemies' flesh. So it is with the Passing. Each believer who makes the impossible journey to the stars is a victory for our people, Aimarrh – just as Pyas prophesied before the elders of Caim.' He grimaced ruefully. 'Perhaps that wasn't the best of examples. They did murder him, after all.'

Aimarrh shook his head. He understood that the older man was trying to humour him, but Pyas was one of the heroes of the Machinist faith. 'That is the point, Engineer Fyan. Pyas *knew* he was going to die, but sacrificed himself for the good of this land, for the greater victory he knew would follow. And even as his apparent defeat led to the establishing of the true faith in these lands, so each successive ascendant proves a victory for our faith out *there*.' He flung his arms out in a gesture that encompassed the compound, the world beyond it and the unknown universe beyond that. He felt emboldened by his words. He could see the Machine's plan as if it were spun from webs of gold and hanging in the air in front of him. He knew, he believed, he *understood*. 'The ritual of Passing, the breaking of the body – it is for a purpose, Engineer. "The treasure of the fruit..."'

'"...is the seed within." Yes, Aimarrh, I know.' Fyan was grinning now. 'I'm glad you've imbibed at least some of my wisdom.' Abruptly, he seized Aimarrh in a crushing hug. 'Your faith is an example to us all. I will miss you, but I am so *proud* of you.'

Aimarrh returned the older man's embrace. 'And I you, my teacher.'

Fyan broke away from the young initiate and moved towards the door. 'I must leave you to your preparations.' His eyes glistened. 'I shall be watching in the congregation. Be at peace.' With that he was gone.

Aimarrh turned to the piles of clothing. Soon the fear would be shed from his mind, even as the mind sheds the body to journey to the stars.

* * *

'It is the will of the Machine that the faith of our people be taken beyond our lands, beyond our world. This is the Mystery of the Machine; that in the canopy of night, in the worlds of the infidel, the minds of the faithful shine forth with a pure brilliance, unfettered by the frailties of the flesh.'

THE IMPOSSIBLE JOURNEY, JONEN,
HIGH MACHINIST IN THE REIGN OF THE QUEEN OF STARLINGS

'Passing formation! On my order... march!'

The clipped steely voice of the guard captain rang out across the compound courtyard. Aimarrh felt a heartbeat of pride and then stilled his wayward mind. He stood in the centre of a five-strong squad of guards. The early afternoon sun glinted off their polished silver armour, and sweat ran down their faces in the stifling heat. But their solemn expressions never wavered as they began to march slowly and deliberately across the courtyard, past the chapels and cloisters, out through the imposing double gates and into the city beyond.

At last, the Passing Parade had begun.

It was a two-mile march to the Sanctuary of Stars in the very centre of Hezrah. The streets were lined with the customary celebrants and revellers, some waving banners with the golden star on black background design of the Machinist faith. Despite their increased frequency in recent months, a Passing was an event around which the whole of the city united in fervent joy.

In the nobles' quarter, with its grand villas and spacious sloping gardens, the small procession was joined by a band of jubilant minstrels, their music a blaring, raucous hymn to the glory of the Machine. Aimarrh felt lifted by their song and also proud that he was so honoured in the seat of the city's wealth and privilege. The broad, clean roads and elegantly dressed residents, who waved and cheered their thanks, were far removed from the dusty streets and grinding poverty of his former home in the Den of Tears. His heart swelled with pride again. To think that he, a beggar's son, had been elevated to the status of initiate, traveller to the stars.

The parade gathered a variety of followers and marchers – flautists and percussionists, jugglers and acrobats, simple folk and servants, beggars and lords. They all, however, kept a respectful distance from the small well-armed group of men and their hallowed charge, who formed the group's head.

At the festival square in the merchants' quarter, the crowds were particularly thick. Extra squads of temple guards formed a narrow corridor through which the parade could move. The markets and stalls were a kaleidoscope of colours and smells. The crowds thronged and pressed forward. Their presence, their constant chatter and cheering, together with the stifling heat, began to feel oppressive. Insects, attracted to the bright cloths and fruit on the merchants' stalls, buzzed lazily around him.

There was a short delay while an over-enthusiastic reveller was restrained from breaking the cordon, as he attempted to reach the parade. Aimarrh watched as a trio of burly guards in the city militia's uniform dragged the protesting man away. The crowd muttered its reproof and Aimarrh sighed, glad that the parade would soon be moving again, and he could...

The narrow, cramped streets crawl with soldiers. The man falls to the filthy ground under a flurry of kicks and punches. He is screaming, protesting his innocence. He has done nothing wrong, he shrieks. He has a wife and children. Still they come on, their faces insane masks of brutal joy. They do not acknowledge the man's words. They do not care. The man on the floor curls up into a ball, face tucked up tight between his knees, but still the kicks and blows come. Steel-shod boots, gauntleted fists. He is crying now.

'Don't let him see! Don't let him see!'

The punishment stops. One of the guards bends down and hisses something in the man's ear. His shoulders shake and he whimpers in response. Apparently satisfied, the guard straightens up, signals to the others and swaggers away towards the government district. As he does so, he reaches out his hand to tousle the hair of a young boy who stands underneath the shade of a makeshift awning. The boy's mother pulls him fiercely to her and he smells the dirt in her rough robes and tastes the sweat of her fear. Then, she releases him as she runs to the broken form of her husband, mewling in the dirt like a wounded animal.

The rasping command of the guard captain brought Aimarrh back to himself with a jolt. His mind was awash with confusion. His father? He couldn't remember anything like that happening. He knew that his father had been a potter, before some sort of accident had lamed him when Aimarrh was a very young boy, but... Where had this remembrance come from? And why had it come to him now?

Flies buzzed uncaringly around his face. Absently, he swatted them away, as the parade moved on to its final stage.

* * *

Kharis watched the parade from the relative comfort of his small shop. The awning provided welcome shade and, with the parade attracting his would-be customers far more successfully than his displays of clocks and ornaments, the shop was nice and quiet, too. Of course, business would pick up once the parade had passed. There were plenty of nobles nearby who would doubtless love to buy a clock for their families as a souvenir of the day, but...

Kharis scratched his grey-stubbled chin uneasily. There was something in the air. Something he couldn't quite put his finger on. He'd watched parades of all sorts over the years. By oil and gear, he'd even been in the crowd that had watched old Felljar the Firebrand become the King of Dust, and there weren't many still trading who could say *that*. There was something different now, though. There were scowls as well as smiles on the faces of the crowd and he'd never noticed as many guards line the streets as he had today. Even the initiate hadn't looked as... serene as they normally did.

Kharis frowned grimly. It was those two strangers that had started it. It had been a slow morning and he'd even considered taking his afternoon sleep early, when the man and the girl had walked in. They'd made a show of looking at his wares for a few moments, the man picking up the cheaper clocks and tutting approvingly, while the girl browsed through shelves of carvings and pottery.

They were different. While it wasn't unusual for strangers - particularly fair-skinned northerners - to visit him, there had been something about those two - the way they carried themselves, their whispered banter, their ridiculous clothes, the girl's unfashionable hair style - that had made him edgy. After an appropriate period of silence in which he had given himself the opportunity of judging whether they were going to make a purchase, Kharis had coughed politely and taken an involuntary step backwards as the man had turned towards him.

'I... mean no disrespect...' he had heard himself mumbling, before reminding himself that this was *his* shop and they were the strangers here.

Crowned by waves of snowy hair, the man's face had been lined with experience and age, yes, but there had been an authority in it that was difficult to resist. Perhaps he had been a counsellor or sage to men of rank once. But, no, there was strength in that face as well as wisdom. This was a man who had *done* things - great things, things that Kharis could only imagine.

He had licked his lips and waited for the man to speak.

The man had smiled. 'I don't know whether you could help me, old chap, but my friend and I were wondering about the celebrations you've just had.'

Kharis had stared. 'What? Oh, the Passing two days ago. You must have missed it, yes? A shame, but there'll be another one in a week or so – perhaps earlier, if the Machine is gracious.'

'The Machine?' the girl had interjected, her brown eyes bright with interest.

So, of course, Kharis had told them. About the Machine, about the parade, about the initiates who made the impossible journey to the stars, about the history and legends of the Machinists and their followers. By the end of the conversation, even the shaded air of the shop had grown unbearably hot and the strangers had somehow leeched every iota of religious knowledge from his mind.

The man had looked puzzled. 'You say the initiates are chosen by the Machine?' Kharis had nodded. 'Yet, from what you've just told me, the vast majority that are chosen are the poor, the dispossessed, the homeless. Isn't that a little strange? Why aren't nobles or merchants like your good self chosen by the Machine?' He remembered opening his mouth to offer a reply to these questions and then closing it again, when he realised he didn't have one. 'And why haven't you, in all the years that this tradition has been going on, heard from one of the thousands who have "ascended" to the stars?' He had stood there dumbfounded, not sure that the turn the conversation had suddenly taken did not qualify as heresy of some sort. He still wasn't sure now.

But the tall, white-haired man and the pretty girl in the strange clothes had left his shop as quietly and unobtrusively as they had entered it, the man turning to favour him with a courteous bow as he did so. Their questions remained, however.

As he looked out at the parade readying itself to move on, he found himself scrutinising the face of the young initiate who was about to make the impossible journey. With an uneasy jolt, he realised that the boy *was* a ghetto child. The noticeably sallower complexion and coarse black hair were tell-tale signs. He observed the removal of the unruly celebrant, the rough behaviour of the three guards who attended him, the polished leather and steel armour of the militiamen lining the parade route – he saw all these things with an unusual clarity, as if, for all his life, he had been wearing a mourner's veil that had only now been removed.

His frown deepened as the five guards at the head of the parade began to move again, escorting the poor beggar boy to his wondrous fate.

* * *

'We are the people of the Machine. Its oil flows in our veins; we march to the rhythm of Its motor; we speak with the roar of Its eternal engine. Hear us, O peoples of the world! We are the Children of the Sublime Mechanism. This world shall be ours, and worlds beyond worlds will tremble at our ascension!'

THE BOOK OF AYBEL THE HERETIC, CH. 3, V.4, 5; THE FIRST BOOK OF THE MACHINE

The Sanctuary of Stars dominated Hezrah's skyline. In this city of low, squat government buildings, packed mazy warrens and sprawling residential estates, a building of any height was unusual and the Sanctuary of Stars - the spiritual centre of an entire continent and of Hezrah, its capital city - was of a vast height. The gleaming tower at its heart, symbolic of the start of the impossible journey, stretched arrogantly into the cloudless sky, seeming to impale the bloated sun on its glass-tipped point.

The rest of the building was no less impressive. White-washed walls reflected the sunlight, and deeply recessed window-slits at regular intervals gave the church the slightly incongruous appearance of a heavily fortified castle, prepared to withstand a siege.

And perhaps that wasn't that far from the truth. Sarah Jane Smith shuffled forward, part of a crowd of worshippers that must, she thought, have numbered at least three thousand. They were orderly and relatively subdued - but then, heavily armed guards usually had a calming influence, didn't they? Sarah scowled, and scratched her arm underneath the rough woollen blouson she was wearing. Another insect bite! Travelling to an alien world with the Doctor invariably involved discomfort of one sort or another. She was determined not to complain, though. If what the Doctor had told her was true, the flies were the very least of these people's worries.

The crowd moved forward again. The Passing Parade had entered the building about half an hour ago. Ever since then, the guards had been allowing groups of ten or twelve worshippers through the high doors that comprised the Sanctuary's entrance. She just hoped she actually got in. Although the Doctor's plan didn't specifically require her presence (and she suspected he partly wished she *wouldn't* be there), he would need as many friendly faces as possible if things went wrong.

She looked around her. It was difficult to see more than a few feet with so many people pressing in, but... There! A flash of startlingly dark eyes, grave and intense amongst so many dull ones, the hint of a grey-flecked beard. Tarris was close by, bent over as if constricted by arthritis. The crowd shuffled forward, the doors got nearer and the former councillor was lost to Sarah's sight. She just hoped that no one realised he had a crossbow underneath his flowing robes. Firepower was another important component of the Doctor's back-up plan in case things went wrong.

The congregation settled into the bare wooden pews and the guards paced quietly up and down the aisles. Aimarrh was only dimly aware of the small sounds and movements around him. His mind was consumed with his forthcoming ascension. He stood alone at the centre of a vast onyx five-pointed star, embedded in a gold-plated floor. At the apex of each point of the star, some five yards away from him, stood each of the five parade guards. Throughout the march and the hour or so it had taken to seat the people, their sombre expressions had not wavered.

Again, Aimarrh felt a stab of pride that their devotion, no less in its way than that of the revellers who had lined the street, was for *him*. He stared straight ahead at the golden doors through which he would soon enter and meet the Eternal Machine to begin the impossible journey.

To one side of the golden doors was a small, raised pulpit. It was from here that the High Machinist, the Eternal Machine's principal spokesman, would deliver his address to the people and then his charge to Aimarrh. The front of the pulpit was carved in the shape of a five-pointed star. Its lectern was fashioned from pure gold, and studded with precious stones.

The congregation fell silent as a High Engineer ascended the steps of the pulpit, and began to lead the people in the words of the fourth catechism. His strong tenor voice rang out in the Sanctuary. The people's voices thundered back. Aimarrh did not lift a hand to wipe the tears from his cheek.

Sarah didn't know the words, but then that didn't really matter. The people around her did and their fervent recitation of them struck her as being both powerful and disturbing - a million miles away from the few insipid Church of England services she'd experienced as a girl.

Their words spoke of worship, and a longing for protection and comfort in a harsh, unpredictable world of violence and death. Sarah swallowed as she realised that this security and certainty were about to be destroyed forever.

* * *

The High Engineer left the pulpit and the High Machinist replaced him. The crowd was still, expectantly waiting to hear his words of encouragement and counsel – a reaffirmation of the special place that the people of the Machine had in this world.

They never came. The High Machinist opened his mouth and chaos erupted on the Sanctuary floor. Guards were rushing towards a section of the congregation at the back of the building. Aimarrh couldn't help but turn towards the commotion and, as he did so, he saw a man, strangely dressed with a shock of white hair, step out of the crowd at the front of the congregation and walk quickly towards the pulpit. Two of the guards around Aimarrh left their positions on the five-pointed star and rushed towards the interloper. Together the three men went down in a flurry of arms and legs. Aimarrh watched, amazed, as the stranger got up from the tangle of limbs, calmly patted down his outlandish clothes and continued on his journey to the pulpit, leaving two unconscious guards in his wake.

Aimarrh sensed a blur of movement at the corner of his vision and he turned to see another one of his guards collapse to the black floor, scrabbling frantically at the crossbow bolt lodged in his throat. Aimarrh looked around him and saw some of the Sanctuary guards locked in vicious hand-to-hand fighting with a group of five or six worshippers. All around the building little pockets of fighting had broken out, while, here and there, the bodies of dead guards lay still in the aisles of the hallowed place.

The congregation was beginning to panic, rushing to their feet with the evident aim of leaving the building as quickly as they could. Aimarrh watched, his mind unable to grasp the meaning of the events unfolding around him. A dark-eyed man with a square-trimmed beard rushed towards him, the dagger in his hand glinting evilly in the sunlight drifting through the sky windows in the vaulted roof. The two remaining guards drew their ceremonial swords and rushed to meet him, barring his path to Aimarrh. The dagger flicked out in a curved slashing movement that took it through a guard's neck and out the other side. The guard fell heavily and lay still, in a slow-spreading pool of blood. The other guard roared his anger and lunged with his sword. The bearded man sidestepped the blow neatly, and the two combatants circled warily over the dead soldier's body.

The black star glistened with crimson streaks. The blood of the guard seeped across the floor towards Aimarrh, and...

He sees the still form of the young woman lying in the rubbish and filth of the alleyway. Her once lustrous dark hair lies limp across her pale face. Her almond-shaped eyes, the colour of chocolate, stare at him, but do not see him. A dog is lapping at the blood hardening around her chest. A halo of flies hovers around her. He runs forward to beat them away from his sister...

'No! Stop this now! You must listen to me!'

Incredibly, the fighting died down. Aimarrh saw the bearded man who had tried to kill him exchange venomous glares with the lone Passing Guard and they both lowered their weapons cautiously.

The man who had spoken was the white-haired stranger. The acoustics of the Sanctuary carried his voice to every man, woman and child still in the building. There was authority in his voice and Aimarrh instinctively understood that it came, not from position and rank like that of the engineers and machinists, but from a lifetime - many lifetimes - of experience and struggle. Perhaps that's why his stern words were suffused with pain as well as passion.

'I wish there were some other way to say this, but... your god, your Machine... is a lie!' The man paused, as if anticipating an outburst of enraged denial, but none came. An uneasy peace had descended on the Sanctuary. For the moment, the stranger had his congregation's attention.

'Over a thousand years ago, your world *was* visited, yes, by an alien life form - incredibly old and wounded from a battle that, were I to try and describe it to you... well, it would probably send you insane.' An approving murmur swept through the crowd. A battle between gods they could understand. Still at the back of the auditorium, where she'd remained when the fighting broke out, Sarah bit her lip anxiously. She knew the stakes the Doctor was playing for - even if the congregation didn't. Yet.

'In a desperate effort to survive, the creature went into a deep regenerative sleep. Even in its dormant state, it reached out with a part of its mind and began to influence this world's development. Over the course of three centuries it fomented revolutions, manipulated kings and priests, inspired heretics and rebels, founded a religion.' The Doctor paused to let his last words sink in. 'I've studied your history. I can trace the divergences and convergences of "chance" and "coincidence" from generations past to this. You have been manipulated. You have been used.'

Someone - and it sounded to Sarah like the High Engineer who had led the congregation in prayer earlier - called out, 'Then if this "creature" has done all this, then it truly *is* a god. It is deserving of our worship and service.'

Sarah winced.

The Doctor gazed at the congregation calmly. He nodded. 'Perhaps so - were it not for the fact that it has systematically lied to you for seven hundred and seventy years. The "initiates" who journeyed to the stars were killed by your god. Their bodies were brutally dismembered. Their minds were sucked clean, as the creature savoured their sense of betrayal, and wallowed in their desolation. There is no journey to the stars - just a cycle of despair and death, time after time after time. And with each successive death it grows stronger, more powerful. In time it will leave this place, and seed itself on other worlds. You must not allow that to happen. You have been told that behind this door' - he gestured behind him to the golden doors that led to the Inner Sanctuary, the vast vault that housed the Eternal Machine - 'lies a machine, a wondrous device that fell from the stars in the time of your ancestors, that can control your lives and the fate of your nation, that can send your race in a glorious adventure to the stars.' He shook his head, sadly. 'I'm sorry, but that is a lie.' He nodded almost imperceptibly, and two men rushed forwards to throw open the heavy doors, and allow the people to see fully into the holiest place of all.

Aimarrh caught his breath at the blasphemy of that action, but his jaw fell slack at what he saw before him. An impossibly complex creation of steel and wire, diamond and gold, filled the ancient vault. Lights winked to highlight controls and switches of unguessable purpose. A steady hum of power pervaded the Sanctuary. The people gasped in awe. It was *true* - not a lie, but a glorious wonderful truth. The Eternal Engine, the Sublime Mechanism - it was real, gloriously, beautifully real!

But the stranger was speaking again...

'What you're seeing is an illusion, an image projected into your mind by a creature of unimaginable mental power.' He took a deep breath and raised a small white box to his forehead. 'Let me show you.' His eyes closed and his face stilled. The lines on his face smoothed and the air around him began to ripple like the surface of a breeze-blown lake. The people stirred restlessly, growing tired of this stranger and his lies. But then things began to change.

The image of the Machine - the unbelievably vast network of conduits and consoles, of whirring fans and gleaming metal prostheses - began to dissolve, fracturing and splintering into scores of discrete bubbles of illusion, which eventually shrank and finally vanished. What their disappearance revealed drew screams of horror and gasps of revulsion from the waiting crowd.

The Inner Sanctuary was occupied, and some of the things that were in it were indeed mechanical; but much of its content was all too organic. Several human bodies, in various stages of decay, lay on the filthy floor, like broken dolls discarded by a careless child. More bodies or parts of bodies hung from hooks on the walls. Insects flew aimlessly around them, engorged on corrupted flesh, and the air crawled with the bitter-sweet stench of decay. At the centre of the vast chamber sat a huge, monstrous thing of slime and filth.

Aimarrh was horrified by it, but he could not look away. The horror of the crowd behind him turned to anger and disgust. The stranger was saying something, but he could not hear it. He was transfixed. The monster's skin glistened wetly with blood and waste. It was impossible to count its limbs, some tentacled, some ending in appendages that snapped and cracked. It had no eyes, but seemed to know that the crowd was there. It began to move, slipping through the slime that surrounded it, dragging itself forward, slowly at first but then with an increasing sense of purpose.

Aimarrh stood directly in its path, but he could not move.

Something slid through his skull and pierced his mind, its touch as delicate as a feather. He heard words, softly, malevolently whispering, *My child...*

It was the stranger who saved him.

'Concentrate!' he urged the crowd. 'This... thing has lied to you for centuries, all the while nurturing your hope and then feeding on your despair. Look at it! It is a creature of evil and death! Take your anger, your horror, your pain and wield it like a sword. Destroy this abomination!'

The monster faltered, its claws clicking in indecision. And then the wave hit.

The horror, revulsion, fury and hatred of almost three thousand people slammed into it like a giant fist. Its limbs flailed the air wildly. A thin, jagged crack opened in its hide and an inhuman, guttural scream echoed around the Sanctuary.

The end came quickly. Someone threw oil at it. Someone else hurled one of the ceremonial lamps. It arced through the air and then Aimarrh was staring at a roaring curtain of fire.

Someone grabbed Aimarrh's arm. 'Come on! We've got to get out of here!'

He stumbled through the throng. No one paid any attention to his distinctive black and gold robes, though some did look twice at the young fair-skinned girl holding onto his hand. Here he was just a part of the frantic panicking crowd, struggling to escape. There was nothing special about him anymore.

Short of breath, coated in sweat and thoroughly dishevelled, he burst into the Sanctuary courtyard. People were milling about, frantically searching the chaotic jumble of faces for family and friends.

The girl turned to him. 'Are you alright?' she asked, her brown eyes searching his face. He did not even know how to begin to answer that question. 'I've got to go and find the Doctor. There's more to be done, I'm afraid. We've got to get over to the palace. There's a revolution to start.' She smiled in what she evidently thought would be a reassuring manner and touched her hand to his cheek gently. 'Things are going to be different now.' She began to pull away, her eyes already scouring the crowd for a sign of her strange, terrible friend. 'Different.'

She was gone, and Aimarrh was alone. He stood in the courtyard of the Sanctuary of Stars, watching a thin wisp of black smoke drift from the top of the Sanctuary tower, as if in gentle mockery of his intended journey. Drained and exhausted, he collapsed to the hard ground, sitting in silence while bit by bit the crowd dispersed, returning to their homes, some doubtless in fearful wonder at the day's events, others perhaps in cautious expectation of the new and 'different' future that was to come.

He felt empty and cold. The sun-warmed ground offered no comfort. The months spent learning the rites and sacred words had been for nothing. The engineers and their teachings had been worth nothing.

Memories shifted in his mind like desert sand and he sank into confusion and uncertainty. There were fragments... His mother's face, care-worn and creased with pain. His childhood on the streets. He had seen a Passing Parade once. It had seemed to stretch on for miles, as if all the people in the city had joined it, dancing and swirling in celebration... bright colours swirling... He had watched from the side of the road, shouting and screaming. He had been so *excited*...

Now he felt nothing. The Sanctuary doors hung awkwardly off their hinges. The once orderly space inside was a mess of smoke and destruction and at its heart was a grotesque, charred shape. It was an ending, but he had no sense of beginning.

The ever-present flies circled him languidly in the cooling evening air. The sound of their grimy wings scratching at the silence unnerved him, but he listened carefully. Perhaps in their seemingly chaotic flight he could find a direction of sorts.

The day lengthened. From time to time, Aimarrh heard sounds of fighting, echoing distantly across the city. Once, he raised his head and saw smoke rising from the government district. Revolution. That's what the girl had said, wasn't it?

The flies seemed to be congregating around him, although they also seemed to be careful not to touch him. He frowned. *My child...* Vividly he remembered the touch of the Machine - of the thing that had been the Machine - in his mind. *My child...* He thought he heard it now, carried on the hissing sibilant wings of the insects around him.

Somewhere in the city, the men of power and knowledge fought for the future of the land and, perhaps, the world, but in the rubble-strewn grounds of the shattered Sanctuary, as the lengthening shadows marked the end of the last day of the old religion, Aimarrh the beggar boy sat perfectly still and attended to the murmuring of the flies.

The Fear

Alexander Leithes

In the main control room of the TARDIS, the Doctor frowns. He paces about the room, staring at the slowly pumping central column. Pausing to throw one end of his scarf over his shoulder, he appears to examine every panel of the console in minute detail - until he spots a single throw switch and a look of realisation creeps across his features, followed by a broad triumphant grin. He flicks the switch into its alternate position and the grin melts away instantly, leaving him looking positively depressed. He grabs roughly at his enormous hat as if to confirm its continued presence, but even the texture of the cloth under his palm seems to cast him into deeper gloom.

The Doctor spins around away from the console, and at the same time drops into a crouch. A small metal dog has crept up behind him, making only a moderate amount of noise as it glides over the incredibly smooth floor. The Doctor cups its head in his hands.

'K9,' he says, a prelude to some momentous statement. K9 whirs and chatters in anticipation, but remains otherwise mute. 'Everything is working perfectly,' the Doctor whispers with an intense stare.

'Affirmative master,' K9 chirrups. His radars spin, though whether it is with delight or irritation it is hard to tell.

'Perfectly,' the Doctor repeats, a little more calmly, rising to his feet as he does so. 'It's all far too positive... I don't like it one bit.'

He looks down. 'K9, can you sense anything unusual?'

As the dog chatters and whirs, cogitating on the problem, the Doctor makes himself a cup of tea. He sips at it, but it does nothing to settle his mind. He peers into the gently swirling brown liquid, gradually being drawn closer to the mug, his eyes taking on an increasingly fixed appearance. He takes another sip.

'Negative, master.'

The Doctor places his mug on the central column, which rises and falls gently. He shakes his head. 'No, this is very bad.'

He tenses, waiting... Nothing happens.

He sighs impatiently then strides to the other side of the console and stands with the tails of his long coat swinging gently to rest, his hands on his hips. Nothing happens.

Except that this time, *nothing* really does happen - suddenly, violently, the Doctor is thrown into utter blackness; an absence of light, sound, even gravity. He feels that sickening, yawning sensation in the pit of his stomach that usually comes while falling, only this time he knows that he is not, as the usual tearing rush of air that accompanies that experience is missing.

Almost as he thinks this, he feels the wind begin to tear past his face.

'Ah, that's much better!' he shouts into the teeth of the gale, baring his own in a broad smile. He now finds he has to hold tightly on to his hat in order to stop it being whipped away into the inky blackness. All the while he can hear his scarf and coat flapping in a distressed manner, but of course he can see nothing.

At first the Doctor feels the usual animal fear that accompanies the sensation of free fall. But very quickly, he begins to find the whole experience quite exhilarating. Naturally, it crosses his mind that he might well eventually fall into something, but he thinks it best not to succumb to wild speculation over things he knows nothing about. These thoughts have barely passed through his mind when he begins to discern vague grey shapes in the direction that can best be described as down, to judge from the direction of the wind.

The Doctor's sense of direction receives further confirmation, as the grey mass draws closer and grows clearer. It is a vast plane of a particularly hard-looking form of granite. As if to relieve the monotony, excitingly pointy extrusions are thrown up periodically from its otherwise flat surface. The Doctor frowns as he wonders how the plain is being illuminated, given the vast distance he has fallen through utter darkness. Then he brightens as he realises that in about ten seconds, judging by his present speed, this worry will no longer be troubling him. He spreads his arms wide, closes his eyes, and beams as he embraces his imminent fate.

The Doctor feels solid rock beneath him, and is startled to discover that his feet are not embedded in his ribcage. He opens his eyes, and instantly wishes he had not. He is now in a cave, roughly one hundred metres in diameter, with no immediately visible means of escape. This is not what has struck him as unappealing, however. The half-dozen or so humanoid creatures are not entirely pleasant, particularly given that they are not entirely whole: each is missing one or two limbs. They whimper and moan as they drag their bodies painfully across the floor. Every missing limb has left behind a torn and ragged wound; no surgeon's work, this. But even this is not the most disturbing feature of the cave. The huge mound of teeth and claws, quivering with furious power is.

The creature raises its red and drooling snout, and sniffs curiously.

The Doctor feels a shiver run through him as he begins to guess how the other occupants of the cave have come to lose weight so dramatically. One of the aliens who has dragged himself furthest from the slavering beast, and by happy chance is closest to the Doctor, looks up at him with pain-filled eyes and speaks in a voice cracked with terror.

'He's smelt you! He's coming! He always wants new unspoilt flesh. He will take you, eat you, as he's eaten all of us! As he's *still* eating all of us!'

This last statement is delivered almost as a screech, but the Doctor is able to understand him clearly enough. Unfortunately, the sound has also enabled the beast to locate the Doctor more quickly, and it is rapidly propelling itself towards him on its six, taloned legs. The Doctor pushes his mounting fear aside, studies the beast for a moment, scans the cave for somewhere to hide then, finding nowhere, wraps his scarf around his head. He is not sure what he hopes to achieve by this; perhaps it is to confuse the creature until it loses interest, or possibly he simply wishes to block out the terrifying vision that faces him.

All is silent now; the noise of the approaching creature has abated. The Doctor waits another ten seconds, then cautiously lifts the scarf away from his eyes. The beast takes his arm off, just above the right elbow.

The sheer intensity of the pain is something for which the Doctor was not entirely ready. He screams as white-hot searing fire rolls up from his bleeding stump, washing through every facet of his mind. He sinks to the floor, panting and rocking, while the creature chews thoughtfully. It then returns to the other side of the cave to sleep off its meal.

The Doctor composes his thoughts with an effort, pushing the pain away to be stored for later study.

'Physician, heal thyself,' he mutters, as he wraps his scarf about the stump. Slowly, he turns to regard the nearest of his fellow amputees. The man stares back at him fearfully.

'I really think we should try and find a way out of here,' the Doctor says, flashing the man a reassuring if slightly pained grin. The man flinches nervously, as if the Doctor might try to bite him.

'There is no way out of here!' he hisses, while furtively glancing towards the beast. The Doctor frowns and is about to suggest an alternative course of action when it suddenly ceases to be his problem. For a second he senses a swirling darkness, but he cannot focus upon an image.

The Doctor now finds himself in a far more comfortable situation. He is sitting in a chair facing a dresser, complete with mirror. He notes happily that his arm is now restored to him, but is puzzled to find that it is rather more wrinkled than he is used to. Squinting back at him from the mirror is a reflection that is also more wrinkled than he is used to: an old man, still obviously his current regeneration, but physically wasted with age. Much of his hair is gone, and his skin is patched with liver spots.

'Hello.' He smiles at this other him, and nods in a friendly manner. The image returns his toothless smile and greeting.

The Doctor decides to explore this new experience and his surroundings, and he attempts to get out of his chair. His arms can barely lift him an inch above the cushion, and he can feel that his legs lack the strength to raise him to his feet. He sinks back wheezing into the chair, which rolls half a foot or so from the dresser, carrying him with it.

'A wheelchair!' He chuckles to himself. 'Hardly my usual form of transport.'

He hears footsteps and voices, and struggles to turn the chair to face his visitors.

'Now Doctor, you know you're not supposed to over-exert yourself.'

This admonishment comes from one of the two young female nurses who have just entered his room. The one who had addressed him is tall, pretty and blonde, while her colleague is shorter with a more mousy appearance. The Doctor nods in gracious acquiescence as the mousy nurse moves behind him to hold on to the handles of his chair. She bends down close to his ear and says loudly, 'It's time for your dinner.'

The Doctor raises an arthritic finger to point towards the door.

'Then onwards, good ladies!' he commands with theatrical grandeur. The effect is spoiled slightly by the croak in his voice. As they wheel him down the corridor the nurses chat to one another.

'Why did you call him "Doctor"?' the mousy nurse asks. 'I thought he was just another one of the patients.'

The blond nurse tuts at her friend's ignorance before explaining. 'He was a great doctor once, but that was twenty years ago. Now we're the ones doing the caring, and all he has to do is relax.'

The Doctor turns his head to regard the blond nurse out of the corner of his eye. 'I am still here, you know,' he reminds her.

'Of course you are, dear,' she says in a professionally soothing tone, before continuing to chat with her friend. The Doctor ignores them both as he considers his situation, theorising about what intelligence may be causing it, and what barriers he can throw up to defend himself.

By now he has reached the dining room, and is gently pushed into place amongst the ranks of the infirm. Looking down he sees a plate of mushy stew, a side order of sloppy vegetables and a spoon.

'Do you think you'll be able to manage on your own, Doctor?' the blonde nurse asks him. He grins at her.

'I'm sure you'd help me if I couldn't,' he replies with a wink. Another thought strikes him; in this state of decrepitude, he should have regenerated by now. Obviously, by some unknown force of will, he is expected to remain in this condition. He is troubled by this thought, thinking he will not like the restrictions this new aged condition will impose upon him. Then he shrugs to himself; he is certain this will result in a plethora of hitherto unexplored experiences.

Without warning, the Doctor's universe makes a jump-cut to another scene. He now sits, his usual healthy, vigorous self, in surroundings that are once again abstractly familiar. The six feet square room he now occupies is a sterile white and every surface has been quilted for his comfort, enjoyment and safety. It is the archetypal padded cell.

Looking down at his now restored body, the Doctor discovers that he is clothed in nothing except white pyjamas. He stands up and looks around. There does not seem to be any sign of a door or window. Even the bright, cold light source seems entirely hidden to him. He walks clockwise about the cell before retracing his steps; he does not, after all, want to get lost. This exercise over, he sits down and waits.

After about an hour, he has begun to guess that this new state is in some way meant to be permanent. The walls seem almost to frown with the effort of just being immutable.

'La.' The Doctor sings out the single note.

'La, la, la.' These three follow the first, and all are of the same duration and pitch. There is now a significant pause before the Doctor repeats the four identical notes again. By the third repetition of the notes it becomes clear that the significance of the pause is that it consists of four rests, equal in length to the notes.

The Doctor maintains this behaviour for what seems like an age, but it is probably only fifteen minutes. Just as he inhales in preparation for another burst he feels a change in the air accompanied by a strange rustling. In one corner of the room an eerie swirling shape has begun to appear. At first a wisp of black smoke spirals up near the floor, growing to become about six feet tall. The apparition, while still smoke-like in form, has the vague suggestion of a shape to it, that of a cowled, humanoid figure. Its voice echoes oddly as if at a distance, or located in another, more acoustically resonant room.

'What are you doing?' it asks, puzzled.

The Doctor smiles and stands up.

'I was composing a song,' he says with a grin.

'But...' the entity begins.

'Yes?' the Doctor inquires, tilting his left ear towards it.

'It only has one note.'

'Ah, but of course!' the Doctor cries. 'Isn't it always best to start off simply and build up from there?'

'What do you mean?' the entity probes, a hint of anger entering its voice.

'Well, I mean once I had fully explored all the interesting facets of the one-note song, I could then have moved on to the dizzying heights of the two-note song! You can see there's an inexhaustible musical realm to be explored here, can't you?'

It suddenly becomes very dark, and the Doctor can almost feel the entity's anger as an increase in the air pressure. He realises that he is not quite immersed in total blackness; he can see he is standing on a slightly reflective, hard floor, but he cannot see any walls or other physical features in any direction. Indeed he is struck by the impression that he is standing upon an infinite plane, although he knows that this is impossible. He notes with some pleasure that he is again dressed in his own clothes, scarf draped around his shoulders, hat sprawling once more upon his head. In spite of the reduced lighting, the Doctor can just make out the swirling shape of the entity. Now it speaks.

'You know,' it says accusingly. 'You know what is happening, don't you? You know why you're here!'

The Doctor frowns and adopts an expression of modesty. 'Oh no, you credit me with too much. I don't even know the name of the entity to whom I'm speaking. I'd imagine you have the advantage of me there.'

'We have no need of names, you and I,' the entity responds.

The Doctor raises an eyebrow. 'But you do know me?' he asks.

'Better perhaps than you know yourself.'

The Doctor brightens upon hearing this, flashing a toothy grin at the entity.

'Really! Then I've no doubt you could be of inestimable service to me. There are so many things I should like to know!' Again the Doctor can physically feel the anger in the atmosphere close about him.

'I, be of service to you! You are so far wide of the mark, you make me wonder if even now you realise what you have done.'

'And this would be one of those parts of myself I don't know, I suppose?' the Doctor asks politely. The entity fumes.

'Do you know why I brought you here?' it roars, while still maintaining the odd, removed quality to its voice.

The Doctor smiles. 'From what you've said, do you think that's likely?'

The entity appears to subside slightly, to become cooler, more controlled.

'Have you any idea the fear you have caused?' it asks quietly. The Doctor is genuinely taken aback by this.

'I have caused you fear?' comes the puzzled question.

'Yes!' the entity responds with venom. 'And not just me, but millions, billions of others throughout time and space.'

The Doctor finds this hard to take in.

'Now look, I know that when I get out of bed in the morning my hair can look pretty frightful, but still...'

'Do not trivialise the suffering of others,' the entity screams. 'Especially when you are their tormentor!'

The Doctor becomes sober. 'I have never terrorised innocents. It is against everything I am.'

'No! It is all you are! All you have done. You are fear's messiah; worse, you are the form made flesh!' After this outburst, the entity calms itself before continuing.

'Have you never considered the consequences of your meddling? Have you never understood the ripples your actions create, spreading and growing to become tidal waves that engulf entire worlds? Entire worlds thrown into chaos as old orders collapse to be replaced by the new. Unemployment, hunger, riots, wars: all these things the common people suffer. All these things they fear to come to pass, and you have created them. Fear. When I say billions, I do not bandy these numbers around lightly. You have forced fear upon all these people.'

The Doctor considers this.

'I have only ever acted against the evil of others,' he states simply.

The entity utters a humourless laugh.

'So, you encourage an uprising on a subject planet in a galactic empire, an uprising that successfully throws off the imperial control. You'd count that one world's freedom as a success?'

'Sounds like a fair day's work to me,' the Doctor agrees.

'But you don't bother to find out the effect that has on the stable, peaceful and prosperous empire spanning thousands of worlds, do you? The economy falters, dissent breaks out, law and order vanish to be replaced by chaos, uncertainty and, of course, fear. Billions of ordinary people, fearing what the next day will bring. And this is but one example, from only one of your actions.'

The Doctor looks concerned, but unrepentant.

'I still must believe it's for the best.'

'And who are you to decide a therapeutic course of terror for the universe?' the entity scoffs, then laughs to itself.

'Still, that is exactly what I intend to administer.'

The light of understanding begins to dawn within the Doctor's mind, a mind that he is taking increasing pains to shield from the entity.

'These trials,' the Doctor says quietly. 'Each one has been an attempt to induce fear within me, correct?'

'Exactly,' the entity replies. 'I wish to trap you in a permanent state of fear.'

'Ah,' the Doctor says knowingly. 'For revenge.'

'For justice!' the entity snarls. 'For myself and the billions of common people like me...'

'Er, excuse me,' the Doctor interrupts, 'but you don't seem all that common to me. All this...' He gestures around him to all that the entity has created.

'Once I was, but for reasons that don't concern you I came to my present state,' the entity says, then pauses. When next it speaks, its voice sounds as if it is barely six inches away from the Doctor's face.

'Or perhaps it does,' it hisses.

'So,' the Doctor continues, 'For "justice" you want to scare me?'

The entity tuts. 'Not just scare you. I want to trap you in a constant state of fear. The fear that traps the lives of those you touched will become your ultimate governor, the force that stays your hand and saves the universe.'

The Doctor nods. 'So, fear of falling, amended to fear of hitting the ground. A further tweak to fear of physical pain or perhaps fear of mutilation; I'm thinking of course of the beast. Then you attempted to hold up a bogey man I've never really faced, old age. Finally, an interesting choice, boredom, confinement, lack of stimulus. Yet none of these seemed able to sustain that which you desired. What went wrong?' he asks.

'You, of course!' snaps the entity. 'You did not react as you were supposed to. In every case you overcame or suppressed your fear. You revelled in every experience and seemed almost to... enjoy them. And even when I removed all external stimuli, you still found a method of amusing yourself!'

The Doctor sighs and smiles. 'Ah well, you're never really alone with a good tune, and besides,' he says gesturing around him, 'the mind is such a wonderfully creative thing.'

'And so I revealed myself to you. It was becoming harder to read any thoughts from you. I must know that one thing you fear, so that I may confront you with it for all eternity.'

The Doctor frowned. 'I've already told you,' he says slyly.

'What?' the entity cries incredulously.

'What my greatest fear is.'

'You have not! What is it?' the entity insists.

'Well, I said I stand against the evil of others.'

'Yes?'

'And we tend to fight against our fears lest we are overcome by them,' the Doctor continues.

'Yes?' the entity repeats.

'So perhaps my greatest fear... is you!' the Doctor says with a flourish.

The entity screams in rage, flies around the Doctor like a whirlwind, then is instantly still. 'We shall see!' it hisses in his ear.

Then the Doctor is careering through an ever-changing landscape of macabre images; creatures leap out, gibbering, to grab at him as he flies over an undulating plain of purple flesh. Next he is submerged in an ocean of blood, while mermaids sing of the suffering he has caused. Now maggots chew at dozens of rotting wounds scattered over his body as he lies on a stony plain, the sky on fire above him. The images change faster now and with it his own physical orientation so that he is literally tumbling through time and space. But for all his disorientation he still does not feel the one thing the entity desires: fear. As the jumble of sensations grows too fast to separate, his only concern is that he might lose...

No. He pushes that thought deep down within him.

Creation stops turning. The Doctor is standing once more on the dark expanse, the seemingly infinite obsidian plane.

'So that was it,' the entity says with satisfaction.

'What do you mean?' the Doctor asks lightly.

'Your one fear is to lose your mind,' the entity answers with suppressed triumph. 'So this is what I will do. I will take away your rational mind, leave you a random insane shadow of yourself. A husk, a caricature of you, with no real meaning. But somewhere in there, screaming, a part of you will remember what you once were. That part will fear its eternal imprisonment, fear the continuing degradation of the legacy of the sane you by the insane you, and fear the harm you might cause others.'

The Doctor struggles hard not to show that this threat has struck home. He turns from the entity and clasps his hands behind his back. Then he looks back over his left shoulder, a familiar, broad, unnerving grin upon his lips.

'How do you know that hasn't already happened?' he asks mischievously.

The entity pauses for a moment. 'Don't play games with me Doctor, I know who I have here.'

The Doctor shrugs. 'And does he seem to you to react in a normal, rational way?'

The entity makes no reply and so the Doctor continues.

'After all, I didn't succumb to any of the usual emotions you'd expect from anyone else put in the situations your mind created. Surely any sane person would?'

The entity is not so easily convinced. 'But I can see your personality, trapped here within my mind. I can remove the rational part I perceive.'

The Doctor holds up a warning finger. 'Ah, but even you admitted that you only have a partial view of this mind of mine. How do you know that it is not merely the shattered remnants of a once noble and logical mind, and that what you perceive as the rational part is just some shoddy glue, holding the fragments together in a gruesome parody of the original? For all you know, somewhere in this mind there is a part that remembers how it used to be and screams constantly for release.'

The entity now wails, and tears of frustration choke its voice. 'I will not be cheated this way!' it cries, 'I will remove it, glue or not, I'll shatter you once and for all time!'

The Doctor runs his thumb and forefinger down his nose thoughtfully. 'I'm sure you could do that,' he says mysteriously.

'And why shouldn't I?' snaps the entity.

The Doctor looks around him once again. 'This is all in your mind?' he asks rhetorically.

'Yes,' agrees the entity.

The Doctor then gestures with his hands from his head to his toes.

'Then *this* is all in your mind as well,' he states.

'No!' the entity screeches, once again whirling about the Doctor before settling down.

'But yes,' the Doctor assures it calmly. 'You cannot deny that I now exist in your mind. What evidence have you that I have any other existence?'

The Doctor feels himself gripped by a giant invisible hand, pinning his arms to his side while lifting him an inch off the ground. He cannot deny to himself how real this feels, and he feels a thrill of fear as he struggles for breath against this constricting force. The entity speaks to him now.

'Do you really think you're not here? I doubt it!'

The Doctor somehow finds the air to speak. 'The issue is not really what I think about this, but what you think, because ultimately that is all there is to this.'

The entity relaxes its grip by the tiniest fraction, allowing the Doctor easier breathing; but it does not allow him to continue speaking. 'You cannot double-talk your way out of here!' it insists. 'I can see you, you foolish little man. You're lying on the floor of your vessel, with that ridiculous metal dog fussing around you. I can see this, and I have you here under my control.'

The Doctor considers this information.

'So are you actually there, physically, yourself?' he asks.

'Not in any physical sense, but then that is not how I exist now in any case,' the entity responds.

'So you can't go over there and give my body a good kick, just to make sure I'm there then?' the Doctor asks.

'No, but this is irrelevant. My senses still show me you are there. I have no worries in that regard.'

The Doctor frowns.

'But you've just admitted that you have no real contact with the physical world. Surely then there must be at least the tiniest grounds to doubt the validity of your own senses, divorced as you are from the real world.'

'No!' the entity roars, gripping the Doctor tightly once again.

'But will you not even listen to yourself?' the Doctor gasps.

'What do you mean, "Listen to myself"?' the entity sneers.

'Allow me to exlain and it'll become clear,' the Doctor requests. 'The only real evidence you have for my lying unconscious on the floor of the TARDIS is the images provided by your senses. These images exist within your mind, yes?'

The entity pauses, thinking.

'Yes,' comes the reluctant reply.

'And the only evidence for your senses are these images in your mind.'

Again, the entity is forced to concede the point.

'And so, in reality your senses and their method of verification are both in fact generated by your mind.'

'No,' the entity growls. The Doctor can see it crouch down slightly, as if it might launch itself at him like a tiger.

'And so everything you perceive, or *think* you perceive is exactly that, just thought. *Your* thoughts. And that doesn't just include those images you believe to exist beyond yourself, the TARDIS and the universe through which it travels, but also those images generated here. These, even you concede, are generated entirely by your mind.'

'No!' the entity whimpers. The Doctor can now feel the hold on him loosen considerably, and his feet are once more touching the ground.

'And if I am, in fact, only existing within your mind then I am, in fact, merely another product of your mind, a fragment if you will.'

'No,' the entity pleads softly. The Doctor can now move his arms, although a little sluggishly as if through treacle.

'And this fragment of your mind has a personality distinct from your own. This is clear since you, or the part of you that identifies itself with you, is arguing, tormenting and interacting with this fragment, named the Doctor. But this naming is only a way of separating one image, one part of yourself from that which you want to believe is you. Any way you look at it, this must be a split personality.'

'No,' the entity whispers. The Doctor shakes himself and finds his movement unfettered.

Now, in the blackness, a rectangular opening of pure white light appears.

'So it would seem that you have two choices,' the Doctor continues, 'Either you can continue with this plan and condemn yourself to an eternity with an insane fragment of your mind...'

The entity sobs.

'...And thereby condemn *yourself* to eternal insanity...'

The entity sighs with grief.

'...Or you can let me walk out through that door.' The Doctor concludes, gesturing towards the blinding white rectangle. The entity makes no further sound. The Doctor wonders if he might now be crushed to the size of a pinhead and he feels then that one thing the entity wants from him, fear. He walks slowly towards the door. No response still from the entity. It seems trapped by fear; on the one hand the fear of losing the Doctor screams at it to act and stop him from leaving, while on the other the fear of suffering the same fate as it had intended for the Doctor stays its hand. In this condition the mind of the entity seems to flicker like a faulty neon sign, trapped between two states, ineffective.

The Doctor looks back once, but his dazzled eyes can make out no shapes within the darkness. Then he passes into the light.

Mauritz

Jonathan Morris

The darkness was so absolute, so intense, I felt that if I were to reach out my hand I would be swallowed up. All I could see was a shifting blur of after-images as my eyes struggled to accustom themselves to the deep, blotted night. The gloom seemed to press itself against me, my skin prickling to its touch. I drew in a breath of clammy air, thick with the smells of corrosion and decay.

A torch clicked into life and its beam swung through the darkness, picking out ever-falling apparitions of dust. The beam drifted across the stone floor and scuttled up a pillar of crumbling plaster, its glow weakening as it crossed the vaulted ceiling, and then brightening as it settled upon the opposite wall. More brickwork, rotten and stained, strangled with creepers and moss. A number of archways, each leading into blackness.

The beam drifted around the chamber, awakening more dust phantoms, gauging the extent of the room. The heaviness of the atmosphere gave me the impression of being far underground. I shivered and put my hands in my pockets as I followed in the Doctor's footsteps.

The Doctor halted and announced in his boom of a voice, 'Shop!'

'Where are we, Doctor?' I asked.

'Literally or philosophically?' The Doctor strode across the floor, his long scarf sweeping the dust behind him. He seemed distracted, hunched in thought.

'Either?'

'Ah.' The Doctor turned his wide eyes upon me and shrugged, breaking into a conspiratorial grin. 'In that case, I haven't the faintest idea.'

'You should know,' I told him. The Doctor possessed a vast intellect – he was the greatest scientist I had ever known – but he could also be frustratingly whimsical. Indeed, he sometimes took a strange pride in his foolishness. My own belief was in logic, in rigorous thought; a belief the Doctor did not share. 'You claim you can control the TARDIS.'

'Just because one can do something, does not mean one should,' countered the Doctor. 'A wine cellar, without the wine? An unoccupied crypt? How cryptic.' The Doctor lifted his head to address the ceiling. 'Hello? Anyone home?' His words echoed back at him indignantly.

I glanced away from the Doctor. Down one of the passageways something flickered, casting flitting shadows across the rough walls. Two lamps bobbing in motion, held by two figures in robes, one tall and stooped, one standing at about my height. They remained motionless, as though watching us, their faces obscured by cowls.

'Doctor – '

The Doctor dashed to my side melodramatically. 'What?'

I shrugged to indicate the passageway, but the figures had gone. The archway led to blackness once more.

'I thought I saw – ' I began, but the Doctor shushed me, a finger to his lips.

I listened. I could hear the sound of footsteps, a steady pat-patting upon the ragged floor. They seemed to be approaching from every direction. I backed towards the TARDIS. The empty archways loomed threateningly around us. The footsteps grew nearer, nearer still, and halted.

'Welcome,' said a voice behind me.

A figure stood between us and the TARDIS. A figure draped in robes, its face hidden by a hood. The habit was of a coarse, woven material, unornamented and hanging in folds. It raised a lantern in one hand as if in greeting.

The Doctor's expression dropped into concern. 'Hello,' he began cautiously, avoiding eye contact. 'You don't know me, but I am...'

'The Doctor,' answered the figure. It had the voice of old man, breathy and hesitant, the words scraping at its throat. It turned its facelessness towards me. 'And Adric.' The figure raised its hands and lifted its cowl to reveal a drawn, lined face, the features set in a downcast frown, the hair thin and moon-white. His eyes were grey and lifeless. He bowed, and smiled, revealing worn, yellow teeth.

'Welcome,' he said, facing us in turn, his expression softening. 'My name is Mauritz.'

Each passageway was submerged in darkness, the only illumination the swinging, oversized shadows cast by Mauritz's lamp. We followed the scuffle of his footsteps up narrow stairwells, the mould-encrusted walls barely a shoulder-width apart, and passed through vaulted chambers identical to the one in which we had arrived, each one in a differing state of disrepair. And at no point did we pass a window, or catch sight of any natural source of light.

The man who led us did not utter a word. Every question the Doctor and I put to him was answered only with a beckoning motion. Occasionally Mauritz would disappear completely from sight, ducking into a side-passage, only to emerge from another passage a moment later. He repeated this trick time and again, seemingly unaware of doing it.

We emerged into a long, dusty hall lined with reading desks and bookcases. The bookcases extended to the ceiling on three levels, each accessed by a balcony, accessed in turn by stairwells. Each bookcase brimmed with tomes and parchments, each bound in a leather cover.

Seated at the desks, what appeared to be monks leafed through the ancient tomes by the gleam of their candles, their identities shrouded in the same anonymous robes.

We moved wordlessly through the library and arrived at a heavy door. Mauritz unbolted the lock and led us into a spartan dormitory. A fireplace was set into one wall, and he quickly set to work on it, gathering up coals and puffing the embers with the bellows until it finally snapped into warmth.

Three high-backed chairs surrounded a wooden table; to one side was a curtain, which I presumed concealed a bedchamber. Again, there was no window.

Without a word, the man ushered the Doctor and me into the chairs. The door creaked open and one of the monks entered, his face again obscured by his cowl. He carried three steaming bowls, set them on the table before us, bowed and left.

I was famished, having not eaten for several hours, and dragged the bowl towards me, feeling its heat tingling against my numb fingers. The soup's steam was rich and spicy, and the liquid contained clumps of white meat. I was about to bring the bowl to my lips when the Doctor shook his head in warning.

'What is the soup?' he asked nonchalantly, sliding his bowl away from him.

'We are provided with a supply of meat,' answered Mauritz.

'Cattle?' said the Doctor.

'We make the most of that which we have.'

'We?' I asked, reluctantly putting down my bowl. 'Who are you? What is this place?'

'A monastery?' suggested the Doctor.

'A place of study. Of contemplation, certainly. You are not hungry?'

I looked again at my soup. Following the Doctor's lead, I shook my head. 'Maybe later?' I smiled apologetically.

'Of course.'

The Doctor stood, the low ceiling causing him to stoop. He ruffled his hair. 'So would you say it was more a university?'

'All will be explained.' Mauritz rose from his chair. He considered for a moment, then smiled in decision. 'If you are ready, I will show you the citadel.'

We found ourselves in yet another vaulted chamber. Treading across the flagstones, I would have believed we had returned to the chamber in which the TARDIS had landed, except that a section of the wall had collapsed to reveal the cloisters beyond. Six monks busied themselves at the wall, clearing away the rubble and bracing the ceiling with wooden joists.

I had been handed a lantern, and walked over to the damaged wall, the shadows snaking away as I approached. The masonry lay in an advanced state of decay, the plaster crumbling to the touch. It seemed strangely brittle. Ground creepers coiled through the cracked flagstones.

A monk cemented a new brick into place, smoothing the edges with plates of wood. I sensed the Doctor and Mauritz approaching behind me, the light of their lamps conflating my own.

'This quarter of the citadel is currently uninhabited,' explained Mauritz. 'And undergoing renovation'.

The Doctor looked bleak. 'No sooner do you put it together, than it falls apart.'

'Indeed,' said Mauritz, covering his face with his cowl and moving amongst the identically dressed monks.

The Doctor took a brick from the pile, weighed it in his hands and then returned it. He looked for Mauritz amongst the monks, and remarked off-handedly, 'Where do you get the bricks from?'

'We make the most of that which we have.'

'Like the cattle?'

One of the monks lifted his cowl, revealing Mauritz's features. 'What we cannot use for food, we employ elsewhere.'

'So nothing goes to waste?'

'Inevitably there is always waste. That is taken to the gardens. Follow.'

The gardens turned out to be a chamber of the same dimensions as the library. The ground, however, consisted of soil, broken up into avenues. Dozens of monks toiled in the murky candlelight, hoeing the earth and planting bulbs. Others harvested the crop, which consisted of spindly growths, somewhere between a mushroom and a coral, that reached to little above knee-height. The gnarled stems and branches of the organisms were covered in transparent grey leaves and sickly, pale pod-fruit. Evidently whatever they were, they did not require natural light for sustenance.

We watched as a monk brushed some dirt over the bulbs and mixed it with compost, the rotten remains of fruit and meat.

'So everything is ploughed back,' said the Doctor. 'Home-grown, very efficient. Don't need to pop out to the supermarket much?'

'No,' replied Mauritz. 'We do not require outside support.'

'Not at all?' I asked. 'But you must, occasionally. You can't just live on this - '

'We never leave the citadel.'

'But *why*?' I removed my hands from my pockets and clapped my fist on my palm for emphasis.

A silence fell over Mauritz as he turned to the Doctor. Whilst I had been talking, the Doctor had strolled over to the monks, watching in fascination as they dug one of the fungus-corals out of the ground. He wandered around them, oblivious to the fact he was trampling over the crop. 'Hello, I'm the Doctor,' he said genially, addressing one of the robed figures. 'So you're on gardening duty, eh?'

The figure did not respond. The Doctor gave a nonplussed pout and turned to another figure. He blocked the monk's way. 'Still, I'm sure it's all worth it, come supper time.' The monk did not respond.

'Not Trappists, are you?' inquired the Doctor as he advanced on another monk. He brushed his nose and grinned. 'If you don't want to talk about it, I'll quite understand.'

The monk ignored him and turned his back on the Doctor. As he did, the Doctor leaned forward and pinched the top of the monk's cowl, drawing it back suddenly to reveal the face.

The monk was an elderly man, hairless, with lined features fixed in a downcast frown, his eyes buried in wrinkles. Black marks freckled his saggy, ghost-pale skin. He was obviously exhausted, close to death.

It was Mauritz.

Or, at least, an older version of Mauritz. This man was at least twenty years the elder of the man standing beside me.

The Doctor dashed over to another of the monks and tugged back his cowl. Again, it revealed the same face, but this time the man was about the same age as Mauritz. He did not seem startled or shocked. He simply gazed ahead, his eyes devoid of expression.

One by one, the remaining monks solemnly removed their hoods. They were all the same man, some little older than Mauritz, some twenty or thirty years his superior.

'Do not be alarmed,' said the original Mauritz. 'I should explain.'

'Cloning?' I suggested as we wound our way up yet another steep staircase. The climb was exhausting, the steps narrow and worn smooth, the walls dribbling with condensation. 'You're all clones of the same man?'

'Nothing so rudimentary.' Mauritz pushed open another door, and we emerged into a vaulted chamber. Again, the chamber was identical to the one in which the TARDIS had arrived, but it had the appearance of having been recently constructed. The plaster that covered the walls was smooth and clean, the lines of the brickwork were fine, the paving stones free of dust or grime. The air smelt clear and cool.

'You know,' remarked the Doctor, rubbing his lips, 'I'm beginning to get the feeling we're going round in circles.'

I agreed. I had a fleeting sensation of *déjà vu*. If I did not know better, I would say that we had been visiting the same chamber over and over again. But throughout our time in the citadel, we had never walked down a staircase, only up. So it was impossible.

'No, Adric, this *is* the chamber in which the TARDIS arrived,' said Mauritz. 'Or rather, the chamber into which your TARDIS will materialise. You see, in this part of the citadel, you have yet to make your visit.'

'What?' exclaimed the Doctor, somewhat over-loudly.

'Time is not an absolute here.' Mauritz walked to the centre of the chamber and gestured expansively. 'This citadel comprises all pasts, all futures. Take this chamber. We can visit this room at any point in its history. The day it was built, or a day later, or a hundred centuries later. Every room, at every point in time, exists within the realm of the citadel.'

I was beginning to understand. 'You mean, you can travel into the future, just by walking into another room?'

'Precisely,' smiled Mauritz. 'We can access any time, in any future.'

'Just a short hop down a corridor and *fa-zam*! you're back where you started, but in the next week?' suggested the Doctor.

'The... geography is inevitably a little more complicated that that, but yes. As you might expect, the more distant the future, the more inaccessible. A thousand years hence may be many miles away.'

'Of course, of course. It's all relative.' The Doctor grinned a wild grin.

'So here we are,' he said, waving his lantern-light across the chamber. 'Standing in the middle of last Wednesday.'

'So *that's* why you said there was no outside,' I breathed, patting my hands together. 'Because in every direction, there is no boundary to the citadel - there is merely more of the citadel, or rather the same citadel again, but at another time. More of the same rooms, extending further and further into the future.' I could barely contain my awe. To stand inside such an achievement of multi-dimensional engineering, I felt suddenly giddy.

'Infinite?' asked the Doctor, as though enquiring about the weather.

'Impossible to tell. But to answer your next question, yes, it is a closed system,' said Mauritz.

'Hence the recycling. No supermarket.' The Doctor wandered the chamber, lost in thought. 'You have to make the most of what you've got, I see, because there's nothing else...'

'It's incredible,' I said, jogging over to Mauritz. I couldn't help burbling with enthusiasm. 'A four-dimensional space, mapped into three dimensions. Of course, mathematically it's quite straightforward...'

'A four-dimensional space?' muttered the Doctor derisively, staring at his shoes. 'Five-dimensional!'

'Five?'

'The Doctor is correct,' said Mauritz. 'The citadel does not merely allow access to one future. It permits passage to *every* potential future.'

'What do you mean, every future?'

'Every probability is played out somewhere within the confines of this building. Naturally, the more remote the possibility, the more remote the region. But,' Mauritz leaned closer to me, fixing my eyes with his, 'take this chamber for instance. In ten years' time, it may have fallen into disrepair, or it may have been adapted for a new use. Both possibilities exist within the citadel.'

'A multiplicity?' I marvelled. 'But how do you do it?'

'The technical explanation is not relevant.' Mauritz collected his lamp and headed for the door opposite. 'Let me show you the new library. Or, to put it another way,' he said, pausing, 'let me show you the library when it was new.'

It was the same library, the same long, solemn hall, the same three galleries of bookcases, but a gust of warm air brushed our faces, and there was no taste of dust, no aura of decay. Hundreds of monks filled the chamber, occupying every desk, scratching away at parchment. Others bustled from bookcase to bookcase, recovering and filing the leathery tomes. Others hurried in from adjoining passageways, heaving in piles of dust-coated books. The chamber echoed with hushed words.

'So you can go to this same library in the future,' said the Doctor, 'see what will be written in ten, twenty years' time, and bring it back here?'

Mauritz nodded.

'And no fines to pay?' He grinned that irreverent grin again.

Mauritz smiled and shook his head.

'You must have a very efficient filing system,' joked the Doctor. 'But what about paradoxes?'

'Yes.' I shuffled forward. 'What if you go into one of the future libraries, take out a book, and in the process of bringing it back cause it not to be written?'

'Every potential future is as valid as any other,' explained Mauritz. 'Paradoxes may either stabilise or collapse.'

'Stabilise?' I couldn't help but assume a note of superiority. 'But that's ridiculous!'

Mauritz did not reply, but his expression disagreed.

'But it's not just every potential library that exists, is it, Mauritz?' said the Doctor darkly, his gaze averted. He nodded towards the monks. I had almost forgotten. Beneath those cowls and robes, they would all be identical copies of Mauritz.

'No,' said Mauritz. 'Every potential future version of myself also exists.'

'Together?' I shook my head in disbelief. 'You mean they... are all future versions of you?'

'Indeed. Learning from each other. Passing on their knowledge. All of them, what I am to become.' He blinked sadly.

I watched the monks in awe. The same man, at different stages in his life. Some hunched with age, others standing tall. Muttering to each other, passing parchments between them, oblivious to the sheer... impossibility of it all.

'For every potential course of action, there will be a future me,' said Mauritz, folding his arms. 'A future that I can learn from.'

'And thus know in advance the outcome of every decision,' said the Doctor delightedly. 'So you can predict events with the benefit of hindsight. How dreadfully cunning!'

'You mean,' I began, clicking my fingers in realisation, 'if you have a choice, you can go and visit a version of yourself from five years in the future, see how things turned out, and compare notes?'

'Precisely. For every choice, every alternative is played out within the realm of the citadel.' Mauritz paused. 'There is one more thing I wish to show you. Or would you prefer... to return to your craft?'

The Doctor and I exchanged glances. The Doctor stared at me with his wide, grave eyes, and I was gripped with a sudden foreboding. I shivered. For a moment, I considered suggesting we go back to the TARDIS. But, no, it was too fascinating an opportunity. We had to see more.

'So be it,' said Mauritz, leading us to one of the passageways. 'If you will join me - '

After an exhausting ascent up another sheer stairwell, we emerged from the citadel and I took in a lungful of rare night air. We ducked through a low archway and out onto a square balcony at the summit of a high building. Above us hung a heavy iron bell in its tower, ropes looping through open floor-hatches.

I made my way over to the balustrade, rested my hands upon its rough, rusted railings and gazed out across the turrets of what seemed to be a vast city. Everywhere there were narrow, vertiginous ledges and flues and bulwarks. Dark, sinister walls dropped away, some smothered in creepers and ivy, others choked in soot. Many hundreds of feet below us they sank into a tide of undulating fog.

Squinting into the distance, I spotted another bell-tower, its zenith rising through the drifting mist. A collapsed, hollowed-out edifice, it was otherwise in every way identical to the tower in which we stood. Looking to the left there was another bell-tower, again identical. And beyond that another bell-tower, and another, and another stretching away to the horizon. And not far distant, maybe a mile away, a bell-tower was undergoing construction.

I walked a complete circuit of the balustrade. In every direction, the minarets and ramparts and roofs continued in a never-ending maze of architectural confusion. A sea of buildings extending to infinity, at first similar in their greyness and bleakness, but in the details, each one unique. Acres of slate and coughing chimney-stacks, roof after roof of every incline and variety.

Something caught my attention at the nearest bell-tower. Standing within it, I could see three unmoving robed figures returning my gaze. Oddly, they were of different heights. Then I spotted more of the monks below, strolling through galleries, making their way up and down flights of stone stairs. Constantly in motion, hurrying from doorway to doorway in a ceaseless, mathematical pattern.

'The citadel,' announced Mauritz.

'It's endless,' I said, glancing up into the cloudless sky. Above us there was a canopy of blackness, scattered with a million untwinkling stars. Utterly still and lifeless. 'The stars...'

'Other possibilities,' said Mauritz. 'Too strange, too distant to reach.'

We stared out into that infinite, fog-laden night for some minutes, and then the Doctor spoke. He rounded on Mauritz, looked him straight in the face, and asked, 'But you still haven't explained *why*. What is it all for?'

'Contemplation. Research. Meditation.'

The Doctor *pah*-ed derisively.

Mauritz continued. 'I created the citadel because I wished – '

'You created all this?' I interrupted.

Mauritz nodded. 'Because I wished to study. To attain a plateau of pure thought. To create the purest philosophy. To reach understanding.'

'I see,' said the Doctor, then held up a hand. 'No. No, I don't. You built all this, single-handedly... to have a bit of a think?'

I decided to explain to the Doctor. 'But, don't you see? The intellectual resources here are unimaginable. Because every potential future-Mauritz can put his learning at the disposal of the current generation... every possible avenue of thought can be covered, studied, and recorded. A feedback loop of knowledge... It's fantastic!'

'Standing on the shoulders of giants,' brooded the Doctor, deliberately avoiding my gaze.

'Adric is correct,' said Mauritz. 'For every problem, every solution can be investigated. I have a hundred, a thousand, a million selves to consult.'

The Doctor remained unimpressed. He took another tour of the balustrade, and stared out into the distance. 'Or, rather,' he said, 'standing on your own shoulders, and pulling yourself up by your bootstraps.' He rounded on Mauritz. 'Don't you get lonely? I mean, here you are, all on your own, all however-many of you?'

Mauritz bowed. 'One is never alone if one appreciates one's own company.'

We had returned to Mauritz's dormitory. My calves ached from our long descent, and the heat of the fire came as a joyous relief. I dragged my chair nearer to the hearth and warmed my palms.

The Doctor slouched in the chair opposite, watching as a monk brought in three bowls. The monk handed me my bowl and spoon, and I inhaled a deep breath of the steaming soup. It smelt delicious. I stirred it and some white meat bobbed to the surface.

Mauritz sat at the table and ladled himself a mouthful of the soup. He looked directly at me as he swallowed, a smile wetting his lips. 'Please.'

I looked at the Doctor, who was staring vacantly as though awaiting some stage direction. I shrugged and brought a lump of the meat to my mouth –

The Doctor launched himself out of his chair and stood upright. 'Of course!' He glared at Mauritz. 'A closed system!'

I dropped my spoon. 'Doctor – ?'

'"We make the most of that which we have",' said the Doctor, hurling each word in Mauritz's direction. 'You don't keep any cattle here, do you?'

Mauritz did not reply.

'No, of course not, you don't need to. Where do they go, the future Mauritzes? Where do they all end up?' The Doctor knocked his bowl to the floor. 'A *feed*back loop! They end up right here, on the dining table!'

'What?' I gulped.

'You eat them,' said the Doctor. 'There's nothing else to eat, is there?'

Mauritz did not reply.

'All your future selves – boiled down to soup. And their skin... dried and bound into books. Their bones, baked to make bricks. This whole place, it's all made out of one thing. *You*!'

I looked down at the bowl. The white flesh I had been about to eat lurked beneath the surface. Human flesh. I shivered and felt a sudden coldness as the blood drained from my face.

'For each of my selves,' said Mauritz at last, 'there are a dozen or more potential future selves. When they die, they are not left to waste. Just as each of my selves learns from each of his future selves, so, when they die, he will draw nourishment from them.' He looked up at the Doctor and his lips parted into a grisly smile. 'Yes. Every brick of this citadel is made of my ground-up bones. Every book in the library is inked in my blood upon my skin. My body fat is used for candles, my hair is woven into twine. And what cannot be used is composted and ploughed back into the soil, to create the plants that provide oxygen and wood. I require nothing. I depend on no one but myself.'

'Well I've heard of self-sufficiency,' joked the Doctor humourlessly, 'but this is ridiculous.'

'At least,' continued Mauritz meaningfully. 'Until you arrived... now I have company.'

The Doctor nodded to me, and I inferred his meaning immediately. He gathered up his scarf, collected a lamp, violently upturned the table, and bolted for the door.

How we found our way back I do not know. We dashed across the library and hurried down the nearest stairwell, grabbing the walls for balance. I struggled to keep up with the Doctor, barely able to see more than the reflected glimmer of his lantern, whilst also taking care not to tread on his trailing scarf. We passed through dozens of vaulted chambers, all in different states of disrepair, some thick with ivy, some collapsed, some freshly constructed. We hurried through the library, its empty shelves draped with cobwebs, its floor smothered in dust, the air still and silent. We dashed through the gardens, some full of monks tending the stunted corals, others filled with ghost-pale trees.

But after another descent down another narrow staircase, we emerged into the vaulted chamber in which we had first arrived. I recognised the patterns of rot that daubed the walls, and our footprints trailed across the musty floor.

The Doctor swung his lamp forward, and in the corner the TARDIS emerged from the darkness. The lamp flame reflected in its windows. A surge of relief filled my heart as we ran towards it.

There was a grinding, churning sound. The light on the TARDIS roof span and flashed. I could almost reach out and touch the surface of the police box as it faded from view. I found myself staggering into the square of floor it had deserted. The sound of dematerialisation hung in the air for some seconds more.

The TARDIS had gone.

Recovering my breath, I looked up, aghast. The Doctor and I had been joined in the chamber by dozens of monks. Some stood tall and stooped, some were about my height. They lined the walls, each of them in robes, their faces concealed by their cowls. They made no motion, and gave no sound.

Another monk entered and lifted his hood. Mauritz. He raised his lantern, its red flame flickering in his eyes.

'Your time machine has gone,' he said.

I exchanged a worried glance with the Doctor. He looked suddenly unnerved, his expression grim. 'We noticed!'

'Do not be alarmed,' said Mauritz. 'As you will remember, the citadel does not merely allow access to *one* future. Every potential future is played out within these walls. Earlier, you had the choice to depart in the TARDIS. There was the possibility you might leave, or the possibility you might stay.' He paused. 'But both alternatives occurred. So... there was the Doctor and Adric who returned to the TARDIS and left.' He gestured towards the empty stone floor. 'And you. *The Doctor and Adric who decided to stay.*'

I took a step backwards, my mouth suddenly dry.

'You will join me. As it shall be, so it has always been.'

Mauritz smiled as all the other monks in the room lifted back their hoods. I immediately recognised the faces.

The monks were me and the Doctor. Over and over again. Some looked as we did now. Others were many years older and had grey hair, and lined faces, and watery eyes.

I saw myself as a man of forty, my skin coarsened with age. I saw myself as a man of sixty, my hair thin, my skin cracked and folded. I saw myself as a man of eighty, bald, my skin blotched with cancers.

And the Doctor - that same face, over and over again, but with the eyes increasingly hooded and dulled, the hair increasingly thin and grey. Wearing an expression of infinite sadness and regret.

'You have always been here,' said Mauritz. 'Here, by my side. Welcome.'

The Comet's Tail

John Binns

As the Doctor stirred into consciousness, it was with some irritation that he realised he had been woken by the sound of his doorbell ringing. Although he couldn't remember as such, he thought it highly likely that he had left strict instructions that he should not be disturbed until much later. It was rare enough that he found any time to sleep these days, and the least he could expect was that he would be able to wake naturally, and at a reasonable hour, rather than with a persistent bing-bong, bing-bong at - he shot a bleary glance to the clock-radio at his bedside - around a quarter past five. It would be a pleasant surprise, the Doctor thought, for people to have just a little consideration now and again.

With an effort he forced his eyes to stay open, adjusted his sight to the darkness. It was a small bedroom, perhaps eight feet by ten or a little more - just enough for his bed, a wardrobe, chest of drawers and a bedside table. The furniture was elegant, Victorian, probably, and there was something about the predominance of mahogany that the Doctor found comforting. Clicking on the bedside lamp, he noted that someone - perhaps a landlady, or a well-meaning cleaner - had clearly tried to make him feel at home, by the use of thick, pencil-drawn roundels over two of the walls. They were a little larger than they should be, not so uniformly placed, and a few had circumferences that veered wildly from the circular in one or two places. But all the same, it was good to know that someone had made the effort.

With the doorbell ringing again - there had been a brief pause, but it was too much to hope for that the caller might have given up - the Doctor hauled himself out of bed, placed his feet into his waiting slippers and dragged on the dressing-gown from the hook on his bedroom door. There was a small mirror at head-height next to the door, in which the Doctor expected to see the long, blond hair of his new regeneration in an unholy mess, and his clear blue eyes bleary and bloodshot with stress and lack of sleep. But as it turned out the mirror showed only a pale grey mist, as if it had steamed up somehow from the inside. Absently he gave it a light tap with his knuckle, as if that might somehow clear the fog - but it didn't, and the Doctor resolved that he would just have to have another look at it later.

By the time the Doctor had made it down the stairs and opened his front door, the speed and frequency of the doorbell-ringing had become decidedly anxious. Alarmingly, as he opened the door to the biting cold, it was not one but more than a dozen callers that greeted him. Many of them, like him, had evidently rushed outdoors in their nightclothes, but some were dressed in the primary-coloured tunics and slacks that seemed to pass for fashion amongst the townsfolk. With barely an exception they huddled together in twos and threes, their diminutive forms - even the tallest was no more than four feet, and that included the crest of blue-green feathers that erupted from his crown - huddled together for warmth.

At the front of the crowd was a reptilian couple, whose neat white coats reminded the Doctor that they were the proprietors of the local pharmacy. The male was clearly flustered, kneading his scaly hands together and blinking up at the Doctor with a pathetically pleading gaze.

'What's wrong?' the Doctor managed, his voice cracking slightly with the tiredness and the cold. The pharmacist couple mouthed an agitated reply, their forked tongues jutting in and out as they spoke. Frustratingly though, and not for the first time, the Doctor found himself incapable of understanding their language, or indeed of hearing it: despite straining and concentrating for all it was worth, the Doctor could hear only silence. Looking beyond them, it was clear that none of their neighbours would be able to impart anything vocally either. Fortunately, after a while a dirty-looking seagull child was able to attract his attention, pointing into the sky to the Doctor's left.

Following the child's line of sight, looking into the direction of the town centre and far above the spire of the church, the Doctor saw the source of their agitation: an angry, blazing shape far above them, outlined against the cloudless, dusk-blue sky by a ragged, white-hot tail. At such a distance the Doctor thought it would be difficult to judge its trajectory, but he was well aware that for the townsfolk there would be little comfort in quoting odds. The comet, for all intents and purposes - and quite frankly, he could give no definite assurance of the opposite - was heading straight for the town.

'Stay there,' he said over the pharmacist couple's heads, in a tone he hoped would be reassuring. 'I'm sure I've got some literature on these things in the bookshop; I'll just get the keys, and we'll go and have a look.' The townsfolk were nodding, their fears abated for a moment, while the Doctor kept two thoughts to himself. The first was that he would never normally have come to the front door without his keys with him, and at that precise moment he had no idea (the bedside table, or in his shoes, perhaps?) where they were. The second was that, although he was confident there would indeed be information on this comet in the bookshop, he was rather less so that any such data would be sufficient to help them.

Once he'd closed the doors on his callers and started up the stairs again, therefore, the Doctor was in a decidedly despondent mood. It didn't help that the landing at the top of the stairs had been altered since he'd last used it, so that he had to make a detour around the second or third bathroom, in order to transfer to the west staircase and continue the journey from there. By the time he reached the second floor it was embarrassingly clear to him that he was lost, not least because he still wasn't entirely clear where he was heading. Fortunately, an increasingly strong aroma of coffee at least gave him something to aim for.

The fourth door on the right at the top of the west staircase was panelled oak, and it was already slightly ajar. There was only a little surprise in the Doctor's mind when he pushed it open and found about half a dozen tables arranged around the room, around half of them seating various young men and women in (at a rough estimate) very late twentieth century dress. A bar area along one side of the room appeared to be serving coffee; the other walls were sparsely decorated with abstract art and bookshelves. In response to that part of his mind that protested that it was simply too early to be ordering coffee, another part of him rationalised that it must now be the middle of the morning.

Still, he was disorientated. He suddenly imagined that he must be conspicuous, standing at the doorway and looking startled, and so he was glad to see the young woman at the nearest table offering him a seat.

'I'm so grateful,' he told her earnestly, as he sat down at the small wooden table. He was gratified to see that the woman had arranged some tea for him, which she pushed towards him in a large china cup.

'I knew you liked sugar,' the woman said, as she indicated the cup with a smooth and delicate hand. 'So I went a bit crazy. There's eight or nine sachets in there.'

The Doctor nodded, and smiled at her: he couldn't argue with that. He took a sip of the tea, which was beautifully sweet and hot. He looked deep into the rich, brown liquid, and was grateful for that moment of clarity and focus as for the tea itself. 'I really think I'm lost,' he confessed, looking straight at the young woman as he said it. She was slim, no more than twenty-one years old, with short dark hair and a smart, navy-blue jacket. She had the air of being a student, perhaps a post-graduate. For the first time, the Doctor noticed there were two neat, A4 ring-binders on the table, one red, one blue, which she delicately moved out of the way of her coffee.

'Don't worry. I think we all feel a bit lost sometimes.' She waved a hand towards the ring-binders, as if to help her make a point. 'Particle physics, for instance. I must have slept through a good twenty minutes of that this morning; either that, or I must be genetically incapable of understanding it.' From the pronunciation of *genetically*, in particular, the Doctor guessed that the woman's accent was South African. She was clearly well-intentioned towards him, and he felt somewhat awkward as he winced and frowned back at her.

'I'm terribly sorry,' he said at last. 'I really don't have any idea who you are.'

He expected her face to fall, a bewildered cry, and he wished there had been a better way to say it. But instead there was a flash of sudden realisation, a bounced-back memory, a waking-up. Her warmth and good humour didn't falter for a moment. 'Gosh, yes!' she exclaimed. 'I'm sorry about that. I'm Matilda. You must think I'm an absolute idiot, buying you tea, rabbiting on about particle physics. You'll have to forgive me, I'm afraid.' She fixed him with a stare as if to make sure he did. 'It's possible I might be eccentric, or peculiar, or at the very least substantially odd. You don't need to talk to me at all, if you don't want. I can carry on with my latte, sitting here on my own until someone more interesting turns up. But I thought I could talk to you. I don't know, but I think it might be something about your face that makes me think it might be pleasant to share a coffee with you.' She seemed to relax suddenly, as her fingers closed around her own giant cup. 'Or heavily sugared tea. You don't mind, do you, really? I promise I'll forgive you if you do.'

The Doctor found himself cradling his own cup quite tightly, as if the girl's moment of animation had been somehow infectious. 'Not at all,' he said with what he hoped was a polite smile. 'It's just that I think I must have got a little sidetracked, somewhere along the line,' he told her. 'I was looking for the library, I think: some... astronomy research.'

'I don't think you've come at the right time,' Matilda said. 'If I've read this term's timetable properly, that is, and it wouldn't be the first time if I hadn't.' Again she waved towards the ring-binders, and the Doctor wondered for a moment whether he should ask her for a copy of the timetable. It would certainly be a help if he was going to be expected to attend lectures, and even more so if he were expected to be giving them.

'I just have a feeling it might be urgent,' he decided to tell her.

'I'm sure it is,' Matilda said, but there was nothing in her response to hint that she properly understood. She took another sip of her coffee, licked the foam away from her lower lip. 'You're never involved in anything that isn't urgent, it seems to me. Gadgets to fix, monsters to run from, planets to save. It's all such a terrible rush. Whatever you do, it always seems to need sorting out at the very last moment, or later. Of course I can't pretend I know what that's like: I spend half my time running away from deadlines, missing lectures; the occasional terrorist alert is the closest I get to the world's problems. But you're out there dealing with them, sorting the universe out. I consider myself very lucky to have caught you for a moment, even if it is bound to be brief.'

Relieved for a moment, the Doctor took another sip of his tea. He noted with some puzzlement, but gratefully, that he was dressed. It seemed likely that he wasn't actually here at all, on reflection. He looked past Matilda to a window in the far wall, through which he could see the comet against a dark green sky. Sitting at a table by the window was an old man, grey-haired, bearded, whose red robes denoted his status as dean of the university. He didn't seem to have a drink, and was instead looking mournfully at a book.

'I don't think I should be here,' the Doctor told Matilda at length. And then: 'I'm not even sure I *am* here.'

Matilda shrugged at that, unperturbed, but then her smile faded for the first time, and she frowned. 'Why not, though?' she asked him. 'Are you sure you have to be somewhere else?'

She was looking straight at him again. Her eyes were wide and vivid green.

He looked away. 'I'm sorry,' he said. 'This is important. I have to try something.' He closed his eyes, and took his hands away from the teacup. In a second or two, he lost all sense of his surroundings, until even the smell of the coffee had gone.

There was a brief moment in which the Doctor was nowhere, and alone. Somewhere in the back of his mind, as if from miles away, he heard the sound of an explosion.

When he opened his eyes again he was in the midst of a crowd, mostly troops he thought (pale green uniforms, machine guns raised), and without exception running, briskly, through a street. He was in their way, clearly, and in the circumstances he thought it best to run as well.

The street was wide and devoid of traffic: he could see now that he was in company with around three or four dozen of the green-clad troops, who were all human and relatively young. Looking at the buildings on either side of the street, and the city square up ahead, the Doctor mentally tagged this as an Earth colony visited by one of his previous incarnations - he didn't remember the name; inevitably, there had been so many over the years - in the context of some invasion or other. Some of the buildings were familiar to him, but grimy and weather-beaten; others were more modern, fashioned in stainless steel, with bright reds and greens shouting out at him. The Doctor reckoned that at least a generation had passed since his previous incarnation had left.

Looking back for a moment, he saw a dozen or so figures bringing up the rear of the troop movement - or, perhaps, pursuing it. They too were humanoid, but they wore sleek body-coverings, jet-black, and perfect mirror coverings over their faces. Each had a medium-length black coat, which flapped very slightly in the wind as they ran; they too carried large, fearsome-looking machine guns. On the Doctor's previous visit these creatures had been instrumental in the invasion's defeat, and silently he prayed to himself that they had not somehow gone rogue. If he remembered rightly they were not robots, but more like golems - constructed entirely from biological material, and programmed genetically rather than mechanically to enhance the colony's fighting potential. They had been called Implementation Units, he thought, originally, but with their customary efficiency the humans had shortened that to Imps.

He looked beyond his immediate surroundings and registered plumes of smoke rising in the middle distance, dirty-grey against a dark green sky. He heard another explosion, fainter and farther away than the first, and wondered absently at the source of the bombardment. Perhaps, he thought, it was of natural origin rather than actual aggression: certainly, there was the comet to consider, or possibly it had been a meteorite. He couldn't see it in the sky, and he pondered the possibility that the object had fragmented and hit - in which case, he couldn't see very much that he could do about it. He wondered if the troops around him knew that he was the Doctor, and decided not to tell them until he knew a little more. Certainly, if this was something to do with the Imps, he didn't much relish the prospect of being blamed.

By now they had reached the market square, and with a shout from the troops' commander the whole crowd came to an abrupt stop. The opposite side of the square was a terrible, billowing mass of smoke, obscuring the bottom fifty feet or so of the cluster of buildings. The

Doctor remembered advising them a generation ago to keep their buildings close to the ground, in order to minimise their susceptibility to any attack from the skies. But clearly, they had ignored that advice: the buildings around the square were immensely tall, modern, ornate and proud. The main building, from which most of the smoke poured, had a spire above it as if it were some sort of church - curious, the Doctor thought, as he remembered it as a secular world.

The troops appeared to be talking amongst themselves: though he strained to hear, it was impossible for the Doctor to make out what they were saying. Somehow or other, the Imps were no longer with them - although, as he strained to look through the smoke at the building in front of him, the Doctor thought he could make out some of them running in and out.

Not for the first time, the Doctor wondered whether there was anything he could do. Meanwhile, he was becoming aware of something tugging at his left sleeve.

He looked behind him, and then down a few feet. It was a young boy, with the eyes, nose and whiskers of a dog: he was pointing, with the paw that wasn't holding on to the Doctor's sleeve, up into the sky. The comet was still there, and it was substantially larger than before. Its tail, still angry and forceful in its intensity, now seemed to blaze above it rather than behind it, hinting that its trajectory was headed towards them.

The Doctor's cottage was just behind them, fortunately, and he looked through its window at the bookshop he now owned and managed. 'I'm sure we can find something in there that can help us,' he told the dog-faced boy, 'if I can only find the way in.' He started to fumble in his pockets, as it occurred to him that he had not intended to bring the dog-boy here, to this world. He shot him an angry look, as if to reproach him for his presence, but if the boy realised what the Doctor meant, he didn't show it. Instead, he formed his right paw into a fist, as if to break the shop window. At this the Doctor's patience snapped.

'We are not breaking in,' he insisted, raising his right index finger as if to make the point. 'This is not just a bookshop, you know. It's more appropriate to think of it as a nursery of ideas. The concepts imagined in these volumes are still growing, developing and connecting with each other. Eventually they could form the foundations of whole cultures.' A new thought occurred to him. 'And besides,' he added, 'in this time and space most of the authors of these books are dead, or perhaps not even born. It's up to me to look after them instead.'

Dog-boy seemed unimpressed. But by now, the Doctor had discovered a large bunch of keys in his pocket, and he fell silent as he looked at them, trying to remember which one opened the bookshop. In the background, he could still hear the troops yelling at each other and a closer, smaller explosion. 'It's one of these,' he said uselessly as he looked in bafflement at the dozen or so keys on the ring. Thinking about it, he couldn't be sure there was a key to the bookshop here, or even that he'd been given one when he'd taken it over. Frustrated, he resigned himself to having to try the keys one by one.

He'd tried three or four of the keys by the time the first Imp showed itself inside the bookshop, sidling up behind the shelves of the biography section, as if trying not to attract attention. It was joined by two more, who moved slowly and calmly into position around the room. They seemed content simply to stand there, facing each other rather than outside or the books - their blank, mirrored faces producing infinities in each other as they did so.

'I think they're guarding it,' the Doctor told the dog-faced boy. 'They don't mean the books any harm.' Equally though, he thought it unlikely that they were going to let him or his companion in. He'd have to think of something else.

Two of the uniformed humans had manoeuvred themselves into position around him. He turned and noted the stripes on their collars, denoting a senior rank, but also that they were absurdly young - one, a boy of no more than fifteen; the other, a girl who looked only slightly older.

'Ah, Doctor,' the boy said. The Doctor thought of asking him how he had known who he was, but somehow it didn't seem proper. 'We've been looking for you.'

'Ah,' the Doctor said in return. Embarrassingly, he discovered he was unable to hide his disappointment at having been found. 'What's the problem?' he said at last, attempting to seem business-like.

'The Imps,' the girl said. 'Three days ago they seemed to lose control completely; they're marauding around the city, stealing as much food and supplies as they can. We think they're deserting.'

'Oh.' Of all the ways to describe such behaviour, the Doctor thought, 'loss of control' probably wasn't the best: if anything control was what they were after, if only of themselves. But still, he applied his mind to the problem, reasoning that though there was little hope of reprogramming them as such, it might be worth trying to detect some kind of command structure as a means of entering into negotiations.

'We want you to wear this,' the boy cut in. Already he and his colleague were moving what looked like giant, off-white blocks of plastic into position around his arms and legs: the Doctor guessed it was some sort of protective armour. He winced as the pad for his right leg locked into position, seeming to mould itself around the limb like an instant plaster-cast. 'It's just a precaution,' the boy continued, unconvincingly, 'to protect you from the Imps. In case of combat, the armour will afford you a hundred times more strength.'

As giant plastic sleeves locked themselves around the Doctor's arms, he nodded grimly at his young comrades. Strength was precisely what he needed, no doubt: there were few problems in the universe that couldn't be solved with that. 'Just one thing, though,' he said. 'I wonder – '

Before he could finish the sentence the Doctor's head was enclosed in a gigantic, hemispherical helmet. Alarmingly, the loss of feeling that had overcome his arms, legs and torso when they had been covered had now extended to his senses. There was not a trace of light available to him, nor a sound; the only thing he could feel was a jet of air coming from somewhere near the bottom of the armour suit, which was ever-so-slightly too warm. *How am I going to move*, he thought, but already he could detect the answer, as he numbly felt his right leg moving forward as if by remote control. With a distinct sense of panic he wondered what weapons the armour carried.

'Don't worry.' The Doctor heard the male soldier's voice crackle into his left ear, clearly switching on an internal radio. 'I'm turning on visual now.'

Sure enough, with a harsh click, a clear image flashed on in front of him, as if a few feet ahead – rectangular, as if he were watching the scene on television. He saw the coffee bar with its tables and chairs in disarray, the patrons – including a shaking Matilda – huddled together with fear in the far corner. Opposite them, there was a vast hole in the outside wall of the room, a halo of smoke and fire surrounding it; the sky beyond was an angry red, dominated by the head of the comet, now very close to them.

The Doctor was aware of the armour carrying him slowly forward, with big, lumbering steps. His feet were so heavy that the floor seemed to shake with his weight. The coffee bar's patrons seemed not to notice his presence, though – except for Matilda, who shot him an inexplicably withering look. As if to say: *Must you*?

There was still very little sensation within the suit, but the warm air he had felt earlier was now joined with another source of heat. In the small of his back the Doctor felt a sharp stabbing of extreme warmth from what he guessed was the armour's engine or propulsion system, possibly charging up. The heat was almost unbearable, as if he were on fire.

The building was rocked suddenly with another gigantic explosion. The Doctor was aware that the floor directly beneath him was burning, but of course he was unable to move. It seemed unlikely that anyone here would be able to get him out of the suit; the dean, by now, had disappeared. He could see that Matilda was screaming.

And then the ground gave way: not just beneath him, but the whole room. There was an unholy clatter as the bookshelves ranged along the walls lurched forward, and hundreds of aged volumes fell hopelessly into space.

The Doctor's visual monitor struggled with the input, as the armoured suit fell through one floor, then two, before crashing face-down into the west staircase.

As the picture cut out, the Doctor was aware only of the intense heat that had flared up in his back growing hotter and hotter. He surmised that the armour must have been damaged by the impact, as a degree of sensation returned to his arms and legs. He was aware then of falling again, sliding to the foot of - again, he surmised - the west staircase, his legs very probably broken.

Alarmingly though, the Doctor's world remained sightless, and silent: for all he knew, the entire building could now be on fire, but in his state he couldn't even see it, let alone do anything to stop it. Meanwhile he was undoubtedly burning, and unable to move a muscle. From in front of him, he could feel another object moving in closer. He tried to move away, but his body was unresponsive.

The object took his arm, somehow getting through the heavy armoured sleeve.

It was Matilda: he could feel the soft wool of her coat under his fingers. Again he tried to move, but there was nothing he could do. The heat was growing all the time, and he could sense somehow that the building had collapsed entirely. It was entirely possible that no one else had survived, and it was just him and Matilda huddled together there in the wreckage. Though he tried to think, there really seemed to be no more options left open to him. He couldn't even say he was sorry.

And so they burned together, brightly, fiercely, and for what seemed to him like forever.

Long Term

Andy Campbell

The Latin master was once again absent throughout the entire period, so Abney had the opportunity to visit the school library to do some research of his own; and it was here that the first peculiar incident took place.

The library was an immense echoing cathedral of a room, with ancient hard-backed tomes crowding the oak bookcases that spanned floor to ceiling on every side. Dust had sifted steadily from the higher shelves to the lower, so that the shelf Abney wanted - the one containing the texts on existentialism - was filthy with the grime of centuries. Each volume he consulted creaked in his small hands, as if ready to disintegrate at the handling.

The boy felt a sense of awe, as he had so often before, at the extent of the library. Emerging from one labyrinth of bookcases, one simply entered another, and then another. There was rarely any difficulty in locating the exit, but there appeared to be no limit to the distance one could walk from it. Abney's deepest excursion into the library had taken him six hours: a little under three hours on the outward trip, a little over three heading back towards the exit. His favourite book, a transcription of J M Barrie's play *Peter Pan*, had once taken him many hours to find, despite the fact that the library was known to possess multiple copies of it, and to store them under a wide range of thematic categories.

It was while Abney was thoughtfully consulting a dusty copy of Sartre's *Huis Clos* that he became aware that he was not alone in the library. Someone had crept in surreptitiously to join him, making small breathy sounds. Turning around, he was alarmed to see that the visitor was not one of his classmates.

'Let me help you, boy,' the visitor said. Abney's shriek made the bookshelves around him tremble, releasing plumes of grey dust into the air. Then the peculiar incident occurred.

Much later, the other boys, led by Parkins, thoroughly investigated the part of the library where Abney had been working. Every surface within fifteen feet of the spot where he had been standing was smeared with some part of the boy. Through careful inspection, however, the boys ascertained that there was enough organic material present to constitute a whole body, so they were able to conclude that cannibalism had not been the motive for the attack. Abney's visitor, it appeared, had appetites of another kind.

The second peculiar incident took place in the mundane setting of the boys' lavatory, located somewhere along a corridor in one of the science areas. The chemistry master being once again absent throughout the entire period, Haynes Junior had taken himself off to the toilet, and was washing his hands in freezing water in one of the chipped porcelain washbasins. Absent-mindedly watching his breath forming clouds in the cold air, he realised that something was amiss; but for some minutes he was unable to determine what it was.

Finally he deduced what was wrong. Of the eight toilet cubicles lining one wall of the room, seven had their doors standing open as usual, but the eighth - the one farthest from the exit - was apparently occupied. Yet Haynes had been in the lavatory for some minutes, and had heard no sound from the cubicle, so had naturally assumed he was alone.

He suspected that he should simply leave, but something about the enigmatic closed door of that last cubicle compelled him to stay. Holding his breath, he made his way steadily across the tiled floor towards it. Still no sound came from inside. Did the occupant know he was here? Was he, like Haynes, keeping silent, for some reason of his own?

Very slowly, Haynes got down onto his knees to peer beneath the cubicle door. Two dark, dirty-looking shoes could be seen through the six-inch gap beneath it. The shoes were unmoving. The boy slowly straightened up again, listening to his heartbeat, hoping it could not be heard outside his body. He gingerly reached out a hand to push against the cubicle door.

For Haynes, time seemed to slow down. He watched his own hand, palm open, moving through the air towards the cubicle door. It seemed to him that the movement took forever, as if he were pushing his palm through layers of treacle. Then, when his hand was within an inch of touching it, the door was pulled abruptly inwards, and he saw what was seated inside.

Later, there was another grim scene for Parkins and the other boys to discover. All eight toilet cubicles, the porcelain washbasins, the fly-spotted mirrors, the tiled floor, the grimy walls, the cracked ceiling, were splattered with the boy's remains. Not the tiniest part of Haynes, Junior had escaped the visitor's attentions. It might have been thought that a bomb had detonated inside his body. Little was left that would even have appeared human on casual inspection.

* * *

The third peculiar incident occurred in the school gymnasium: specifically, in one of its various gymnasia, for there was more than one, and no one could say for sure how many. The mathematics master was once again absent throughout the entire period, so Karswell and Humphreys decided they would go and take some vigorous exercise as a welcome alternative to their endless studies.

The gymnasium was disconcertingly vast, but over the years the boys had grown used to it. It no longer occurred to them as strange that it was impossible to see from one end of it to the other with the unaided eye. It now seemed only natural that it should possess not one but hundreds of vaulting horses, not just a few but thousands – perhaps hundreds of thousands – of assorted barbells and dumbbells. Who knows what demand there might be for exercise apparatus in a sizeable boys' school? The gymnasium was dark, too; one would have said it was candlelit, had there been any candles in view; and the shadows stirred endlessly, dark shapes on dark wood.

Karswell was climbing a rope, while Humphreys observed his progress. It was a feat of both daring and endurance, since the rope extended into the nebulous upper shadows of the gymnasium until it was lost from view. The rope had to be attached to the ceiling in some way, but the ceiling (this had also come to be accepted without question) could not be seen, so that the rope might just as well have been hovering and swaying under the supernatural influence of an Asian mystic. Heedless of this, Karswell continued his climb.

As Humphreys lost sight of Karswell in the dark upper reaches of the gymnasium, he started to feel anxious. The ascending boy's grunts of exertion faded into silence; Humphreys hoped his friend had left himself enough energy to get safely back down. There was a pause, lengthening until Humphreys's anxiety began to turn to fear.

'Is all well up there?' he called. His accent was all elegant received pronunciation. 'Karswell?'

Humphreys strained his ears to catch any reply his friend might make. What he eventually heard – or rather felt, as a minute vibration in his inner ear – was an infinitely distant cracking sound, reaching him from somewhere high, high above his head, from somewhere amidst the dark sky of the ceiling.

A sudden terrible certainty gripped Humphreys, a flash of insight of a kind he had recently been experiencing more and more often: somehow, someone was up there with Karswell. Someone who dwelt in the upper reaches of the immense gymnasium, uncurling to greet the boy as he ascended into the dark.

Humphreys managed to comfort himself: the distant cracking sound had been ambiguous, perhaps even a product of his imagination; there had been no cry of distress; Karswell was perfectly capable of looking after himself; his own fears were irrational.

Now there was movement above, dangerously fast. For a sickening moment Humphreys was sure that Karswell was tumbling back down towards him. He strained his eyes upwards into the gloom. But what fell back down the length of the rope, drenching Humphreys from head to foot, was not Karswell at all, but a shower of tiny human fragments.

Humphreys was discovered later by Parkins and his other classmates, physically unharmed, but in a state of psychological disarray that promised to be permanent.

The schoolroom was steeped in slowly moving shadow. Darkness flowed up and down the wood-panelled walls, in and out of the inkwells of the battered wooden desks. On the ancient blackboard, carefully chalked in block capitals, was the message:

Dr Sampson is unfortunately unable to be present for today's physics lesson, due to unforeseen circumstances. Please continue making preliminary notes for your essay entitled 'Economy, compatibility and plausibility in quantum mechanical formalism.'

Presently, a most incongruous sound welled up from nowhere to banish the silence of the schoolroom: a ghostly suggestion of the twiddle and bleep of electronic systems, more and more deeply submerged beneath a rhythmic grinding scrape. As the grinding swelled to a bellowing crescendo, the air flushed dark blue and resolved itself into a standing cuboid, solidity flooding through it. With a terminal crunch the noise ceased, and the object stood imposingly a few feet in front of the blackboard, obscuring the chalked message.

Perhaps the young-looking blond man who emerged cautiously from the box appeared less incongruous in the schoolroom than his vehicle. With his long fawn coat, neatly edged with red trim, his cream pullover and his striped trousers, he might well have been no stranger to academia, certainly not to a cricket pitch.

The man watched curiously as a line of a dozen uniformed schoolboys filed dutifully into the classroom from the corridor outside. Wood scraped noisily on wood as the boys took their seats, each before his own desk. Some of the seats, the man observed, were empty.

For a long time there was an uncomfortable silence. Finally one of the boys asked courteously: 'Excuse me, sir. Are you the physics master?'

The man was gazing thoughtfully around the classroom, taking in each of the expectant young faces in turn. Each of the boys appeared to be aged about twelve or thirteen. 'I'm afraid not,' he replied carefully, as if anxious not to disappoint. 'I'm a – Doctor.'

'Excuse me, sir?' asked another of the boys. 'Has the physics master perhaps been detained?'

Peering around the gloomy classroom, the Doctor now noticed the message chalked on the blackboard. 'It appears he has. I'm sorry you've been dragged here for no reason.'

'Don't worry, sir,' a third boy said kindly. 'It happens a good deal, as far as I can recall. And I'm quite sure he will have left plenty of work for us to get on with in his absence.'

'Yes,' the Doctor confirmed, still reading the chalked message. 'Yes, naturally.'

'You could perhaps give us a little test, sir?' asked a fourth boy, a pleasant-looking lad with an untidy tangle of red hair. His suggestion was followed by a chorus of enthusiastic approval from the others.

'What's your name?' the Doctor asked the boy.

'Dennistoun, sir.'

For a moment the Doctor appeared nonplussed. Then with a sudden burst of inspiration, he exclaimed: 'Physics! Very well, Mr Dennistoun – explain quantum field theory.'

'Sir, it's an inclusive theory of interactions between fundamental particles, with each type of particle represented by appropriate operators that obey the laws of commutation. The particles are the quanta of fields in just the same way as photons are the quanta of the electromagnetic field.'

The Doctor gazed into the boy's eyes for a few moments. Then he turned to another of the classmates. 'What's *your* name?'

'Anstruther, sir.'

'Very well. Mr Anstruther, define entropy.'

'Sir, it's a term in classical thermodynamics: a measure of the extent to which the energy in a system is available for conversion to work. Statistical mechanics interprets the increase in entropy in a closed system to a maximum at equilibrium as the consequence of the trend from a less probable state to a more probable one. Consequently, the predicted heat death of the universe – '

'Thank you, Mr Anstruther.' The Doctor turned to another of the boys, this one bespectacled, his left cheek riddled with acne. 'And *your* name?'

'Poynter, sir.'

'Mr Poynter, what can you tell the rest of the class about neutron spectroscopy?'

'Sir, neutron spectroscopy is an experimental determination of the intensity and change in wavelength of the neutrons scattered in a particular direction when a beam of monoenergetic particles are incident on a crystal. It's an obsolete method for studying lattice vibrations.'

'Obsolete?'

'Yes, sir.'

After a long and thoughtful pause, the Doctor addressed another of the boys, a handsome but anxious-looking lad with curly blonde hair and dark green eyes.

'And *your* name?'

'Parkins, sir.'

'Mr Parkins, what is the year?'

'Sir, it's a measure of time corresponding to one complete revolution of a planet around its parent star.'

'No, Mr Parkins,' said the Doctor patiently. 'What year is it *now*?'

Parkins faltered. 'The same year it's always been, sir. I mean...' His voice trailed off in confusion.

'Can *anyone* tell me what year it is now?'

There was a long silence. The boys began glancing uncertainly at each other, then back at the Doctor.

'Abney was the real specialist in metaphysics, sir,' somebody offered finally. 'But I'm afraid he's dead.'

It was one of the most cordial receptions the Doctor had received in some time; the boys made him most welcome. They shared sandwiches and orange juice with him in the school's refectory, although they had to admit, with some embarrassment, that they did not know where these refreshments came from. Food and drink were always in ready supply in the refectory, yet to the best of the boys' recollection, no kitchen staff had ever been seen.

'Tell me, boys,' the Doctor said cautiously, 'have you noticed anything strange about your school?'

Again the boys exchanged uncertain glances.

'Strange?' asked Parkins.

'There are all the usual amenities, sir,' said a skinny boy called Dillet, rather defensively. 'The laboratories are extremely well equipped, and the library contains every work imaginable.'

The Doctor sipped his orange juice. 'That's a lot of books,' he observed, mainly to himself.

'*Every* work imaginable,' Dillet emphasised.

'I imagine the playing fields are quite splendid,' said the Doctor cheerily. 'Do you like cricket?'

'I've read a great deal about cricket,' Poynter commented eagerly.

'But have you *played* it?'

'Where, sir?' Poynter asked.

The Doctor was staring curiously into the boy's eyes. He now discerned for the first time that something was wrong with them, but could not for the moment place what it was.

'The playing fields, Mr Poynter,' the Doctor said. 'Outside.'

'Outside...' said Poynter slowly.

'I've discovered something rather odd,' said the Doctor. 'I should share it with you. Consider it a physics problem.'

The boys waited eagerly for this new test of their knowledge.

'It's just this,' said the Doctor. 'My, er, vehicle performed a routine environmental assessment on landing. She - it - surveyed the architecture of the building we're in.'

'Really, sir?' asked a chubby boy named Paxton with polite interest.

'Yes. And unusually - how can I put this - my vehicle was unable to determine the size of the building. It doesn't appear to have perimeters. Which I thought was a curious paradox, especially since I've been able to rule out instrument malfunction.'

The boys looked bemused.

The Doctor took a bite of his sandwich; it was delicious. 'Let me ask you something else,' he said. 'When was the last time one of your teachers actually turned up for a class?'

This seemed to strike a chord for some of the boys. 'It's a curious thing, sir,' said Dennistoun. 'I know the Latin master has been absent a great deal recently - and the geography master - and the art master. In fact - ' His eyes narrowed. 'Do you know, sir? At this precise moment I can't actually recall a single lesson that *any* master has been able to attend. I try to think back, but before a few days ago, it just seems a blur.'

Some of the other boys were nodding vigorously, in sympathy with Dennistoun. But Parkins was just watching Dennistoun thoughtfully.

'We work hard, sir,' said Anstruther. 'We study endlessly, by ourselves. 'But I'm not sure about teachers. We wait for them, but...'

'But they never come?' asked the Doctor. 'Never?'

'But that's ridiculous!' Poynter exclaimed.

'Yes, isn't it?' mused the Doctor.

'Be that as it may,' said Parkins, 'we've got bigger problems.'

And he told the Doctor about Abney, and about Haynes Junior, and about Karswell. When he had finished his account, the other boys looked pale with fright and disgust at the memories it had revived.

'How many of you are there in this school?' asked the Doctor. 'After these three deaths?'

'This is everyone,' said Parkins, gesturing around the group. 'I mean, all except Chiddock. He was here with us a while ago. I'm not sure where he is now.'

In normal circumstances the Doctor would have asked why such a vast school was necessary to accommodate a dozen or so boys, but he and the boys now recognised that Chiddock's unexplained absence represented a more urgent priority. An atmosphere of foreboding enveloped the group.

'He'll still be here in the refectory,' said Poynter. 'It's - large. He won't have left it.'

The Doctor and the boys rose from their chairs. The refectory was, it appeared, L-shaped. They moved around the corner of the room into the adjoining area. There was no sign of the missing boy, just more tables and chairs, and another corner, with the promise of even more seating space beyond it. The Doctor experienced a curious sensation that he was losing his bearings; what *was* the shape of the room?

The group were making their way cautiously through a third identical seating area when they heard Chiddock's high-pitched scream. What most sickened the boys was their own lack of surprise; the scream, they now realised, had been inevitable.

'Quickly!' the Doctor cried. He and the boys ran, until at last they found, in yet another section of the refectory, the remains of young Chiddock. For the boys, it was one more surreal nightmare, an unrestrained study in red paint. For the Doctor, it was one more boy he had failed to save: strangers or friends, the guilt was the same.

'He's everywhere,' breathed Dennistoun, meaning Chiddock.

The Doctor was breathing hard. He looked at Parkins. 'I need to speak to you,' he said.

'I've seen many things,' the Doctor told Parkins in the prefects' room. 'But I've never seen anything quite like this. I must have your help if I'm to understand what's going on here.'

For a while Parkins said nothing, his dark green eyes gazing into empty space. 'I like to make up stories, Doctor,' he said at last. 'Something to do, to while away all those endless lessons with no teacher. Perhaps you'd like to hear my best story?'

'Yes,' the Doctor said. 'Very much.'

'The way I view it, Doctor, with over ten to the twenty-two planets in this universe alone, every conceivable situation is certain to arise at least once. Wouldn't you say?'

'Go on.'

'You'll like my premise, Doctor. At least I hope so. Imagine a culture that's very advanced. Really, *really* advanced. They have all the usual technologies, of course: genetic engineering, artificial intelligence, faster-than-light travel, extraplanetary colonies, the standard things. And then imagine them a thousand years further on, and then *another* thousand years beyond that. Approaching the asymptotic ceiling for scientific and cultural development. Are you picturing them, Doctor?'

'I am.'

'Now imagine them after another *million* years. All the above technologies have been improved further, then abandoned as primitive mysticism, superseded by technologies for which other cultures wouldn't even have words. But one thing still haunts this culture: the problem of evil. After a million generations honing their own cerebral perfection, they find they still have murderers, they still have rapists, they still have anarchists and terrorists and gang-lords. Built into their evolutionary heritage, you see. Their prehistoric ancestors were insatiably territorial, and so are they - in the deep ancient parts of their brains that the cerebrum has nothing to say about.'

Parkins's voice was becoming hypnotic. The Doctor gazed steadily into the boy's eyes.

'What does this culture do about the problem of evil? Naturally, they have long ago abolished capital punishment as an archaic barbarism. But for a species with deep technological powers, there are alternatives. Let's suppose their psychometric testing is so acute that they can identify twenty, thirty, or forty years in advance who's going to grow up to be the most dangerous criminals. And suppose they can arrest the development of future criminals in childhood. Nothing so crude as a time loop: the children go on living, breathing, thinking, speaking. And they're intensely clever, like all the other children on their world. They just don't get any older. Ever.'

Parkins paused. He and the Doctor faced each other without words for a while, their three heartbeats pulsing quietly against the silence.

'Naturally, the authorities can't just leave these children to drift around society fixed eternally at the same age while their brothers and sisters, and their brothers' and sisters' children and grandchildren, get older and die. A special place for them has to be found. Somewhere made just for children, where they'll feel at home. An environment where they can remain innocent for all eternity, and never grow up to do the vicious things they would have done. What do you suppose is the ideal place for highly intelligent children, Doctor?'

A long pause supervened. Finally, the Doctor asked: 'How long have you been here, Mr Parkins?'

'I really don't know, Doctor. An unspeakably long time, I think. Or maybe even longer. Long enough to work out everything I've just told you, without a great deal to go on. I think this place has been in equilibrium for a very, very long time. Until now.'

'Until my arrival?'

'No, Doctor. I'm not naïve enough to blame you for the events that have been happening here, just because your arrival has happened to coincide with them. Although I imagine a traveller like yourself gets quite a lot of that kind of thing.'

The Doctor smiled. But behind his smile, he was already thinking hard. 'I'm going to have a little look around,' he said.

The Doctor moved through semi-darkness. It had taken him hours, all his psychic senses prickling, to track the visitor to a vast echoing chemistry lab, an unknowable distance from the schoolroom where the TARDIS had materialised. The room might have been an aircraft hangar, attached to another, attached to another, attached to another. The Doctor could not recall ever before having seen a room with a horizon. And to the horizon, the laboratory bristled with an apparent infinitude of test-tubes, glass jars, bowls, retorts, Bunsen burners - some of these lit - as far as the eye could see, and far, far beyond.

The Doctor swallowed. As he watched, something was emerging, with a curious stooping gait, from the nearer shadows of the lab. In the flickering light of the Bunsen burners, it resolved itself into a shambling humanoid shape, and then into the figure of a grotesque old man, clad in an ill-fitting brownish suit, its face hideously deformed by age. The Doctor imagined, with a sudden chill, what effect the sight of it must have had on young boys, *perpetually* young boys, accustomed only to youth and vitality, forever and ever. Despite himself, he closed his eyes against its image.

But when the visitor said 'Doctor', the sound of its voice was like the dry tearing of ancient paper, and the Doctor opened his eyes. The figure shambled forward. The Doctor recoiled with a surge of revulsion at the foetid smell of its baggy clothes.

'What do you want here?' he asked. 'Why are you killing these children?'

In response to the question, the wrinkled face began to transform. Its contours writhed and stretched. The jaw-line distended, forced outwards by the pressure of lengthening teeth; the eyes turned yellow and the cheekbones folded back. 'I've got reason,' said the tearing-paper voice, emanating no longer from the creature's mouth but from deep inside its body. 'I'll show you.'

The figure advanced upon the Doctor, its body succumbing to progressively viler deformities. But even as it superficially relinquished its human shape, long talons extruding from every part of its stubby forelimbs to embrace the Doctor in the flickering yellow light of the lab, it remained somehow mundane and familiar, and for the Doctor that was the worst of it; for it was still not a monster, just a hideous, *repulsive* old man.

Talons wrapped around the Doctor's shoulders, and obscenely extended jaws folded around his neck, but he received no bite. Instead he smelled the brown stink of its breath, and felt his mind abruptly flooded with images, unnaturally clear. A vast structure, a soaring technological wonderland, breaking apart in multiple explosions. Falling bodies, burning, whirling in the air. Cries of panic. Sobs of despair.

'See what *should* happen,' breathed the creature. 'Anguish beyond measure. Three thousand souls up in - *smoke*.' The last word was enunciated so sharply that it was accompanied by a spurt of foul liquid against the Doctor's cheek.

Then the creature unfurled its grasp, and the Doctor was free to watch it shuffle back into the farthest shadows of the laboratory.

'I've seen what it is,' the Doctor told Parkins in the biology room. 'And I believe I know what it's doing here.'

'I don't understand why it didn't kill you,' said Parkins.

'I witnessed an attack on a hydrogen plant,' said the Doctor. 'A terrorist strike. Thousands died in the fire and the explosions.'

'Who's responsible?' breathed Parkins.

'That's the hard part, but I think you know the answer already. I don't think this atrocity actually happened. But it was *going* to. Which is rather the point.'

Parkins lowered himself onto one of the wooden benches in the lab, slowly covering his face with his hands.

'I think what's been killing your classmates is the corporeal expression of something that one of you *should* have grown up to do - probably thousands of years ago - if you'd been allowed,' said the Doctor. 'This event *knows* it should have happened. No doubt it feels cheated of its existence by your society's novel penal system. And now it's trying to intrude into reality, and expressing its aggression in the only way it can.'

'But why is it just *us*?' Parkins exclaimed. His usual composure had completely deserted him, and now there was only a child's petulant desperation in his voice. 'Why didn't it kill you too?'

'It probably recognised that my mind would be a suitable vessel for its message,' said the Doctor slowly, as if thinking aloud. 'Despite all your intelligence, your race isn't psychic. Mine is. This thing wants you to know exactly why it's here.'

'Before it kills us all.'

'Yes,' said the Doctor gently. 'I expect so.'

'You've travelled through the universe, Doctor. Isn't that true?'

'Yes.'

'And witnessed many creatures, many life forms?'

'Some, yes.'

Parkins gazed straight into the Doctor's face. The Time Lord now realised that the boy's dark green eyes looked impossibly ancient.

'Can you help us to kill it, Doctor?' Parkins asked.

The Doctor stared back at him. Minutes passed, and more minutes. But above all else that he had studied, Parkins had learned patience.

At last the Doctor said: 'There is a possibility. But there's a serious chance it won't work.'

'Well, we have to - '

'And if it *doesn't* work,' continued the Doctor, 'we'll have problems you haven't even dreamed of yet.'

But somewhere in the dark and endless corridors of the school, an unwanted visitor was still moving, and breathing, and slavering. And both Parkins and the Doctor knew there was no longer a choice.

It was time to implement the Doctor's scheme. All the remaining boys were gathered with him in the prefects' room.

'Concentrate,' said the Doctor to the assembled circle of schoolboys. 'Your minds are filled with power. You've been honing your mental abilities in this place for thousands of years. It's time to use them.'

The boys concentrated, each staring intently at the large circle that the Doctor had carefully chalked on the wooden floor. As they focused their minds, each of them contributed something different, as the

Doctor had instructed; a unique gift from each boy, harvested from his own dark potential. From Poynter, serial rape on his home world. From Anstruther, genetic terrorism on Scavenius. From Wraxhall, gang warfare on Kory Prime. From Garrett, blood smuggling on Dispo. And more, and more.

The boys' thoughts originated as flickering electrochemical impulses, dancing along the intricate neural pathways of their brains. But soon their thoughts extended beyond their skulls and out into the cold of the room, deftly reshaping the molecules of the air.

The boys watched as a shape began to form over the Doctor's chalk circle: a pool of cream-coloured light hovering in the humming air. The shape solidified, unfolding into an upright human skeleton, four feet tall. As the boys recognised their handiwork, their attention faltered; the outlines of the skeleton wavered, light refracting haphazardly around it.

'Concentrate!' urged the Doctor. 'You have one chance. You must not lose it!'

The boys concentrated. Spurred on by this visual proof of their success, each one poured all his thoughts into the diminutive shape materialising in front of them.

Now the small skeleton was awash with blood. It poured out from nowhere, flooding over all the bones simultaneously, racing around the curvature of the ribs, over the arms, down the spinal column, over the pelvis and down the legs, flowing across every surface until no white bone was visible at all. Muscles sprang up in leathery red sheets, folding into place, wrapping themselves against the bones.

'Concentrate!' insisted the Doctor.

The boys concentrated. Ligaments snapped into position, crisscrossing tendons flickered into dark gaps and dragged muscle to bone. Organs bloomed pink and white behind the ribs. Clouds of grey fat puffed up around the thickening chest, the hips, the thighs. Eyeballs blossomed in the sockets, a pink tongue wriggled out between the sprouting teeth.

'Concentrate!' cried the Doctor.

The boys concentrated. Pale skin slid out over every surface, meeting and sealing; light brown hair fluttered up out of the scalp. Finally the small figure stood complete, a naked male child. Soon its nakedness was covered by clothes that seeped out of the air to enfold it: white shirt, black trousers, dark blue blazer. Even a school tie, identical to those of the other boys, looped itself around the slender neck. Its face was angelic, but not even the Doctor felt able to meet its gaze.

'Get out of here, boys,' instructed the Doctor as the small figure began to stir in the chalk circle. 'That concludes the lesson for today.'

'Get ready,' said the Doctor to the boys a few minutes later. They were standing in the main corridor that reputedly led from the senior common room to the drama hall. Here, the school's unnatural geometry became wholly apparent. It was a corridor that started ordinarily enough, with a wide polished wooden floor, elegant wood-panelled walls, and a high ceiling; but one dizzying glance at the vanishing point in either direction betrayed its infinite length. The Doctor recognised immediately that the architecture of the corridor did not permit of its having an end; for Parkins and the rest of the boys, it was as if the Doctor's company had lifted the veils from their eyes, and they saw now what had previously eluded them, that the structure of the school was quite, quite impossible.

Some metres along the length of the corridor, their new classmate was wandering, beginning to explore his infinite new world: the slight, frail figure of a uniformed schoolboy, fruit of the Doctor's ingenuity, composite of the boys' inner darkness. He was peering silently around at the walls, the floor and the ceiling, appearing lost, vulnerable and frightened.

Then, as the Doctor had predicted, another figure appeared: first as an infinitesimal point in the vanishing reaches of the corridor, far beyond the newly created figure, then swiftly growing, approaching. It resolved itself with unnatural speed into the shambling shape of a stooped and hideous old man.

The visitor was expert at sniffing out youth. The fresh smell of the newborn schoolboy, wandering aimlessly in the corridor, was intoxicating in its nostrils. The Doctor and the other boys watched breathlessly as it approached. Despite the Doctor's presence, the boys experienced a thrill of primordial terror. Their one bitter consolation was that it would reach their new classmate before it reached them.

'My *strong* advice,' said the Doctor, his voice high-pitched with anxiety, 'is not to look.'

No one obeyed. They were transfixed by the sight of the approaching old man as it finally relinquished any pretence to humanity. All its limbs were deforming at once. Everywhere claws were sprouting, sharp tusks unfolding, ribs splitting through the grey skin and baggy old suit to extrude from the creature's body as a multitude of flexible stabbing weapons. The head became flattened and bestial, dominated by the mouth, a nest of jagged fangs leering with obscene appetite.

'Three thousand souls,' the thing rasped; the sound of its voice made the boys whimper.

But the new boy seemed not to notice it, even after it spoke. Instead the small figure continued to wander in the corridor, never far from the same spot, oblivious to the approaching, slavering creature.

'Are you lost, boy?' the creature said, addressing the small figure. As the Doctor and the others watched, the creature closed the remaining distance between itself and the boy. One of its forelimbs flashed out, suddenly elastic, sprouting killing talons as it sped through the air. At the last possible moment, the small figure turned sharply to stare straight into the creature's eyes.

'I said *don't look*,' said the Doctor more firmly.

His advice still went unheeded. Parkins and the others looked, as the little boy's eyes turned cold yellow, staring unwaveringly into those of the creature, which faltered in its tracks, for the first and only time. Impossibly, a sound that might have been a whine of fear issued from somewhere in the depths of the creature's throat.

The little boy just had time to flash an angelic smile into the creature's face before he too began to change, faster than the creature had done, and into something more hideous. The two entities struggled, embraced and intertwined in continuous fluid transformation; they struggled as opposing forests of snapping mouths.

For the onlookers, the battle was beyond belief and beyond bearing. The Doctor would have liked to extend some comfort to the boys; but as so often, his pragmatism had been all he had to offer.

As the critical point was reached, the two opposing entities fused into a single vast writhing organism, reeling and raging in the corridor. The physical strain of the battle was too much for it; it could not withstand the tidal forces of muscular pressure slamming and colliding within it; and it fractured and came apart in a roaring explosion of spraying blood, fragments of skin, splinters of bone, twirling shreds of organic material. The air was filled with a blizzard of flying pieces; the Doctor, Parkins and the other schoolboys were drenched in it.

After a long and sober silence, Parkins said quietly: 'Thank you, Doctor.' And the boy smiled up into the Doctor's eyes.

And that should have been all.

But after the customary grateful goodbyes, back in the TARDIS console room and a million million miles away, the Doctor was troubled by two thoughts that turned him cold. He would not share them with Nyssa; she was too upset, still mourning Adric's death.

If all the boys' potential evil had been poured into the little boy that they had united to create, could it be that the boys themselves were now left sinless? That would be unthinkable, for then their eternal confinement would be without reason.

And worse, could the dark power of a potential future event be so simply destroyed? As the Doctor pictured the endless gloomy corridors of the school, its classrooms and its dormitories, its libraries and its laboratories, its creaking wooden furniture and the shadows that crept around them, it seemed impossible to imagine the place delivered from evil. How much more likely that somewhere in that infinite labyrinth, something cold and carnivorous would be taking shape again, dreaming of meeting schoolboys in the dark, while the boys themselves continued waiting patiently for lessons they would never receive.

Soul Mate

David Bailey

Tegan looked at the woman again, frowning. Anna was smiling though, clasping her hands together almost in glee. She was facing the other way, bobbing up and down on tip-toe, trying to see out of the grubby window-pane that made up the top half of the door. Light from the neon on the wall of the corridor outside spilled through the window. Anna was breathing fast and hard, and Tegan could hear every breath, every excited wheeze.

She tutted and sighed, but Anna paid no notice. Tegan looked about, hopeful that she could find something - anything - that might help her escape.

But the room was more or less bare. The simple plaster walls were stained with filthy water. At her feet lay a blanket, drab green, damp and dirty from a lifetime spent on the gritty stone floor. It was too much like a prison - which, she supposed, it was, even if that wasn't its original function. The only real furniture - apart from the chair Tegan was tied to - was a simple single bed, carelessly rammed up against the left-hand wall, its head towards the door.

Tegan coughed, her throat dry and sore. When had she last had a drink? 'When are you going to let me go?' she asked, her voice creaking with thirst.

Anna still didn't look at her, her attention caught entirely by the empty corridor outside.

'I said - '

'I heard you,' Anna suddenly trilled.

'Well?'

'I think you know the answer, Tegan.' Anna turned to face her, smiling a serious smile. She was pretty, Tegan could tell, but it had been a long time since she had taken any pride in her appearance. Her blonde hair fell in lank, greasy knots, drooping past her shoulders. From the dark smudges on her cheeks and forehead, it looked like she hadn't had a wash in weeks - and the smell when she got too close only confirmed Tegan's suspicions. But even so, her blue eyes sparkled with life, darting this way and that from second to second. Her full, twenty-something figure was worthy of jealousy. And when her full lips parted and she flashed that smile, Tegan almost felt sorry for her plight.

Tegan shifted her wrists in their bonds, waggling her fingers and tensing and relaxing the muscles in her arms to keep the blood flowing through them. She couldn't see her hands, tied behind her back as they were, but she was sure they were red and plump - she could feel her pulse making them throb.

Almost sorry for her, yeah. But not almost enough.

Nyssa trotted alongside the Doctor as he strode expansively across the floor of the docking bay. It was a huge room, a bare metal ceiling hanging over them like a bleak storm cloud. Their footsteps shattered the silence like gunshots. To one side, a small spacecraft lay, cracked open like an egg, wires and twisted metal spilling out onto the concrete floor.

The Doctor stopped next to it, swept back the tails of his jacket, put his hands in his pockets and quietly whistled to himself.

'That's that, then,' said Nyssa, as she slowed her pace and came to a stop next to him. Even from a quick glance, she could tell it was beyond repair. A raft of circuits hung, blackened and burnt, from the nose of the craft and one of the engines swung uselessly from the rear. Its hull was torn open, jagged steel dulled with the first signs of rust. The air on this planet was full of moisture, and it had already taken its toll on the craft's wounds. 'It's amazing there were any survivors at all,' she added.

'There were plenty, according to Anna,' the Doctor pointed out. He took two steps towards the ship and rested his hand on the cold metal. 'But all of them got away.'

'All except Anna. We'll have to help her, then.' Nyssa looked up at the Doctor. 'We'll have to help her get away.'

He slowly turned to face her, a sad smile crawling across his face. He took a deep breath and replied, 'Yes, indeed. She should go back to Earth, really. Back home.'

'Can't you at least untie me?' Tegan asked, shifting in the chair to gain some semblance of comfort. 'I mean, if you're so intent on keeping me here…'

Anna fell into a crouch, then hustled across the floor, all the while smiling and looking deep into Tegan's eyes. When the woman's face was mere inches from Tegan's own, she whispered, 'No, no, no. You'll just do what everyone else did. You'll forget about me, you'll run, and you'll escape.'

Tegan swallowed hard, her dry throat resisting the motion. Anna's breath was stale and unpleasantly hot.

'That's what everyone does, you see,' Anna continued, kneeling on the filthy blanket. 'That's what this place does. Makes you forget. They went, off they went...' She turned her face up to the ceiling, but her gaze was focussed far beyond. 'They went and they forgot about me, never came back. Bye-bye!' Anna giggled.

'But where would I go?' Tegan pleaded. 'You said yourself, there are no working spaceships on the planet, and there's next to no atmosphere outside. I'd be stuck in the complex - I couldn't run anywhere.'

Anna shook her head, frowning. 'You don't fool me, no, no. You got here. The Time Lord and the Trakenite brought you here. Somehow, somehow... They'll take you away.'

'You're right,' Tegan mock-sighed, shrugging. Anna squinted at her. Time to try a different tack. 'They'll be back for me soon, though. They'll wonder where I am, and they'll come looking for me.'

'No,' Anna stated, her voice firm and loud.

'They will. You know they will. And when they see what you've done, they won't want to help you.' Tegan was talking in a sing-song way, her voice lifting at the end of her words - it was as if she was threatening a little girl with nothing more harmful than 'no sweets if you don't do your homework'.

'No,' Anna said again, jerking her head to one side. She stared hard at the window, listening. Tegan followed her gaze but there was no one on the other side of the door. Slowly, as if she was frightened the sound of her joints moving would attract attention, Anna turned back to her. 'They all forget, Tegan,' Anna whispered, her voice like a breeze tickling the leaves of a tree. 'All of them. Soon, they won't remember you at all, and they'll leave you. They'll go away.'

Anna leapt upright, almost stumbling as she knotted her feet up in the blanket. She shook it free, then scuttled back over to the door. Resting her forehead on the window-pane, she hissed to herself, 'Away, away...'

'And what if they do?' Tegan snapped, sick of trying to humour Anna's strange behaviour. 'Then where will you be? Still stuck here like before.'

Anna chuckled. 'Not like before, Tegan. Now I've got you.'

Wonderful, human you.

You can't imagine what it's been like, living here all alone. Well, I call it living, but what's life without a reflection? What's the point without someone to share it with?

Your friends – they're no good. They're not human. And imagine that: imagine being whisked away by them to heaven knows where. They did it to you once; they'll do it again. I've seen what aliens do. You probably had the most normal life imaginable. A home, a family, friends, a job. You had everything, and they took it away from you when they took you away from it.

What did they do? No, no. I can imagine. Did you scream? Did you struggle and cry? Did they threaten death? Oh, I know. I know what they're like.

I watched while they tore my colony, my friends, apart and left it all for dead. They weren't the same – the aliens that came here, they weren't the same people who took you. But I bet it happened the same way. I bet you screamed, and fought and died like they did. I stood there, hiding in the shadows, while they marched dozens of our people onto their ships and took them away to...

I don't know. Away. They took them away.

Six years. Six years, I've been here alone. It's a damn good job this place had food stores and supplies enough for two hundred people. But man cannot live on bread alone. You can't live on much, alone.

I dreamed about this. I'm sure it's not quite turning out the way I imagined. There was more sunlight in the dream, for a start. I haven't seen the sun since we landed here, you know. No windows – I mean, I know the atmosphere's a wreck, but really. What were they thinking?

And I wasn't sent here to go outside. I'm here as support for the mining crews. A medic. Much use that was when my friends and colleagues were cut down by those monsters. I didn't even know where to start. At least the hospital unit had a good incinerator. I may have been desperate for company, but I wasn't about to share the colony with a heap of dead bodies.

Every one. I had to drag every one, from every ruined corner of this place. I had to shoulder each rotting corpse, lug it into the bin, and push them down the chute. Light the fire. Watch them burn. Smell them burn.

So, no. No sun. And it seems awfully dark in here, too, right now. I can see the light through this window – can you see it too? – but that's just one of those nasty neon things plugged into the concrete wall. Can you see it? Maybe I should move you round, clean this window a bit, let you see it. I wish you could see it.

Maybe then you'd laugh and giggle and hold my hand, like you did in the dream. Maybe, bathed in light, you'd tell me everything is all right, and you'd tell me that the aliens would never come back, and that we were safe here at last.

I wish you could see the dream.

'Where *has* she got to?' The Doctor was drumming his fingers on the TARDIS door, peering over Nyssa's shoulder. Nyssa craned her neck to follow his gaze, but saw only an empty, dusty corridor leading away from the corner of the docking bay.

She turned back to look at the Doctor and smiled. 'I'm sure she won't be long. She and Anna seemed to be getting along so well, they're probably just doing...' Nyssa's words trailed off, and she furrowed her brow and looked at her feet.

'Human things?' suggested the Doctor.

Nyssa laughed quietly. 'Human things.'

'This is ridiculous!' Tegan yelled. 'Nyssa! Doctor!'

'Shut up!' Anna wheeled round, spittle flying from her snarling lips and her eyes wide circles of white. 'What do you think you're doing?'

Tegan was taken aback, struggling with her words for a second. 'What does it look like I'm doing?' she gasped. 'I'm trying to get help!'

Anna stalked across the floor towards her, pushing the blanket on the floor aside with her foot. 'They won't help you,' she growled. 'They'll have forgotten you already. I watched them go, Tegan. I watched them leave, and they didn't come back.'

'What?' Tegan said. 'You saw the Doctor leave?'

Anna shook her head, suddenly grinning. Her eyes flitted from one corner of the room to the other. 'Not your friends, silly.' She giggled. 'All the others. I watched them go. They forgot me, Tegan. Everyone forgets. Do you still not understand?'

Tegan tensed everything, pushing her feet against the floor. Her muscles tore against the ropes that bound her hands and legs to the chair, and slowly she rose from her seat. She couldn't stretch more than an inch or two off the chair, but the determined movement obviously unsettled Anna. The other woman took a slight, almost imperceptible, step back, and a look of confusion troubled its way across her face. 'The Doctor won't forget me, Anna,' Tegan whispered. 'It's only a matter of time, you know, before he finds me. And he can be a hell of a lot more terrifying than those aliens who killed your friends.'

Anna's jaw worked the air for a second. She raised a clawed hand to the shard of her head and scratched her hair violently.

Tegan pressed the advantage. 'Right now, he'll be telling Nyssa to look for me,' she hissed. 'He'll tear the place apart, he'll turn it upside down until he finds me. And then...'

'Then?' Anna stammered. 'What? Then what?'

'He'll take me away.'

The woman screamed, running back to the door, her fists wheeling through the air. 'No!' she yelled, thumping the window. 'You can't go! You can't!' Thump! Thump thump thump! Anna was battering the glass, and it was shaking in its frame.

A trickle of dust fell from the edge of the window-pane. Tegan watched it drift to the floor and smiled a thin smile. 'It's going to happen, Anna,' Tegan said, her voice strengthening with a growing confidence. 'He'll find me, and he'll take me, and then we'll go and leave you here again, all alone.'

Anna yelped even louder, her mouth stretched back in anguish. Her fists pummelled the window, pushing it back in its frame so far that a chunk of putty dislodged and dropped to the floor. 'He's forgotten you! You're staying here!' she cried. 'You're staying here!'

Tears were beginning to make little lines of cleaner skin on her grubby face. Her eyes were scrunched closed, and every muscle in her body was tensed into taught knots. Still, Anna lashed out at anything – her blows were going wide now, and her knuckles grazed nastily on the door frame, leaving a smear of blood behind. Now that blood was being transferred to the glass, as she began to batter the window once again.

Tegan laughed, and was almost frightened by what she heard. She was being wicked, deliberately malicious, but it was the only way. 'No, Anna,' she said. 'I'm as good as gone already.'

With a final shriek, Anna flung herself at the door, arms outstretched in front of her. Her wounded hand struck the wall, and the weight of her body following it pushed it out to the side, a streak of bright red tracing the hand's path across the plaster. Anna's other hand hit at exactly the point where the bottom edge of the window met its frame and – Tegan almost yelped with delight when she saw it happen – went through to the other. The window had been knocked loose.

Balancing for a second on Anna's wrist, it slowly tilted backwards into the room.

Anna slumped to the floor, jagged sobs shaking her body. She bunched herself up into a little ball at the foot of the door.

The window tipped further, and fell free, bouncing off Anna's back. And then it belly-flopped on to the floor. First one crack, then another, then hundreds – shards of glass danced across the floor, flying this way and that, away from a silvery cloud of dusty particles.

For a second, Tegan could do nothing other than just stare at the sight of her success. But she knew she wasn't there yet and, although Anna was still collapsed in a heap of tears, she didn't have long. Exhausted and frightened as she was, Tegan summoned every last shred of her strength and started to rock her chair.

It's better in here. Not in the room, silly. And certainly not in this complex. In here. Sure, I'm alone again, but at least I'm alone by choice – and it's not like anyone could join me here, even if I wanted them to.

The sun's in here, and all my friends. And you're in here somewhere, in the bit of me that makes the dreams. I could look at you there now, but I'm not sure I want to see it again right now. I want to look at your face in the dream, make sure you look just like I'd hoped. But I suppose it doesn't matter. There's everyone else. I can look at them instead.

They look back, here. They remember me. Most of them are even smiling.

As the side of the chair crashed into the middle of the broken glass, Tegan had to hold her neck very stiff to avoid her head slamming onto the floor. She breathed steadily and deliberately for a second, composing herself, and stared carefully at her perpendicular view of Anna. The woman was rocking slightly, and Tegan could hear her murmuring quietly to herself. She couldn't make out the words, but whatever she was talking about, it was keeping her happy – she could see the tiniest smile ticking at the corner of Anna's mouth.

She's lost it. Perfect.

Carefully, Tegan twisted her wrists painfully against the ropes and sent her fingers out to search the floor. She could feel them rubbing against the tiny particles of glass, and she was sure blood was beginning to flow from her fingertips. Within a few seconds, though, she happened upon the sharp edge of a chunk of glass. She pushed her fingers harder, willing them to find the other edge, and before long her index finger and thumb were bracing a sizeable makeshift knife.

Ever so carefully, Tegan pulled up with her index finger to flip the glass into the palm of her hand. She grasped it as soon as she could – but too hard. The glass slid into her skin, and she felt blood pour along the glass and onto her fingers. From that moment, it was a battle between holding the glass so lightly that it didn't cut any further, but tight enough so that it didn't fall from her grasp, all the time also battling with a fierce pain like a fire tearing through her hand.

She turned the shard - the gash in her hand screaming its agony with every tiny motion - until its tip caught against the knot around her wrist. For God's sake, Tegan, don't get clumsy now.

There was only so long you could play with the Doctor's tools, Nyssa thought, before you got bored. She'd stood at her workbench for half an hour now, examining each piece of equipment in minute detail, making herself very sure that everything was in working order. At least, she reasoned, if the Doctor himself was none too keen on things running smoothly in the rest of the TARDIS, she could keep this little corner of his kingdom in tip-top condition. But enough was enough, she decided.

She left a few instruments still unchecked, and walked through to the console room. Pushing open the door, she found the Doctor leaning over a section of the console, his arms bracing himself uncomfortably as he peered into one of the screens. He had a look of total absorption, moving only to suck his fingertip gently. Then he made a little grunt to himself, nodded and tapped the screen.

'Is everything all right, Doctor?' Nyssa asked.

'What?' he asked, looking up and blinking as if he was waking from a deep sleep. 'Oh. Oh, yes. I was just plotting a course to the nearest Earth colony.'

'For Anna?' Nyssa walked over to join him and peered at the screen.

'For Anna, yes. It's an awfully long way to the nearest one,' he said, pointing at some indecipherable glyphs on the monitor. 'It's no wonder no one came looking for her.'

'Then it's a very good job we managed to find her.'

'Well,' the Doctor said, scratching his head awkwardly. 'It's not as if we were looking, was it?'

'No, indeed,' Nyssa agreed. 'She's very lucky.'

'Hmm.' The Doctor let his hands fall to his side, still staring at the monitor.

'Is something wrong, Doctor?'

'No,' he said. He gaze was like concrete - set on the little screen, and its slowly tracking coordinates. 'Well, not exactly. It's just...' He pointed at a lump of numbers scrolling across the top of the screen. 'See this?'

Nyssa nodded, and slowly, cautiously, suggested, 'The coordinates of this planet, yes?'

'Yes. And our current position in time.' He tutted. 'And that's the odd bit.'

Nyssa stared at the numbers, but they meant nothing to her. 'I'm sorry, Doctor, I don't understand.'

'Well,' he said, sighing and looking straight at her. 'The nearest colony really is a *very* long way away.' He fell silent, glancing back at the screen again.

'Doctor?' Nyssa stared up at him.

'Come on,' he said, his voice deep. 'We'd better find Tegan.'

Tegan ran as best she could down the corridor, but her legs were suddenly gripped by a bout of pins-and-needles. She could still feel the ropes around her ankles, although she'd cut them loose about five minutes before. Now the blood was rushing back, it felt like she was walking on clouds - painful, crampy clouds.

She leant for a moment against the wall, under a shattered neon tube. She looked down at her hand, watching the blood pulse away from the clean slice through her palm. Carefully, she tugged off her T-shirt and rolled it up. She wrapped it round her hand and gripped it as best she could - she was no medical expert, but any bandage was better than no bandage at all.

From where she stood, she could just see the crushed remains of the last space ship in the docking bay a hundred yards ahead of her. From behind, she could still hear Anna's sobs drifting through the still air of the corridor.

Free at last, Tegan shuddered and sighed. Taking a deep breath, she smiled to herself. She was finally going to get away. The happiness of this thought was the most perfect happiness she'd ever known - but only the very next moment, she was proved wrong.

The very next moment, the Doctor appeared.

Nyssa ran to Tegan's side and gently guided her arm over her shoulder, supporting her as they walked to join the Doctor.

Tegan was grinning, and Nyssa noticed that tears were trickling down her face. As they reached the Doctor, Nyssa slowly helped her to sit down, her back against the grey plaster wall. She took Tegan's wounded hand in her own, and carefully peeled away the bloody fabric of the T-shirt. She winced as she saw the open, fleshy cut, and looked up at the Doctor.

He knelt down and took Tegan's chin in his hand. He lifted her face to his and, smiling, asked, 'Are you alright?'

Tegan laughed, but it came out more like an exhausted gasp. 'I knew you wouldn't forget.'

The Doctor stared at her quizzically for a second, then grinned. 'Anna?'

Tegan sniffed and swallowed, nodding.

'Where is she?' he asked.

She tilted her head back down the corridor, in the direction from which the sound of crying was still coming. For a second, they all listened to the thick choking noise Anna was making, snotty sobs and moans.

The Doctor stood up, and stared down the passage to the open door. 'Nyssa,' he muttered, 'look after Tegan for a moment.'

Slowly, he paced down the corridor. Nyssa watched him go, cautiously approaching the darkness around the doorway. 'He needs a torch or something,' she whispered to Tegan. 'It could be dangerous down there.'

'Dangerous?' Tegan laughed. 'Hold on. What did you say? A torch?' She looked up, squinting along the corridor to where the Doctor stood, just outside the doorway. On the opposite wall, the neon light was a battered and cracked shell, covered with a thick layer of dust. 'It shouldn't be dark there,' she said. 'There should be a light.'

'I imagine,' shouted the Doctor from the doorway, 'there should be a lot of things down here.'

The sobbing had stopped.

Awkwardly, Tegan struggled to get to her feet.

'Careful!' chided Nyssa.

'Just get me down there,' Tegan said, sternly.

Shrugging, Nyssa stood and reached down for Tegan's hand. Once she had helped her stand, Nyssa guided Tegan as she stumbled down the corridor to join the Doctor. As they got to his side, Tegan pulled herself out from Nyssa's gentle hold and leapt past the Doctor into the room. There was the bed. There was the blanket. There was the chair, lying on the floor, and the tatters of the ropes from which she'd cut herself free. And there was the shattered window-pane - dozens of shards of glass, each covered with the same thick dust that lay over everything else.

Other than that, nothing. The room was empty.

They'd found a sun-lounger somewhere and brought it into the console room for her. Tegan lay back on it, with Nyssa perched by her knees, and tried to take in what the Doctor was saying.

She shook her head and raised a bandaged hand to her forehead to shield her eyes from the bright lights in the ceiling. 'Say it again,' she demanded.

'The attack on the colony happened centuries ago. Relative to when we arrived, anyway,' the Doctor explained. This was the fourth or fifth time he'd been through it, but he was being uncharacteristically patient in trying to help Tegan understand. 'The humans were driven from this sector of the galaxy in the early years of the war, and mankind never went back.'

'Right,' Tegan said. 'So...'

'So there couldn't possibly have been anyone there,' Nyssa said. She was being perky. Tegan couldn't stand it when she was perky at times like this.

'But we saw her, Nyssa!' Tegan snapped. 'She tied me to a blasted chair and threatened never to let me go!'

'A trick of the light?' the Doctor said.

'Be serious, Doctor,' Tegan said with a sneer.

'Some sort of geophasic memory, a temporal hiccup.'

'Geophasic?' Tegan laughed. 'I bet that's not even a word.'

The Doctor grinned down at Tegan.

'I swear,' she growled up at him, 'if you patronise me...'

The Doctor, still smiling, sighed. 'It's hard to explain. Sometimes, big things happen in the real world - in the universe we live in. Usually, the universe shakes them off, and they pass quickly into history.' He started to pace round the console, staring into space. After a brief pause he continued. 'But sometimes events are so big that they dent other planes. The space-time vortex, hyperspace... It doesn't matter what they imprint but once it's done, the shape of that dent can sometimes be reflected back on to normal reality.'

'But how does this reflection happen?' Tegan asked, shaking her head. 'I mean, what does it use as a mirror?'

The Doctor clicked his tongue a couple of times. 'Well, usually, space-time events like this are attracted by technology that can cross these planes.'

'Like the TARDIS?' Tegan thought she might be getting it.

'Yes.' The Doctor sounded unsure. 'Except...'

'Except what?'

'Well, the TARDIS just isn't big enough to work as this kind of... mirror, as you put it. Not when everything's working fine, which it is. Well, as much as it ever is.' He patted the edge of the console, then wiped a speck of dust from its surface.

'Well, if it wasn't the TARDIS,' Tegan asked, 'what was it?'

'All right,' he sighed, his hands flapping by his sides. 'I can't explain it.' He puffed air into his cheeks and let it out in a noisy hiss. 'A dream.'

'A dream? Now this is just getting ridiculous!' Tegan cried. 'First of all, it's a dent in space-time, and now it's a *dream*? Could a dream do this?' She waved her bandaged hand at him.

'There are all sorts of psychological tricks that the mind can play on itself,' the Doctor offered, raising his own hands to calm her down. 'You were stuck in that room for a couple of hours, and there was a lot of broken glass around. If you'd been hallucinating...'

'So, now *I'm* the mad one?' Tegan gasped. 'You saw Anna too, remember?'

'We all thought we saw her, yes.'

Tegan huffed angrily, and looked the other way. She hadn't been dreaming, she knew it. Anna had been there.

The Doctor continued, his voice softer. 'Whatever we did see, whatever psychic event did this to you, it didn't have as great an effect on either myself or Nyssa. Somehow, it got into your mind more easily. Maybe it recognised something in you that the two of us just didn't share.'

'Like what?' Tegan sulkily replied, still looking away from him.

'She was from Earth, Tegan,' the Doctor said, his voice steady and low. 'Maybe it was easier for you to sympathise with Anna's plight. I mean, it's only human.'

I was right, I knew I was right!

You're there in the dream. And the sun's back, too. It's bright here, shining. Everyone is around us, all my friends. And they're all smiling, happy to see us again.

And it is you - I can see your face this time, and you're just as I remember, just as I dreamt it. Stay with me, won't you? Don't go. Just us, Tegan. Just us, in the dream.

Whiskey and Water

Marc Platt

The shock of the water tore at the Doctor's lungs. Ice cold, ripping out his breath, freezing his muscles, penetrating his clothes and dragging him down. He thrashed out wildly. Nothing under his feet, no straws to grab at, only the tight grip of the grey, green water round his body, up his nose, smacking at his eyes. Only the churning boom in his ears.

The water closed over his head for the first time and his curling, yellow locks spread out like a golden halo, or so he liked to think.

And he wondered if perhaps this endeavour had all been a mistake.

The Doctor shut the TARDIS's outer door and took a deep breath.

There it was. The smell of spring. Long afternoon sunlight and the scent of pine resin suffused the air. A stillness under the giant redwoods so complete that he fancied he could hear the buds whispering beneath the spongy earth, and the snore of a chipmunk in its winter bed. The immense wilderness of California still dwarfed the first mosquito bites of so-called civilisation. The Doctor pulled his embroidered cloak around him and set off, none too purposefully, for a stroll.

At the foot of a bluff, a broad stream blocked his path. It gleamed yellow under the sinking sun. A row of stakes planted at intervals rose out of the water as if the stream had broken its banks. The Doctor edged closer and half-stumbled over a dark shape slumped on the ground. A bag of weathered canvas. Close by, a small pickaxe lay abandoned, and at the water's edge, a black metal pan.

He dabbed a finger into the water collected in the pan's base and felt a grainy deposit. It glinted as he held his finger to the light.

'Forty-Niners,' he declared and glanced at his watch. 'Nineteenth century Argonauts drawn to the Motherlode, feverish with the lust for gold.'

Amongst the jumble of clothes and tools in the bag, he found a crumpled deed written in smudged ink and numbered three four two. It entitled the owner, one John Pengelly, to three feet of mining rights on Ajax Creek for the sum of one thousand dollars. And there was a folded, well-thumbed letter written in pencil on coarse paper, most of which was barely legible:

My dearest Annie,

I were so glad when your letter... Your words... home real... prove as Cornwall ain't just a place I... of...

Something splashed behind him. The black shape of a man, the collar of his long coat pulled up and his wide-brimmed hat pulled down, was marching up from the stream. He must have crossed the water in a single bound.

'Good evening.' The Doctor extended a hand. 'I was concerned in case you'd lost your belongings.'

The figure snatched the letter from the Doctor's grasp. He swayed as he clutched it to his breast. His clothes were running with water. His bony fingers were cold. Two eyes glittered in the dark under his dripping hat. And he smelt like a stagnant pond.

The Doctor wondered what to say. *Well, if it was private, I suppose I must apologise*. Or better, *Any luck with the panning*? But settled on the decidedly lame 'Are you alright?'

The man gave a cry of misery. He doubled up in some sort of agony and then ran, knocking the Doctor backwards as he headed into the woods.

'No, wait!' The Doctor was up and after him like a shot, but the man moved quickly for one who was stumbling so much. And as he ran, he croaked out the words of the letter. No need to read them or even look at the paper; they were all too clearly scrawled on his heart.

'My dearest Annie, I were so glad when your letter found me. Your gentle words made home real again and prove as Cornwall ain't just a place I dreamed of. Californy's a wild place. There's trees broad enough to make a house inside. And there's bears and elks so big they'd never get in our door. And I seen real Injuns. They's like wild men with ruddy brown faces who covers themselves in furs and sticks feathers in their hair.'

He paused, sobbing and casting about for a way to go, allowing the Doctor to catch up and grab his dripping sleeve. 'John? John Pengelly? Is that you?' It was like a trigger. The man spun and released a fresh stream of gasped words into his captor's face. His own face was grey and sunken behind his sodden beard. His eyes dazzled like the sun on water. And his anguish was growing.

'Give little Jack and Cherry their daddy's love. Maybe they still remember me. I guess they ain't so little now either. Sweetest Annie, I spent a whole summer at dry diggins in Hangtown with scarce a nugget to show for my labour. But there's word... word of a new strike at Ajax Camp up north in Sierra County. They say the water runs with gold there. Men's dancing in the streets of Sacramento. So several hundreds of us set out for Ajax meaning to stake claims before the winter sets in.'

It's spring now, thought the Doctor, not daring to interrupt. Spring already, so the letter never got sent. The letter that was now torn and crumpled, a wet rag in John Pengelly's fingers. With a cry, the man wrenched free and barrelled away again. And his tirade continued for all the forest to hear, easy for the Doctor to follow in the shadows. And from somewhere near, another sound: the drumming of hooves.

'There's gold there by the bagful they say. And when I made the fortune they promise I'll pay for your passage out to the new land Annie. And there'll be rings on your fingers and trinkets to make you a lady in a fine house in Cisco.'

He faltered, crashing through brushwood, almost in grabbing distance of the Doctor. And the hooves were nearer. Driven fast.

In a patch of sunlight some way ahead through the trees, the Doctor saw the swaying shape of a stage coach drawn by four straining horses.

'Don't come, Annie!' choked John Pengelly. 'Go home! Get back home!' And he stepped into the coach's path and under the horses.

The creatures screamed and the coach lurched violently to a halt, throwing the driver from his seat above. From inside came a yell and a loud curse in a woman's voice. 'Holy Jesus! I knew I should never have left Grass Valley!'

The Doctor ran forward, but somehow in the turmoil of struggling horses, the figure he had pursued from the stream had vanished completely. He turned to the driver, who was sprawled on the ground clutching his head, blood seeping between his gnarled fingers. 'Where's ma hat?' he kept saying, his other arm flailing back and forth.

The Doctor turned and found himself squinting up the stubby barrel of an elegant silver pistol. The handle was inlaid with mother-of-pearl and the hand that held it was framed by coffee-coloured lace.

'Did you see him?' asked the Doctor.

'Did I see who?' The voice had a faint Irish lilt. There were gold rings on the well-manicured finger that tightened on the trigger. He caught a scent of roses.

'The man I was chasing, of course!'

A face appeared beyond the hand. A handsome woman, her dark hair piled high under a smart business-like hat. She glared suspiciously at him. 'What sort of outfit is that? If I'm going to be robbed, it'll be by an outlaw with better dress sense.'

'I assure you I have no intention of committing a robbery.'

'How very disappointing.'

The Doctor shuffled with irritation inside his kaleidoscopically coloured coat and drew his cloak around him. To his annoyance, his assailant was now talking sidelong to the driver. But the gun was still angled in his direction. 'Hank. Hank! Get up! We've got to get moving.'

The man shook his head in dazed confusion and muttered about his hat.

'Mild concussion, I imagine,' suggested the Doctor, but the woman ignored him.

'Mr Crabtree!'

'Miss Lola?' A man's face materialised in the window of the stage coach. A countenance like a timorous clerk, with a voice to match.

'Get out here, Walter, and help me get Hank inside. We're expected in Ajax before dark.'

The prim little man descended, edged past the Doctor and started tugging at the driver, but the invalid's weight was too much for him.

'Allow me.' The Doctor ignored the pistol and made a theatrical flourish of lifting the driver and depositing him inside the coach. For the first time, he noticed the initials L M embossed in gold on the coach door. He turned back, smiling broadly and announced. 'How do you do? I am the Doctor and I believe we are going the same way. Miss erm... Lola?'

'A quack?' she said. 'Out here? What are you doing? Chasing patients?'

'Not exactly.' He felt for the rolled deed in his pocket. 'I have property to return.'

'Get in, Walter. I'm driving.' She nodded towards the coach. 'And you, Doctor. But don't give my pianist any trouble. He's a sensitive type. I'm not sending back to Cisco for another.' She gathered her skirts and clambered up to the driver's perch, where she was plainly not amused to find the Doctor already seated and waiting for her.

'A pianist? So you must be some sort of artiste. A singer, perhaps?'

She snatched the reins from him and urged the horses into a trot. 'Singers are for minstrel shows. You won't see me blacking up.'

The Doctor frowned. 'Then you play an instrument. A violin? A banjo? A saw?'

He was plainly annoying her. From somewhere she produced a whip and took it out on the horses. 'I'm a danseuse. A Spanish dancer.' And her Irish lilt became more pronounced.

'Ah, the fandango. How…' and he searched for polite words. 'How exotic. Particularly for the hard-bitten denizens of a mining camp.'

She was turning the whip in his direction. Ahead he saw the lights of several cabins glimmer in the dusk.

'Not the fandango!' she exclaimed. And even he noticed her ample bosom swell. 'My dancing is famed across Europe and America. I've appeared before the Tsar and the King of Bavaria was my consort. I am Lola Montez!'

'Good grief. Not *the* Lola Montez?' said the Doctor, unimpressed. 'Wasn't King Ludwig forced to abdicate because of you? And don't the French call you *La Grande Horizontale*? Well, well. What a career. Aren't you rather slumming it in these parts?'

'Off!' yelled Miss Montez. 'Get off my Goddamn stage!' And she raised the horsewhip.

The Doctor jerked backwards and lost his balance.

As he fell from the coach, he saw whirling wheels and tasted dust. He was unsure if the stars were in his head or in the sky above. But they were golden.

The Doctor gasped for air as his head broke the surface. The icy water was grainy. It was catching in his throat. And as his head went under for the second time, the little grains of gold danced before him, in and out, round and round, in a mocking parody of the famous Spider Dance of Miss Lola Montez…

The ego! The extraordinary ego of that woman! From habit, the Doctor automatically disliked anyone with such a high opinion of themselves. But such petulant behaviour from a so-called lady astounded him. Talk about living up to her reputation. He'd heard of the string of liaisons that Lola Montez had notched up across Europe: Alexandre Dumas, the Viceroy of Poland, Franz Liszt (the demon lover reduced to a nervous wreck). But he had no idea that Lola had headed West. Go West, young man indeed! They had probably all fled her charms. And she, having exhausted the supply in Europe, was obviously in hot pursuit! Well, really!

Dark was settling in as he hobbled up the hill into Ajax Camp, past rows of squat log cabins, dusting himself down as he went. He squinted in the gloom at a skein of gold that glinted faintly on his hands. He ignored the stares of weather-beaten old-timers with nothing better to do than stop in their tracks when they saw him. And he stopped only to take in a poster nailed to a wall:

AJAX SALOON AND FANDANGO HOUSE

THIS FRIDAY EVENING
FOR ONE PERFORMANCE ONLY

DIRECT FROM EUROPE

THE COUNTESS OF LANDSFELDT

MISS LOLA MONTEZ

WHO WILL PERFORM HER FAMOUS
SPIDER DANCE!

$1 ENTRANCE FEE PER PERSON

NO CUSSING, SPITTING OR BRAWLING

Spider dance? Was that meant to be a tarantella? Or just a fandango by another name? No doubt the discerning dance critics among the grizzled miners of Ajax Camp could tell the difference.

He rounded a corner and saw a crowd gathered in front of a building with the painted sign *Ajax Saloon and Fandango House*. There were whoops and cheering. Hats were thrown in the air. And the object of the crowd's adulation stood on the boardwalk before them, arms outstretched in triumph, lit by the glow from the saloon.

'Give us a dance, Lola!' they cried.

'Later, boys. You gotta pay first!'

More cheers. Her mousy pianist, Walter, looking decidedly uncomfortable, stood behind her. Then another figure, a dapper man with a bushy moustache, a black top hat and tailored coat took her arm and led her inside.

Immediately the crowd turned and ran, every man for himself, across the street to a building signed *Assay Office*, where scuffles broke out as they tried to re-assert the queue disrupted by the arrival of the famed celebrity. With much yelling, a little man in a dark tunic and cap was ejected by the throng and ran, his pigtail flying, for cover along the track.

Close by, a horse whinnied with fear. Two shadows stood in the dark at the side of the saloon. Unmoving, their eyes glinted like nuggets of gold under their pulled-down hats. The Doctor caught a smell like stagnant water. He clutched at his inner pocket. In his indignation, he had entirely forgotten the claim deed of the man by the stream. He returned the stare of the two figures. Something was wrong. Something cold and unearthly that needed explanation...

'John Pengelly? Are you there?'

The shadows were stock still.

Out of the saloon came the sound of the most completely ill-tuned piano imaginable. The Doctor winced at the dissonance. And the figures were gone, dissolved into the dark. He sighed and headed inside.

The cacophony from the piano stopped. A card game in the corner froze. Everyone turned to stare across the smoky room. A dozen races, all of them human. Wind-dried faces, most of them melancholy, all of them tired. Muddy boots and blue woollen shirts. And the Doctor realised he was the only one in the place without a beard.

'Good evening,' he said to the massed audience. 'Perhaps you can help. I was looking for a man called John Pengelly.'

Thc silence thickened.

Then with the scrape of chairs, several of the miners rose.

'Who wants to know?' said one, a surly Mexican. And the men advanced.

'*I* do,' declared the Doctor and stood his ground. 'He's tall, dark, unhappy... and soaked to the skin. And I have something of his to return.'

'All fancy, ain't he?' growled a lank-haired fellow. 'All done up in his boiled shirt.' And he rubbed grubby fingers on the Doctor's lapel. 'You after our gold, Mister?'

'I most certainly am not,' declared the Doctor.

'Reckon he's after impressing Miss Lola,' muttered a third.

The sound of more scraping chairs. The Doctor found himself forced backwards against the bar. 'Frankly I have more important matters to attend to!'

'He's insulting our guest!' shouted a Frenchman.

'Give him a lesson in manners!' yelled an Italian. And a dozen hands reached for their victim.

'Boys! That's enough!' A sharp voice cut across the hullabaloo. The crowd opened to let the sharply suited man who had escorted Lola inside stride through. 'There's a lady upstairs. D'you want her to think she's in a rough house? Now leave the gentleman alone.'

But they waited to see the outcome. 'He's after our gold,' insisted the man with lank hair.

'Your gold's just fine.' The soft southern drawl, albeit filtered through the bushy moustache, oozed a charm of sorts. 'It's all safe under lock and key in the Assay Office.'

The level of hostility edged down, but the crowd remained and stared. Under such scrutiny, the Doctor was oddly relieved to meet someone else without a beard who wasn't Miss Montez. His saviour extended a hand - a ring on every finger. 'How d'you do, sir. I must apologise for my clientele. Two guests in one day, you see. That's a lot of excitement for all of us.'

'Indeed,' the Doctor observed and introduced himself.

'A doctor? With some travelling show, I take it?'

'Certainly not!'

'Well, your first drink is on me.' He gestured for his bartender to place a full tumbler of whiskey in front of the Doctor. 'I'm Job Clemens, owner of the Ajax Saloon.'

The Doctor eyed the smeary glass with its pale caramel-coloured liquor. He'd rather have had a tomato juice, but the crowd was hanging on his decision. He lifted the drink and sniffed it. It had a vague peaty smell, but not strong. Tiny grains drifted in the body of the whiskey. 'It's watered down,' he said.

'That's the way we drink it at Ajax,' said Job Clemens.

The crowd was edging in again. Politeness, not always the Doctor's favoured option, seemed for the best. His hosts looked eager for a lynching. He took a deep breath and knocked back the drink in one.

A resounding cheer from the miners. Hoorah for good old Boiled Shirt!

Hhooo! The Doctor clutched at the bar. No wonder they called it firewater. It was burning down his throat like a slow fuse, right the way to his stomach. The suspended grains sparkled and fizzed in his mouth. His sinuses zinged. His eyes watered. 'Excellent,' he spluttered and waved the glass aloft.

Another cheer. The ghastly piano started up again - flat as a two dimensional pancake, sharper than Miss Lola's tongue. The card game resumed. For lack of female company, several pairs of miners started to dance a spirited polka together. The Doctor turned back to Job Clemens and found another full tumbler beside him.

'Tell me, Doctor,' said Mr Clemens. 'What's this property that you're returning?'

'I will when I find the rightful owner.'

'Do you have it with you?'

The burning of the whiskey had died to a few embers, sufficient to give the Doctor a warm glow of comfort. He produced the deed from his pocket and handed it over. The drink had been decidedly moreish, so he took a sip from the new glass and regaled Clemens with his story.

The saloon owner nodded. 'Pengelly. Yes, I remember... if that's his real name. But there ain't an Argonaut in the county who won't be called something different when he gets back home.' He smiled under his moustache. 'Still, it sounds to me like he won't be needing this anymore.'

The Doctor reached for the deed, but Clemens pulled it away. 'And since you were the finder, I'll be glad to give you first refusal on a resale.'

'Resale?' The Doctor tried to be indignant, but an aura of well-being was suddenly glowing inside him. 'John Pengelly is not dead.'

'Lapse of contract. And as proprietor of the camp's Assay Office, I have the right to reclaim the mining rights.' Clemens's smile became a grin. 'Don't say you're not interested, Doctor. A three foot stake on the richest source of alluvial gold ever found? Why it's so plum full of gold, it never even froze over when the rest of Sierra County was under six feet of snow. We've been panning it all winter long.' He leaned forward confidentially. 'There's no need to pay now. You'll soon be rich enough to buy more. *And* get yourself a new set of clothes.' The Doctor was astonished to find himself tempted by the offer. But Clemens went on: 'Better snap it up fast. The word's out and it's spring already. Soon the trail up from Sacramento's gonna look like the main street to the promised land.'

The Doctor took another gulp of whiskey and pondered for a moment before asking, 'If I find Pengelly, will you return the deed to him?'

Clemens slapped the bar in irritation. 'It's time you paid for that drink.'

'For one thousand dollars, I assume. Is that the going rate?' The Doctor had to concentrate to stand upright.

'If you don't like my offer, then the boys'll show you out of town.'

Suddenly the chairs were scraping back again. The music stopped. The mob was closing in and there was no clear route of escape.

'Mr Clemens!' Lola Montez was making her way across the saloon. She had a face like retribution and the crowd parted before her like the Red Sea for Moses. Several miners removed their hats. She pointed towards the battered upright piano in the corner. 'Is that the only instrument you have?'

'Why yes, ma'am.' Job Clemens oozed an extra dose of charm. 'We had it carted up here special from Sacramento.'

She was clearly unimpressed. 'I knew I should have brought my violinist. At least he has his own fiddle.'

'Ma'am?'

'I have my integrity as an artiste to defend. And so does my pianist, Mr Walter Crabtree. So find another piano, 'cause there'll be no dancing to thc cacophony from that jangle box!'

The miners started to mutter uneasily. Job Clemens rubbed his chin. 'Looks fine to me, Ma'am. Just getting it up the trail cost us a tidy sum.' He turned to the bartender. 'Jim, a drink for Miss Montez.'

Lola shook her head. 'That's Countess to you, Mister. And *looks* have nothing to do with it. It's plain no one here has an ear for music.'

'Old Abe here. He plays the tongs real tuneful,' called a voice from the crowd.

Lola ignored the old timer who shuffled forward with a toothless grin. 'No piano. No show. I knew should have stayed in Grass Valley.'

The threat was clear in Clemens's voice. 'Countess. You signed a contract. And you're gonna honour it. The boys here, they've paid good money.'

'Well, *I* ain't seen none of it!' And from her skirt, she somehow produced her horsewhip.

The Doctor beamed expansively over Job Clemens's shoulder. 'Might I make a suggestion?' He ignored the mass look of disdain that came in his direction. 'I think you'll find that all the pianoforte in question needs is a spot of tuning.' He produced a tubular key from one pocket and a tuning fork from another.

Clemens looked to Lola for agreement. She eyed the tumbler of whiskey that was set before her. 'I drink my whiskey neat. This is watered down.'

'That's just what I said,' agreed the Doctor and headed slightly unsteadily for the piano. There was another hearty cheer for Boiled Shirt, who had saved the day.

An all-enveloping glow of benevolence filled his hearts as he extricated various unlikely items of lost property from the piano's innards (sixty two old cigar butts, eight dollars seventeen cents in loose change, three dead mice, a small pickaxe, an item of gentlemen's undergarments) and set to work on re-tuning the neglected brute.

While he worked, a steady supply of tumblers of whiskey, presents from grateful prospectors, were set in his reach. At first, he listened to the banter behind him. Lola Montez appeared temporarily appeased and was flirting outrageously with her audience, smoking a cigar and regaling them with tales of when she danced at the Paris *Opera* and threw her garters to the audience. Then she retired to her room to compose herself.

He was beginning to like the taste and the effect of the liquor. He enjoyed the way it seemed to dissolve away pressing problems - probably some sort of mental corrosive - but who cared? He was quite amused that he would have a terrible headache in the morning - it didn't seem to matter. As he worked along the keyboard, flattening sharps, sharpening flats, he found ways to set his giggles to little tunes on the left hand. And in the tumblers, the little grains glittered and spun in a dance of their own. Bewitching, beguiling as the liquid seemed to separate, water from whiskey, and the water tried in little waves, more like jumps, to escape from the glasses. The whole room seemed to be joining in the dance, swaying and tipping, spinning on one toe like a swan princess at the ballet.

He was vaguely aware of an argument between Clemens and the little man he'd seen expelled from the Assay Office queue earlier.

Probably Chinese. Words like *deeds* and *brothers* and *tricks* and *liar* were dancing in his head. *Damnable coolie! Get out of my saloon!* Oh, dear. *Tempers fugit!* And then he was making up an anachronistic ragtime based on a Chopin prelude. And there were other shouts and dark golden-eyed phantoms in dripping clothes moving round him. And a smell like a stagnant pond. Crashes of overturned tables. Breaking glass. And more yells. And the Doctor joined in, thundering out the tune on the piano, singing *If ten green bottles should accidentally fall* as if his life depended on it. Until the spinning floor whirled up in a wave of darkness to engulf him...

And the Doctor golloped up another noseful of water and went under for the third and final time...

The big bass drum in the Doctor's head roused him with a relentless but limited repertoire of thumps. He felt dizzy. The skin on his hand was dry and parchment-thin. Talk about dehydration; he felt like the shallow end of the Aridian Desert in the dry season. He struggled up, crunching broken glass underfoot and groped his way to the bar looking for water. The large china jug was empty. A hole had appeared in its base as if the contents had burrowed its way out.

It was only then that the Doctor noticed the state of the saloon. Tables were up-ended and chairs broken. A window was smashed and one of the swing doors was half off its hinges. It was daylight and the place was deserted.

Something moved. In the broken mirror on the back wall, he saw a dark blue shape crouching under the bar top. The reflection of a pair of sleek brown eyes stared at him in the glass. He lunged over and hauled the figure into the light. 'Gold fever! Gold fever!' it shouted and struggled in terror.

It took a full minute for the Doctor to calm the little Chinese and get him to talk. At first, all he could describe were the dead men with golden eyes who had smashed the place up. They had come through the door in a great wave. And amongst them were his dead brothers.

But the Doctor frightened him too. 'How do you speak Mandarin? No white man in America speaks Mandarin!'

'"Within four seas, the world is my home,"' the Doctor suggested. It was a proverb he'd once found in a fortune cookie, but it seemed to calm the poor chap enough for him to relate his own story, although he still shivered and his eyes were never still, looking for danger.

His name was Chum Jian and he had come to California from

Shanghai with his brothers. They bought up diggings that other Argonauts reckoned were exhausted and cleaned the left-over gold dust out of them. They had bought claims on the gold stream from Job Clemens and were doubling their fortune each day.

Before winter came, he had travelled to Sacramento for supplies, but the snow set in early and the trail back was impassable until spring. When he finally returned to Ajax Camp, there was no sign of his brothers. And he'd discovered that Job Clemens had resold his brothers' claims, whilst keeping all their bags of gold dust in his own safe at the Assay Office. Clemens had threatened Chum with a gun. 'He's crazy, that one. He's got gold fever the worst and the all others caught it from him. And you...' He looked down at the Doctor's dried hands. 'You got it too.'

The Doctor tried to concentrate through his pounding head. He stared at his reflection in the mirror across the bar. His face had a grey, withered look like old fruit. But his eyes were still blue, not gold. 'You say you saw your brothers?'

Mr Chum swallowed hard and went pale. The Doctor put a hand on his shoulder. 'Was it in here?'

Chum looked at the floor and nodded. 'They came in here with the others.'

'The others?'

'The other dead men with golden eyes. Some of the miners ran away. Clemens ran too. I hid.'

'And the rest?'

'Herded them up like goats and took them.'

The Doctor was bemused. 'But they left me alone?'

'You were playing the piano. They stood around you and listened until you stopped and fell over. Then they took the prisoners away.'

A shudder coursed down the Doctor's spine. 'That's an image I can do without.' He looked deep into Chum's eyes. 'I am very sorry about your brothers, Mr Chum. I will do everything in my power to save them.'

Chum bowed his head. 'I fear for their celestial spirits.'

'As well you might. Do you know where they went? What's the betting it's somewhere near that stream?'

'I went to the stream, Doctor. To look for my brothers. But it has moved.'

'Moved? How can a stream move?'

'It has changed its course. It is moving closer to the camp.'

The Doctor scooped up the water jug and peered through the hole in its base. 'No wonder it's dry in here.' He rubbed his flaking hands and still felt decidedly woozy. 'A bit like standing in a tinder box, don't you think?'

Chum shrugged. The Doctor slid himself over the bar and perused the whiskey tumblers stacked ready for washing. In the lowest glass in a stack of three, there was about a spoonful of water, shivering and leaping, unable to escape from its prison. The Doctor set it on the bar top and he and Chum watched its frantic efforts.

'Doctor!'

They looked up. At the top of the stairs stood Lola Montez, dressed in a ribboned, voluminous skirt and petticoats. Behind her stood Walter Crabtree, her pianist, peeking nervously around her waist. 'Doctor? Get me out of here!' she shouted.

'Easier said than done,' he called back.

'I'll barricade myself back in my room.'

The Doctor flung out a generous hand. 'No, no. Come down. It's quite safe in here... for the moment.'

She started down the stairs, warily, one at a time. 'Are you still drunk?'

That brought him up short. 'I have never been intoxicated in any of my lives.'

And he was only swaying slightly.

Lola turned to Mr Crabtree who was still lingering at the top of the stairs. 'Walter, find some horses and we'll get out of this place.'

'I'd stay here if I were you, Walter,' interrupted the Doctor. 'Unless you want to get yourself shot.' He edged up to the doors and squinted outside. Across the street, the windows of the Assay Office were blocked on the inside with piled furniture. Protruding from two broken panes were two thin rifle barrels.

'Mr Clemens! Is that you?' he called. 'You can't sit it out for ever. We need to talk.'

One of the rifles cracked an answer. It splintered the door frame by the Doctor's ear and cleared his head no end.

'You're all crazy!' complained Lola. 'I'll show him who's in charge.' She was waving her pistol and heading for the door.

Before the Doctor could stop her, she was brought up in her tracks by Walter Crabtree. The once timorous pianist darted into her path. 'Miss Lola. Stop right there!'

'Out of my way, Walter.'

'No, Lola. You can handle a rowdy audience in Cisco, but not out here. These are crazy men. Gold fever'll drive them to anything. Now you just listen to me. Let's sit tight and work this out.'

Lola took a sharp breath. 'Ordered about by a Goddamn accompanist!' She picked up a chair and threw it across the saloon. Then she primly dusted down her costume and sat at a table.'So? What do you propose we do?' she said quietly.

'Thank you, Walter,' muttered the Doctor. And the pianist smiled shyly.

They sat round over empty glasses and discussed their predicament, the Doctor repeating Chum's contribution by way of translation. It seemed that the *dead men* were driven by a fever for gold, the bulk of which was in the hands of Job Clemens, and which they were determined to get back. But the Doctor was neither convinced of their motives nor even of their demise. He set the stack of tumblers with its captive water in front of them. They watched as the tireless liquid tried to escape.

'Why didn't any of you succumb to the fever?' the Doctor asked.

'I do not drink this,' insisted Chum.

'Me neither,' said Walter.'Not before a performance.'

'And I drink my whiskey straight,' said Lola.

The Doctor stared at the glass. 'Exactly. Only I drank the water. Fortunately I have the sturdiest constitution and was able to resist.'

'And Clemens?' asked Lola.

'He doesn't drink it either,' said the Doctor.'His madness is entirely different.The real question is, what does the water want?'

No one laughed.They just watched the angry liquid in the glass with mounting gloom.

'I want to go home,' said Chum.'Back to my family and the rice fields and the bamboo forests.'

'Home?' said Walter. 'I grew up in a little clapboard house, east, in Tarrytown by the Hudson. And there were chipmunks and red cardinals in the trees.'

'I've a house in Grass Valley, open to all,' said Lola.'But my only real home is out there in front of an audience.'

They turned in unison to look at the Doctor.'How about you?'

He sighed. 'I've had plenty of homes. But none I'd be comfortable settling in. Perhaps I'm still looking. I'm not sure I ever knew the meaning of the word.'

And for a moment, he was chilled to the bone. He saw millions of points of light, pinpricks of gold and ice streaming around him against the cavernous darkness of space. 'Home,' he intoned, his voice trembling. He looked embarrassed and dabbed a finger to his eye.

'Excuse me. I'm losing water again.'

With a crack, the stack of tumblers finally overturned, rolled off the table and smashed on the floor. Everyone jumped back. 'Don't touch!' shouted the Doctor, as the splashed water gathered its droplets to itself and flowed like quicksilver for the door.

Out onto the street, across the dust, towards a long stream of golden water that was snaking inexorably up the slope through the camp.

'It's coming!' shouted Chum. 'Coming for us!'

They stared as the slow tide halted and spread sideways across the track. Its surface rippled and broke, and from its shallows rose, one by one, a line of deathly silent Argonauts. Shadowy even in the sunlight, they slowly trudged forward, dripping gold droplets in the dust as they advanced.

'The dead are rising. It's judgement day!' wailed Walter Crabtree.

'No,' muttered the Doctor. 'I think something just wants its property back.' He turned towards the Assay Office. 'Mr Clemens! Me again. You can't fight this. You'd better think about handing over your gold.'

A rifle levelled at the Doctor, but he stood his ground.

'No deal. We have our lawful rights!' Job Clemens's voice was cracked with fear.

'Give me five minutes,' the Doctor called back.

'Tell *them* that,' was Clemens's reply.

The Argonauts were closing slowly on the office, ignoring the saloon. The Doctor turned to Lola Montez. 'We need to distract those men.'

'What?'

'They're not dead, just driven by the needs of something that doesn't belong here. But they've still got deeper instincts. Things that are close to their hearts. John Pengelly still needed the letter he never sent home.'

Chum nodded. 'And they listened when you played the piano.'

'No accounting for taste,' the Doctor added. 'Miss Montez, can you perform your dance now?'

Walter was incredulous. 'What? To an audience of dead men?'

Lola Montez pursed her lips.

'Please!' begged the Doctor.

'Well, I've played to less animated houses,' she admitted. 'Walter? You said you'd never heard a piano tuned so pitch perfect.'

'But, Miss Lola...'

'Just do it!'

As Mr Walter Crabtree sat at the piano, flexing his fingers, the Doctor strode to the door. 'Gentlemen!' he thundered to the trudging

Argonauts outside. 'We are proud to bring you a display of Terpsichorean treasure! A panoply of priceless pirouettes! An event of essential arachnophobia! I give you the one and only Miss Lola Montez and her celebrated Spider Dance!'

From the piano, now beautifully tuned, came a lilting seguidilla, a slow tune above a rhythmic repeating base line at once suggestive and tempting, reminiscent of the rolling dusty slopes and streets of España.

The effect was immediate. The Argonauts turned in their tracks, slowly shuffling their way up through the broken doors into the saloon, where they stood and stared golden-eyed at the performance before them.

Lola Montez slowly moved across the floor, swinging her hips to the music, giving sidelong glances through fluttered eyelashes to the gathering throng. Then she gave a little flick of irritation. Then another, as if something was amiss. The music became more animated as she started to lift first one skirt, then a petticoat, then another, in search of the irritating creature loose in her underclothes. And in the process, she was revealing a lot that was higher than her ankle.

Subtle, it was not. But it was enough to delay the imminent massacre. As Lola pranced back and forth, stamping on the floor at the imaginary spider, the Doctor slipped out onto the street. He waved to the Assay Office. There was no answer. He looked down the trail towards the golden stream. It was advancing steadily, hissing and splashing as it came. Lifting its surface in little waves like claws.

Nothing for it. He had to understand. He stepped off the boardwalk into its path, and threw himself purposefully into its icy shallows.

He was drowning. The water tore out his breath and surged into his body. The bitter cold gripped him both inside and out. Particles of gold spangled in his nose, throat and brain. He was dragged in deep, lost in the thoughts of a lost orphaned being. So, so far from its belonging. The gold danced before him in kaleidoscopic patterns making thoughts and ideas in the gaps in between. He saw glittering rings of ammonia ice where it swam, fluid and uncrushed by the cruel forces of gravity, high above the watchful, loving presence of its yellow-grey mother world.

And he understood how a meteor storm had smashed into the rings of Saturn, tearing it away from its home, and how it had wandered lost and confused through the empty darkness until it spilled down through the burning, burning air of the hot Earth and lay helpless on the hard surface, while little alien creatures toiled endlessly to steal away its golden thoughts and strength.

'I don't know how to help,' he thought. And from the creature came back an understanding of its own. No malice, no ill will. Just a need to understand and survive. And the tune the gold was dancing to was *Ten Green Bottles*.

The Doctor got tired of drowning. He stood up and blew the water out of his nose. He was soaked, revitalised, both inside and out. The stream, the amoebic flumeling, was still as glass, but he could see the gold currents flowing under its surface: uphill above and downhill beneath. As he tramped out of the shallows, he saw Job Clemens and his men coming down the street to meet him, guns at the ready.

'*You're* doing this,' Clemens shouted, madness dancing in his eyes. 'It's *my* gold! *My* future!' He raised his rifle, aiming squarely at the Doctor. 'Goddamn swindling, two-timing... You ain't having it! Go to Damnation!' But he fell backwards with a cry, shooting the sky, golden water creeping around his ankles.

The flumeling rippled and a little wave lifted Job Clemens and settled him on its surface. He moaned as it rocked him on the swell; flowing into him, cradling him, ever so gently, to death. The other men ran for their lives.

Then it heaved itself into a mighty breaker. The Doctor threw himself sideways as the deluge surged up the street, turned sharp left at the Assay Office and engulfed the building like a giant eating the tiniest morsel. Planks, furniture and glass whirled inside its shifting shape. And many, many cloth bags, which tore apart to release swirling clouds of gold.

The creature was swelling into a huge golden watery globe. As it rolled away up the street, it scattered debris in its wake. Discarded jetsam of its reclaimed strength. The Doctor heard it gurgle and splutter appreciation as it went. And he understood that it was heading north, away from the sun, drawn to the magnetic pole where it might at least be cooler, if never, ever really cold.

And the piano music, perfectly tuned, coming from the saloon, reached its climax. There was a hearty cheer. Three mighty cheers in fact, for Miss Lola Montez and her intoxicating Spider Dance.

The dead men, far from dead now, emerged from the saloon, slapping each other heartily on their backs with many a huzzah... and stopped to stare with clear blue or brown eyes, in disbelief at the shattered remains of their Assay Office. And amongst their number stood the familiar shape of John Pengelly.

The Doctor slipped inside before the questions started and saw Chum talking excitedly with his lost brothers. They returned his long and deep bow.

'I hope you're satisfied,' said Lola Montez.

The Doctor raised a smile without fear of his dry face cracking. 'Lola, you were matchless. Unique.'

'That's certainly true,' she agreed.

He looked awkward. 'Ah. I imagine you want paying.'

She was fingering her horsewhip again. He flinched... ever so slightly.

Then she threw back her head and roared with laughter. 'Paying? Why I never had such an appreciative audience. You know, I haven't toured for a while. Maybe I should start again.' She batted her eyelashes in most provocative manner. 'How would you like a job as my manager? And I have a protégé, you know. Little Lotta. She could appear with me. She's only six and plays the banjo.'

The Doctor smiled weakly. Home, any home, was not really his cup of tea. But occasionally it was very agreeable to visit. He made the politest of excuses and left by the fastest route.

The Death of Me

Robert Shearman

'Chloe! This time I've got it!'

As a rule, most people don't die saying anything clever. No, worse than that - most people don't die saying anything even remotely *interesting*. Even bearing in mind that the majority die in their sleep, so they're hardly in a position to articulate anything more meaningful than a snore, that's a pretty poor showing. If they are conscious at the time they meet their maker, more often than not it's a scream. A scream of terror. Or of pain. Or, most tediously of all, a fatuous, idiotic, I-never-realised-that-was-a-live-wire, oops-I-seem-to-have-run-out-of-motorway, dear-me-what's-that-thudding-in-my-chest-I-should-have-listened-to-my-doctor-and-dropped-the-diet-of-fried-lard, *surprise*.

Arthur couldn't find anything at all surprising in death. And he was determined that his last words were going to be something pretty profound as well. Witty. If not witty, then heroic. If not heroic, then at least something better than the scream his wife always gave.

'Chloe! Where are you?'

Of course, he knew where she was. She would be where she would always be. Just as he spent his days in the guest room leafing through a book of quotations, so she spent hers in the kitchen on a hard wooden chair staring off into space.

She looked up at him as he came into the room. But she contrived to look at him in such a way that he couldn't be sure it wasn't a complete coincidence, that she just happened to be on the point of looking up anyway, and that his entrance had nothing to do with it. She'd been practising, and was getting rather good.

'Just listen to this.' He beamed with pride. 'It's perfect. It really is.'

He cleared his throat and grinned. Chloe began practising one of her other looks - the baleful discouraging one.

'"It is a far, far better thing I do than I have ever done. It is a far, far better rest that I go to, than I have ever known."' He struck a heroic pose, grinned at her again. 'Well, what do you think?'

Chloe looked into the face of the man she'd married - oh, so long ago now her eyes watered at the thought. She looked right into his eyes, then at his nose, his mouth, the flaps of stubble that made up his chin. She silently asked herself, as she did every day, whether she would prefer to divorce him or give him children. Not that it mattered, of course. There wasn't time for either. But, you know, if there was, just for *fun* – which would it be?

'It's too long,' she said finally.

'No, it isn't,' he said.

'All that in your dying breath? Not a chance.'

'Yes, there is,' he said. Though he knew she was right, really.

There was silence.

'It might be alright,' he pleaded. 'If I used a few breaths up on it *before* my dying breath. If I took a good long run up before I started.'

Still the silence. He stood there, grinning a little at her, showing his teeth just that fraction too much. Begging for her to agree with him. With an inward sigh, Chloe realised she'd choose the divorce. Never mind. Perhaps the next Chloe might love Arthur better. Perhaps she'd opt for children instead.

'I could always go and choose another,' he said lamely. 'If you don't think that will suit.'

'It'll have to do,' she said flatly. 'There isn't time.'

He opened his mouth, as if to argue. It would be pointless, Chloe knew – he never won an argument. Arthur seemed to realise this too in a rare moment of perfect clarity, closed his mouth again, and sat down on the chair opposite her.

'I wish you'd choose last words for yourself some day,' he said quietly. 'It seems such a waste. To go with a scream.'

She wasn't looking at him any longer, back to staring at the kitchen walls. If he hadn't known better, he'd have sworn she hadn't even heard him.

They came for Henrietta first. As he always did, Arthur wondered whether the poor thing had a clue what was going on. She died without protest.

Next they came for Chloe. A tapping at the window, slow fingernail on double glazing. She left her husband without a look. She died screaming as usual. It might have been in terror or pain, but it certainly wasn't in surprise.

Then it was Arthur's turn. He only reached 'far, far better thing' before he admitted Chloe had been right all along – well, she was always right, wasn't she? He was dead before he'd finished the first sentence. Before he'd even got to the good bit!

Never mind. He'd choose a better quotation tomorrow.

The tapping at the window that signified their doom took place when the clocks struck midnight precisely. So it was something of a shock to Arthur and Chloe when, at the very imprecise time of seventeen minutes past eleven in the morning, they heard a knock at the door.

'They've come early!' Arthur looked at his wife with an expression very close to fear. 'But they never come early!' Chloe's face stared implacably back at him.

The day had begun normally enough. The couple had woken up in bed side by side, and proceeded to check that each other's limbs and external organs were in the right place. (They always were, but Arthur always enjoyed the ritual examination, and secretly dreaded that one day Chloe would ask to put a stop to it. He'd have been surprised to learn that Chloe secretly dreaded Arthur would one day ask the same thing.) They had then got up in silence, washed in silence, dressed in silence. In a voice as close to silence as she could make it, Chloe told Arthur she'd go and fix them breakfast.

They always had an egg each - Henrietta would provide a couple and leave them in the garden shed for Chloe to collect. This morning there were three. Chloe could hardly believe it. In fact, for a while she didn't believe it, and stared numbly at it waiting for the impossible object to vanish into thin air. When it hadn't, after nearly a good half hour of her best disbelieving stare, she'd picked it up and taken it into the house with the other eggs.

Chloe and Arthur couldn't decide what to do with it. Should they toss for it? Should they share it? Should they just ignore it, and what it implied? Chloe resented it, not so much for disrupting her daily order, but for necessitating a conversation with her husband. This new existence couldn't have got off to a worse start.

Or so she had thought. But there it was again, someone knocking. The Crisis of the Extra Egg was all but forgotten, as husband and wife went to answer the front door.

'Hello,' said the visitor - who shouldn't have existed, but dogmatically, emphatically, did - 'I'm the Doctor.'

'Are you anything to do with the extra egg?' blurted out Chloe.

The Doctor was a plump man of unruly curly hair, clothes with more colours than Arthur had ever seen, and a face so used to witnessing strange wonders that abrupt questions about eggs didn't even make it flinch. Arthur giggled nervously at him.

'Eggs, no, I wouldn't have thought so. I've come to stay! This is a bed and breakfast, isn't it?' He pointed at the sign reading 'Bed and breakfast'. Neither Chloe nor Arthur spoke. 'And you have vacancies, don't you?' He pointed at another sign reading 'Vacancies'. Still nothing from his hosts. Unperturbed, the Doctor continued,

'Excellent. I'd like a single room, with the best view you've got, and no newspaper in the morning.'

'We don't have a view,' said Arthur.

'Ah. And the newspaper?'

'We don't have newspapers either.'

'Good. So we're halfway there then. Well, that suits me. Wouldn't be able to see anything through this fog anyway, would I? Could you let me in, please? I really would like to get out of it.'

Arthur moved aside, Chloe still hesitated. 'How did you get through the fog? No one can get through the fog.'

'We haven't had a guest for years,' said Arthur. 'Years and years and years and years.'

'As long as that?' asked the Doctor. 'How do you make a living?'

'Living doesn't really come into it!' He laughed at his joke. The Doctor didn't get it. Chloe just rolled her eyes and groaned.

'The fog,' she repeated firmly.

'I don't know,' said the Doctor. 'It is rather thick, isn't it? Would you show me my room? Don't have any luggage, don't believe in the stuff. Just a bed for the night, maybe two, until the fog clears. And any breakfast you've got going would be most welcome.'

Even the Doctor's face frowned in surprise when Chloe opened one hand to reveal an egg, ready boiled in its cup. 'Yes,' she said. 'I think this was meant for you.'

It was a good boiled egg; the yolk was not too runny, and not too hard. It was an egg boiled by an expert. The Doctor felt unusually embarrassed as he ate it, every mouthful he chewed watched intently but uncuriously.

'You both live on one egg a day?' he asked.

'That's all Henrietta provides.'

'And who's Henrietta?'

So they had shown him Henrietta. It was quite an occasion for her, brought out from the shed to the house where her masters lived, but she took it all in her stride and barely uttered a cluck.

'Henrietta the hen,' laughed Arthur. 'Do you see? Do you see?' He was clearly quite fond of the bird, and gave it a gentle hug. After which, even Arthur admitted, there was really precious little anyone could think to do with it, and it was taken back to the shed.

'And what do you drink?' the Doctor had said.

'There's water in the taps. And we grow vegetables in the garden. They're not worth eating, thanks to the weather. But if we stick them in the blender, we can make juice out of them.'

'It's a very odd set-up,' said the Doctor politely. 'Don't you think?'

Chloe and Arthur exchanged glances - the first time, the Doctor noticed, they had directly looked at each other since he'd arrived. 'Well,' said Arthur eventually, 'it is a little odd. But you get used to it.'

'We did,' said Chloe.

The Doctor wanted to talk to Chloe some more, but Chloe explained that she'd had quite enough talking for one day, and intended to spend the rest of both it and her life sitting in the kitchen staring off into space. So it was left for Arthur to show the Doctor his room.

'I think it's the best room in the whole house,' enthused the portly little man, as he shepherded the Doctor over the threshold. 'It's where I like to spend the day reading.' The Doctor hoped he wasn't getting in his way. Arthur assured him that he wasn't, then changed his mind and admitted he was, just a little bit, but it didn't matter, he could read his book somewhere else, couldn't he?

'And what are you reading?'

And, shyly, proud, Arthur let him see his book of quotations. 'I love it,' he said. 'It's what I love most in the whole world. Even more than Henrietta.'

'Even more than your wife?'

'Oh, absolutely. Look,' and Arthur eagerly flicked to some well-thumbed page, 'these are some of my favourites. So witty. So heroic! So useful for selecting what my dying words shall be. Tell me, Doctor. Deciding what you're going to say before you finally peg out. Is it something you give much thought?'

'Well,' said the Doctor carefully, 'at the end it's good to know the moment has been prepared for.' And he sipped at his carrot juice.

'Quite so! Chloe doesn't see that at all. She's missing out, isn't she, Doctor?'

The Doctor hadn't finished. 'But I'm not sure it's something you want to spend too much time thinking about. Do you? Better to live your life. Don't you think?'

Arthur giggled at him nervously. 'To tell you the truth, I haven't done all that well with *life*. Marrying Chloe, eating eggs - it's not been what anyone could call a roaring success. So I'm determined at least I can get my death right. The right words, the right posture. You understand, Doctor?' His voice dropped to the plaintive tone Chloe knew and loathed so well. 'I don't want *everything* I do to have been a failure.'

The Doctor didn't know what to say. So he gave him a half smile and a non-committal nod. For Arthur it was just the encouragement he needed. 'Thank you,' he said gratefully. 'Do you know, I might try a bit of poetry this time.' And he was gone, shutting the door behind him.

The Doctor didn't get anything useful out of Arthur and Chloe for the rest of the day. Both were far too absorbed in their work, quotation quoting or middle space staring, and weren't going to change the rituals of a lifetime for him. He considered leaving and trying to find the TARDIS, but he knew it was hopeless; the fog he'd landed in was so thick he'd lost his ship as soon as he'd stepped out of it, and if anything the fog was even thicker now. He spent the afternoon lying on the bed in thought; and when it turned dark, he rolled over on to his stomach and thought a bit more.

The fog began to clear just before midnight. The Doctor was surprised at how quickly it did so. Like a floodlight set upon the garden and only the garden, the moonshine cut out a large hole in the gloom, which was perfectly round and perfectly unnatural. That was startling enough. What startled the Doctor further was what he saw illuminated in it.

Hens. Hundreds of hens.

It was not a big garden and yet, somehow, it was able to hold all these birds. The grass was covered with them, all the hens squeezed tightly together, standing side by side in ordered rows. The only area left untouched was the small patch of green just outside the shed door, and it was at that that all the hens were staring directly, the eldest at the front, the youngest at the back. There was an expectant quiet. And then the eldest hen of all hopped out of the group, ambled to the door, and rapped on it deliberately with her beak.

That expectant quiet again, just for a few seconds. Then the shed door opened and Henrietta stepped out. If a hen could look resigned to its fate, then she did so. She walked towards the gathered throng, and waited. She didn't have to wait long. As one all the other birds fell on her, clawing, pecking, biting. Chewing. Ripping.

The Doctor struggled with the catch on the window so he could - what? Do what? Tell them to stop? Scare them off? He looked away from the killing as he got the window open. By the time he looked back all the hens were gone, the murderers and their prize. But he still cried out. He still had to cry out.

Because where the hundreds of hens had been, there now stood thousands of Chloes, tens of thousands of Chloes. Pointing at the back door to the house, as one of their number tapped on the kitchen window with her fingernail. The garden was filled with Chloe and nothing but Chloe, a seething mass of disillusioned housewife.

'Don't do it! Stay in the house!'

But the door opened, and the sour faced woman joined her ghostly sisters. The Doctor was running down the stairs even as he heard her dying scream.

He burst into the kitchen. Arthur stood there, tense, as if waiting in the wings before his big entrance. He smiled a little shamefacedly. 'Always goes with a scream,' he said. 'Seems such a shame, but it's up to her.'

'Don't go out there,' panted the Doctor. 'They'll kill you.'

'Oh yes,' agreed Arthur, 'but I've got a great speech to go out with.'

'Stop. Talk to me. Tell me what's going on.'

For a moment the Doctor thought he was going to do so, but Arthur had opened his mouth only to begin a lament from *King Lear*. With a whoosh of poetry he was outside and dead.

The Doctor rushed out after him. Standing there were an incalculable number of Doctors, all unsmiling, the colour drained from their coats. A Doctor for each day he'd been alive, the most recent at the front, getting younger and younger into the distance. He thought he could spot glimpses of his previous incarnation behind them all, but he may have imagined it - those Doctors were impossibly far away. Millions and millions of Doctors, all in a garden measuring no more than a hundred and fifty square metres.

He was so appalled at the sight of them that, by the time he thought to ask them what they were doing there, they had already killed him.

'I like Shakespeare best,' confided Arthur. 'He's my favourite. He's always got great death speeches.'

The Doctor had heard Shakespeare's last words, the real ones. They weren't heroic and they weren't in iambic pentameter. 'Why not tell me what's going on?' he said gently.

Unwittingly, the Doctor had precisely echoed the actions of his hosts when he woke up that morning, and checked that his body was complete and intact. He had then been down for breakfast to find an egg waiting for him - Henrietta had laid three once more. Chloe hadn't been surprised this time; evidently their new guest was here to stay.

'We were given some sort of explanation at the time,' said Arthur. 'But it's such a long time ago.'

The Doctor made the best impression he could of encouraging patience.

'As soon as we are born, we begin to die. Each day millions of our cells decay.'

'To be replaced by entirely new ones. It's the renewal process that keeps us alive.'

'No,' said Arthur, with a firmness that surprised even him. 'Every day a large quantity of our bodies is lost forever. Of what we consider to be *ourselves*. Within a week we're walking about with new cells, new skin, new organs, we think we're the same people, but we're *not*. We're not. A significant portion of us is completely different every time we get out of bed each morning, the rest of us rotted away somewhere, never buried, never honoured, never even remembered. We all live and die, live and die, live and die, each day back and forth, live and die onwards and forever more.'

The Doctor was listening hard. Arthur seemed a bit embarrassed by his own fervour, and giggled a little to break it. 'Most people are lucky. They never notice. They never have to notice. But Chloe and I do. Chloe and I are the only ones to witness it. Someone has to. We experience these daily deaths, so no one else has to. In a way, I suppose,' he suggested a little bashfully, 'it makes us a bit heroic. Doesn't it? Saviours of the world.'

The Doctor considered this in silence for a while.

'That's the most ludicrous thing I've ever heard,' he said at last.

At midnight on the second day the Doctor stood in the kitchen with Chloe and Arthur. 'I'll go out there,' he told them. 'I'll talk to them. Whatever deal you think you've done with Death, I'll break it for you, persuade them to give you up.'

Chloe was unimpressed. 'They'll simply kill you again.'

'With any luck, if I go in your place, I'll take them by surprise. I'll have time to plead your case.'

The Doctor was right. They did seem surprised, seemed to pause for a while. And he did a lot better than Arthur had ever managed, and got a full three sentences out before they tore him to pieces.

On the third day the Doctor tried to talk to Chloe. She pointedly ignored him, sitting in the kitchen staring off into space as she always did. His rebuttal was to sit directly opposite and stare at her. After eight hours, she finally spoke.

'I wish I loved Arthur. Or hated him. Either way, I'd know where I stood, wouldn't I?'

The Doctor smiled sympathetically. This annoyed her.

'We had to make vows at the wedding. Till death do us part. No way out, this man you met and cared for and hoped you'd fallen in love with - really hoped it was love, that it was the real thing - you'd sworn you'd be with him forever. But if I'd known... If I could have guessed... just how long forever was...' She looked at him directly, and the quiet pain and anger in her eyes made the Doctor look away. 'Can you imagine what it's like to choose someone as your life-long companion - and then realise you're *really* stuck with that? You'll never be able to walk away, never be able to leave them?'

'No,' said the Doctor softly. 'Most of my companions leave me.'

She looked away from him again. He wondered whether it would be another eight hours before she spoke to him again. As it turns out, he was lucky. It was only two.

'When I was a girl, I was so frightened of death. Do you know? My dad used to say there were two sure things in life - death and taxes. But I misheard him. I thought he meant 'taxis'. And throughout my childhood I refused to get into one. Screamed my head off if anyone tried to make me. I somehow thought, if I could avoid taxis, I could avoid death too. I could live forever. I'd rather,' she said, 'travel by bus.'

She sipped at a juice drink, which the Doctor had grimly concluded must have been made from leeks.

'Ironically, my dad was knocked down by a double-decker. Which put paid to that theory.' She sighed. 'Till death do us part. I just wish, with all my heart... I wish I could be frightened of death again.'

Gently the Doctor touched her hand. 'I'm still frightened of it,' he confessed, a secret rarely shared.

She glared back at him with envious hatred, and drank her leeks.

I won't leave them, the Doctor vowed to himself. This sacrifice they make is too much. I'll try again tonight, offer to take their place if I have to. These poor ordinary people deserve their lives back. *I won't leave them*.

On the fourth day, the Doctor tried to leave them. He set off in the fog to find the TARDIS. It didn't matter in which direction he set out, he always finished up back at the bed and breakfast. This naturally made him quite angry.

That night he didn't make the ghosts a courageous speech of self-sacrifice. He tried instead to tell them that whatever was going on here, it had nothing to do with him. 'Take them!' he shouted. 'Just let me go!' And the Doctor died again, held down by the Doctor he'd been yesterday and the Doctor he'd been the day before that, with the deed carried out by maybe half a dozen Doctors from the previous week, with all the other Doctors he'd ever been pitching in by shouting encouragement.

Some time during the fifth day, Arthur decided he'd stop sharing his quotation discoveries with Chloe, and began seeking out the Doctor instead. On the seventh day he came up with a bit of Gerard Manley Hopkins. 'It's not actually about death,' he admitted, 'but it's really, really depressing. Do you think it will do?'

The Doctor took the book of quotations and threw it out of the window. Arthur didn't take the hint, and went downstairs to retrieve it. So the Doctor had to snatch the book back, tear it up, and then throw it out of the window again.

'They're not yours!' he shouted at the bemused little man. 'Say what you want when you die, I don't care. But at least have the decency to use your own words, not those written by people a thousand times more articulate and imaginative than you!'

Arthur began to cry. But it was precisely because he *wasn't* articulative or imaginative that he had to use other people's words. He'd never have glory of his own, he had to borrow someone else's. Was that really so very wrong? He was saviour of the world, after all.

The Doctor apologised. And told him that maybe the next day when they all came back to life, the book would come back too. But it didn't on the eighth, and it didn't on the ninth. On the tenth day Arthur gave up hope, and began spending his time staring off into middle distance like Chloe did. But whereas her expression was always sharp and determined, Arthur's face sank into the sort of despondency a puppy's wears when you stop throwing it sticks.

Arthur never really trusted the Doctor again. Each new Arthur was born with the suspicion of the last, and resisted the Doctor's attempts to cheer him up with promises of epitaph suggestions accumulated from seven hundred years of watching people die in extraordinary circumstances. 'No thank you,' he'd say.

About the time the Doctor was born again for the fourteenth time, he took to spending the time lying on his bed counting the stains on the ceiling. It wasn't so much a decision he took, just something he began to do. Down with the egg, then up to the bed and the stain-counting. Every day he'd hope to find some he'd not spotted before. Every day he failed, and counted four hundred and six exactly. By day seventeen, he began marking the ceiling with stains of his own, so he'd have something new to look forward to tomorrow.

On day twenty-two he broke his eggshell a little too forcefully. And on the night of day twenty-three, was really quite amused to see the yolk stain on his murderer's sleeve.

On day forty-one the Doctor had had enough. He told Arthur and Chloe as much over breakfast. He hadn't spoken to either in over a week.

'I don't see any way out of this,' he said bluntly.

'Of course there's a way out,' said Arthur placidly.

The Doctor spilt his egg yolk again. 'What?' he croaked.

'When your dead selves come knocking,' explained Chloe, 'you just *don't go out*.'

The Doctor looked at them both in frank bewilderment. 'And you didn't think of doing this before?'

'Why would we want to?' asked Arthur. 'That way we wouldn't be special. This way we're heroes. Isn't that right, Chloe?'

Chloe shook her head. And spoke softly, so she could barely be heard. 'This way my marriage *means* something.'

At midnight the dead came calling. Henrietta was happy to die again. After all, life or death, it was really pretty much the same to her.

Chloe and Arthur were both itching to leave. But the Doctor had spent the day debating with them, imploring them, finally begging them as he kneeled on the kitchen floor. 'You've got to take charge of your own lives,' he said. 'You've got to make that choice.'

'But we made a choice already,' Arthur had said. 'We made the choice to have no more choices.'

But Chloe didn't argue with the Doctor. She knew she had already lost. As long as she refused to discuss her marriage, to confront its pointlessness, to make that daily choice between divorce and children anything but a bit of fun, she was strong. Now she had admitted it to herself, it was all over.

By one o'clock the ghosts stopped tapping at the window, and looked at each other in almost comical confusion.

By half past one, Chloe and Arthur had begun to talk to each other. They hadn't spent the night together in living memory. There hadn't *been* a night for them to spend together. So they talked. They could ignore the other whilst they still had death to look forward to. But how could they fill the silence now they knew it wasn't going to end? They talked, for want of any better idea. The Doctor helped them at first, suggesting a few conversation topics, but tactfully withdrew by quarter past two.

By three o'clock they were making love. It wasn't great. But it was better than either had expected.

At ten past three precisely Arthur told Chloe he loved her. By quarter past three he was asleep. At ten to four, Chloe whispered to her sleeping husband that she'd try to love him too. And then spent the next two hours awake, eyes wide open, as she considered the implications of that promise, and whether she was relieved or disappointed Arthur hadn't heard it. His arm lay across her chest until half past four, after which he farted and rolled over - Chloe was too deep in thought to notice.

By six o'clock the fog had cleared. By nine the Doctor was dressed and ready to go.

'The rest of your lives are your own now,' he said. 'Remember that.'

With the fog gone, Chloe could see that the little bed and breakfast was on a rather nice little street, really, with lots of nice little houses surrounding it. She had always known that, she supposed. A little pub across the road. At no more than two minutes' walk away, an Asda supermarket, just a little one, but she had no reason to doubt that it would adequately serve her grocery needs. And just beyond that, a blue police box.

'I think you're going to be alright now,' he said, smiling, and then he was on his way. He didn't look back once, although Arthur still gave him a cheery wave. Then he gave Chloe a hug, and held her close.

Chloe watched the blue box vanish, but her thoughts were elsewhere.

Arthur's hand was on her shoulder. Protective. Possessive. She looked at his eyes, his nose, his mouth. Those chins. She asked herself once again whether she'd prefer to divorce him or give him children. With a sudden thrill of terror she realised that now the decision actually *mattered*. She was overwhelmed by the sudden responsibility of it all. Divorce? Children? Perhaps both? In any order she chose! It made her reel with the possibilities, her entire life stretched out before her. She sat down on the pavement.

'Darling? Are you all right?'

She'd think about it later, she told herself. She didn't have to decide now. Her racing, panicked heart slowed to a regular pace. That was better. Go back inside the house. Make breakfast, eat Henrietta's eggs. In fact, come to think of it. Eat Henrietta. Why not, kill her, roast her body, chicken for dinner, yum yum, that would be a change. They didn't need her any more, did they? She could walk to Asda from now on for her eggs. For more than eggs, for whatever she wanted, they'd have lots of things, lots and lots and lots. All that choice.

She felt quite faint again. Pull herself together.

She decided to sit down on the pavement, and was quite annoyed to find out she already had.

'Darling? What's wrong? Darling? Darling?'

Darling, oh dear, was that what he was going to call her from now on? She looked into Arthur's worried face, and smiled at him. Relieved, he smiled back, showing his teeth just that fraction too much. Kill Henrietta, she thought, that was the plan. Kill Henrietta, roast her and eat her, have kids, go to Asda, divorce Arthur. That was the plan. It was all right. It would all be all right. That was the plan. All of it, all would be all right.

From Arthur's smiling toothy face came one question. 'Which of us do you think will die first?'

She didn't know.

They went inside. And she prayed for fog.

This is My Life

The Seventh Doctor (as told to William Keith)

A Rani once, mad as a hatter,
Decided to blow up strange matter.
A devious plan -
Kidnap every great man -
I was of course one of the latter.

Next I took Mel to the Towers
The stairs to the top took me hours.
If you went for a swim,
OAPs did you in.
Remind me to send Pex some flowers.

The first all-American rocket
Collided with Bill Haley's Comet.
Lonesome boy Billy
Scoffed Delta's royal jelly
Now he's green - but it's love, so don't knock it.

An offer she couldn't refuse
Froze Dorothy out of her shoes.
Ace set off the nitro
Like some kind of psycho
And joined me, though mentally bruised.

I lured Daleks back to Coal Hill
In the year they invented the Pill.
I dug up the Hand,
Drank sweet tea, and planned -
Rice pudding just makes me feel ill.

Next up were some happiness Nazis
I fought for the right not to party.
I talked down a sniper;
Like a sadness Pied Piper
You might say I invented blue Smarties.

And then I met Shakespeare's dark lady
She tried to make out I was shady
I know what I'm knowing -
My jazz is straight blowing
And it's long past the Cybermen's heyday.

A wolf-lady locked behind bars?
The Ragnarok Gods needed stars.
Midst symbols and runes
I played with my spoons
While Kingpin and Ace blew up cars.

I met UNIT protecting a rocket.
With battery-powered toys in my pocket
I went to a pub
And ordered some grub,
Put Morgaine in a cell and said Lock it.

I gave my friend Nimrod a tooth
It was all to teach Ace about truth.
My companion and Gwen
Dressed like posh gentlemen
Light cracked up and blew off the roof.

I didn't tell Ace why I'd brought her
To where vampire girls swam in the water.
I used her as my pawn
But she'd never have been born
If she'd not saved her grandmother's daughter.

Survival is knowing what's right
It's not about learning to fight.
It's good to belong
But you must know what's wrong
Or you might just grow claws in the night.

And finally, here in Vancouver
The Time Lords have sent me to hoover
The Master's remains -
Hope they don't block the drains
A drug gang! No room to manoeuvre!

Gazing Void

Huw Wilkins

Autumn in Encardia City had turned the footpaths into deep drifts of leaves that crunched underfoot as the Doctor walked slowly through the streets. A cool wind twined through the ornate Corinthian columns of the old Imperial buildings, and accelerated unfettered along the regimented blocks of post-revolutionary architecture. Here and there the even facades were interrupted by charred and gutted ruins or artillery-blasted debris yet to be cleared away. In the distance the sounds of pomp and ceremony he had just left behind could be faintly heard, interspersed with an occasional roar of applause.

As he came to the sidewalk of Via Cherenkov, the Doctor paused. The wide road ran straight through the heart of the old city, lined on each side by aged trees and wide pavements designed to accommodate the crowds cheering for the great parades of a century before. Today though, it was empty and silent but for the wind. For a moment the Doctor remembered it as it had looked at the end of the Hundred Days, filled with thousands waving the old Imperial banner, or the modern republic flag with the arms of Jeremiah Maru-Stahl sprayed over or just ripped whole from the cloth.

The Doctor carefully walked out into the centre of the wide road and gazed down its length where, almost out of sight at the point of perspectives meeting, he could see the grey loom of the parliament building. Maru-Stahl had built it from the razed debris of the Imperial palace after the first revolution, allowing it to inherit a peculiarly archaic and graceful aspect at odds with most of its contemporaries.

Turning the other way the Doctor saw the road's surroundings open up into green parkland centred on a vast black granite column. Scaffolding and translucent plastic covered most of its height, obscuring and subtly amplifying its bulk. The plinth on which it sat had, years before, shouldered the cyclopean marble statue of Maru-Stahl that the Doctor could just remember glimpsing once before the city's inhabitants had torn it down and ground it to dust beneath their feet and hammers.

The bottom of the column was lit briefly by an intense flash of light as some piece of heavy equipment sparked against the stone. The Doctor knew that behind all the sheeting men were still hard at work carving the last few of half a million names into the granite surface.

Sighing, the Doctor turned aside for a moment and gazed down at his feet, the steam of his slow breath wreathing him in a brief mist before curling away with the breeze. As he looked down he noticed, as if for the first time, a discreet medal attached to the velvet lapel of his jacket. He lifted a hand and gently unpinned it, turning it over and over in his fingers as he held it up for a better look. The ribbon was a glossy black silk, edged with white and terminated top and bottom with silver bars. From the lower bar hung a slim silver disc, its edges wreathed with engraved laurels surrounding a field of a hundred tiny stars.

The Doctor glanced at his watch and, after a moment of thought, dropped the medal into a pocket and began to walk towards the monument. He shrugged his coat closer around his shoulders and, slipping one hand in after the medal, held the cool metal disc tight in his fist.

As he walked, the tails of his velvet coat flapped playfully around his knees, keeping a regular beat in counterpoint to the clicking of his shoes on the hard flagstones that made the pavements of Cherenkov. The old buildings that flanked him peeled away gracefully, revealing wide wings of green parkland, formally landscaped in the old Imperial style. The wind, now unobstructed, redoubled its strength, teasing strands of the Doctor's long hair across his face. He ignored it and spared the carefully tended flowerbeds barely a glance until he arrived at the base of the monolith.

Behind the plastic sheeting around the scaffolding he could see indistinct figures moving and hear the whine of machinery working. He walked around the circumference until he found an opening and slipped inside. A tall man in work fatigues noticed his arrival and stepped back from the stone wall, slipping a slim chisel into a loop on his belt.

'Hey,' he called. 'This is a closed site.'

The Doctor walked over to him, taking a scrap of paper from his pocket. He stood silently in front of the workman and carefully wrote a name on the paper with a heavy silver pen. When he was done he held it out to the man.

'I have another name for the monument,' he said.

The workman looked sympathetic. 'I'm sorry, but if the name belongs on here it's probably already been carved. Would you like me to check the database for you?'

'It won't be in the database,' the Doctor said. 'Offworlders weren't on the lists.'

'I'm really sorry, but I can't just add names,' the man said in a placatory tone. 'There will be space left over and you can petition the committee for its addition after completion.'

The Doctor reached into his pocket, pulled out the medal and showed it to the man.

'Add it now,' he said quietly.

The man looked at the medal, then the Doctor's face. The oblique light shining between the sheeting picked out a faint scar that ran along his jaw and down across his neck.

The workman nodded silently and took the scrap of paper.

The Doctor stood silently on the ornate marble floor, eschewing the use of the artfully arranged chesterfields, and drank in the carefully restored Imperial opulence in the lobby. Discreet signs painted to blend in with the overall colour scheme politely directed visitors through panelled oak doors to the various wards or up the sweeping staircase to the administrative offices. As he turned a slow circle he tried vainly to remember what the building had been before being converted to a hospital. Some grand ducal winter palace, most likely. He remembered it well from the last days of the second revolution though, its thick walls shielding hundreds of terrified civilians from the fighting as the militias drove the final remnants of the DGSI troops from the city.

'So, how does it feel to be the only offworlder to be named a Hero of the Hundred Days?'

The Doctor jumped slightly at the sound of the voice, and turned to see a slim middle-aged man of about his own height standing a polite distance away. He was dressed in a dark, conservative suit, fastidiously creased and cut, though perhaps in the style of a few years before. His hair, remaining only as a fine fuzz around his temples, was greying evenly in contrast to the distinguished streaks of white though his beard. His face was finely wrinkled, more so now since it was smiling broadly.

The Doctor returned the smile and embraced the man gently. 'Elias,' he said warmly. 'It's good to see you again.'

'And you, Doctor,' he said. He stepped back from the embrace, leaving his hands on the Doctor's shoulders. 'You look well. God, how long has it been now?'

'Four years nearly,' the Doctor replied. 'Not since Nova Croix.'

Elias nodded slowly. 'I remember,' he said. He hesitated and looked away. 'Did...' he stammered.

The Doctor shook his head. 'No. The DGSI armour column cut us off from the hospital. There was no way,' he stated simply.

Elias sighed deeply, a slight catch to his breathing, then straightened up and smiled again. 'Still, enough of this. I'm glad you were able to come.'

The Doctor patted the old man's shoulder and returned the frail smile. 'Let's get some tea and you can tell me why you asked me here.'

'Yes, come up to my office.' Elias ushered the Doctor towards the staircase with a sweep of his arm. As they ascended the Doctor noted the walls were bare but for subtle stains indicating the places where once great paintings had hung.

Elias noticed his gaze. 'Most of the pictures had to be taken away for restoration,' he said. 'I'm afraid all too many of them were damaged beyond repair.'

The Doctor nodded silently. 'I'm sure you'll find ones to replace them,' he said as they crested the first floor.

'Eventually,' Elias said, leading them across the wide landing, newly carpeted in a sumptuously intricate weave. He opened a dark wooden door on which was a discreet plaque that read *Doctor Elias Greenwood, Director* in unassuming white lettering. He stepped inside, beckoning the Doctor after him.

The room was still furnished in a delicately contrived Victorian style, an imposing desk set before wide windows facing into a carpeted area with more informal comfortable seating around a carved stone fireplace. The Doctor wandered over to the window as Elias busied himself in one corner with a kettle and airtight caskets of tea-leaves.

Beyond the window the park behind the hospital rolled away for almost half a mile, its edges surrounded by a dense border of trees that shielded it from the city beyond. Over the top of the foliage the tops of the taller buildings could be seen and, in the distance, the black loom of the granite pillar on Via Cherenkov.

The Doctor turned back into the room and watched Greenwood carefully measuring scoops of expensive leaves into a finely decorated teapot. He walked slowly around the director's neatly arranged desk, pausing to look briefly at two photographs set on its corner. Each was a quite formal portrait of a woman: one old, perhaps the same age as Elias; the other young. Both frames were simple black borders.

The whistle of the antiquated kettle startled the Doctor and he looked up to see Elias fussing with two delicate porcelain cups on a tray. He poured the boiling water into the pot and dropped its lid into place with a clink. 'Almost ready,' he called over his shoulder.

The Doctor went over to the informal area and took off his coat. He made to toss it onto one of the spare chairs, hesitated, then retrieved the medal from inside and slipped it into the watch pocket of his waistcoat. He let the garment fall into a crumpled heap on the smooth brown leather and took another seat for himself. Elias shuffled over a moment later and carefully lowered the loaded tray onto a low glass coffee table between the chairs. Once he was sure the cups were safe he plopped himself down opposite the Doctor.

'So, how does it feel?' he asked.

'How does what feel?'

Elias's eyes darted heavenward for a moment. 'To receive your award. Less than seventy have been awarded in total, and only one to someone not born on this planet.'

The Doctor nodded and looked up at the ceiling for a moment. 'I haven't really thought about it,' he said. 'After all, I've only been a Hero of the Hundred Days for a few hours.'

'You should be proud,' Elias said earnestly. He reached out and began pouring the tea, a cloud of aromatic steam rising between them as he did so.

'I don't know,' the Doctor said quietly. 'It didn't feel like something to be proud of at the time.'

Elias paused, choosing his words. 'You helped free a whole planet, Doctor. Maybe you have to be a native to appreciate it fully. I can remember the time before the first revolution. I saw them both happen.'

'Perhaps you're right. I only ever saw how things were after the first revolution. I can barely imagine what it must have been like before to sweep a man like Maru-Stahl to power.' The Doctor leaned forward and set his cup down on the table. 'I helped because I thought it was the right thing to do, not because I had suffered like the rest of you.'

'All the more reason to feel pride then, I think. You who would stand and fight on principle rather than because you had to.' Elias reached up with his free hand and tapped his jaw. The Doctor's hand unconsciously mirrored his, tracing the slim scar on his face. 'You knew the cost too, Doctor.'

The Doctor looked away. 'Nova Croix was nobody's finest hour,' he murmured.

'It began the Hundred Days,' Elias stated. 'Without it we would still be living that nightmare.'

The Doctor made no reply. Elias finished pouring the tea and the two men drank in silence for a while.

Finally the Doctor drained his cup and set it back on the tray.

'Why did you ask me to come here?'

'I need your help, Doctor. We need it. We need your expertise.'

'As what?'

'As a doctor. I have a patient I've failed to help. We thought perhaps someone with a wider education than our old universities were allowed to provide might have some insight we had overlooked. When I heard you were here I sent out a messenger straight away.'

The Doctor looked at Elias curiously. 'You have nobody else on the whole planet to whom you can turn?'

'I wouldn't say that, Doctor,' Elias said slightly defensively. 'But your arrival was too good an opportunity to pass up.'

The Doctor nodded. 'Very well then. I'll do what I can to help. Who is it?'

Greenwood hesitated for a fraction of a second. 'It's Jeremiah Maru-Stahl.'

The Doctor tossed the thin file onto the desk. It landed with a slap, the gust of air ruffling the neat piles of paper on Greenwood's desk. 'Interesting reading,' he said.

Elias pursed his lips. 'I wish I could show you some more positive results. We're hamstrung by not being able to get better medicines.'

'Are supplies still that limited?' the Doctor asked, turning to stare out of the window.

'Less than they used to be, but it's still difficult to get the more complex pharmaceuticals manufactured in sufficient quantities for everyone. I should take you through the public wards, Doctor. They're full to the brim. Deep trauma cases, mostly, thanks to the DGSI interrogators.'

The Doctor nodded. 'Tell me about the paintings,' he said.

Elias opened the file and riffled through the pages. 'Yes,' he said thoughtfully, 'here we are. Doctor Nguyen tried introducing Maru-Stahl to it just over a year after he was admitted here. He had been an amateur artist before the First Revolution, you know.'

'I know,' the Doctor said. 'I read the file. Tell me what you think, Elias. What's your insight?'

'It's all in the file, Doctor.'

'I see,' the Doctor murmured. He turned back into the room and paced slowly across the deep carpet. 'What's his attachment to them, I wonder?'

Greenwood riffled the file again. 'We thought it was a coping mechanism. He couldn't deal with the loss of his power when he was deposed and created a fantasy world in which he still rules, where he's still powerful.'

The Doctor glanced quizzically back at his friend, then walked slowly to the window again and resumed his even stare through the glass. 'I had assumed he'd been executed after I left,' he said quietly. 'I can't believe he's still alive.'

Elias leaned back in his chair and spun it around to face the Doctor. 'A lot of people felt the same way after the Hundred Days.'

'I have little wonder.'

'The provisional government took the decision to try him for his crimes though. They said there had been enough summary executions by the DGSI.'

The Doctor nodded. 'That can't have been an easy decision.'

'No. A mob tried to break into the military prison where they had him. I'm sure they would have lynched him given half the chance.'

'And what happened to the trial?'

'He wasn't fit to stand. It was obvious even to a layman that he was seriously disturbed. The suicide attempts alone were enough to have him moved here for expert care.'

The Doctor gazed blankly across the parkland for a few minutes, then pursed his lips thoughtfully. 'The elections are soon, I believe,' he said.

'Well, eighteen months away still, but everyone knows they're coming. The first free election ever on this planet.' Greenwood sighed. 'It's an amazing thing to contemplate.'

The Doctor nodded slowly. 'I imagine the provisional government wants to deal with Maru-Stahl before then?'

Elias shifted in his seat. 'They do, yes. I've been asked to give his treatment top priority.'

The Doctor turned around and took the patient file from Greenwood's hands. He leafed through the few pages inside again and handed it back. 'How long has Maru-Stahl been here now?'

'A little over three years.'

'And what will they do if he cannot stand trial?'

Elias grimaced and shrugged his shoulders. 'I honestly don't know, Doctor, but whatever it is, it's probably better than he deserves.'

The Doctor took a deep breath and struck an attitude staring at the ceiling. He exhaled slowly and glanced back at Elias. 'I'd better have a word with him then.'

The door to the room must have been close to a hundred years old, but now was so coated in layer upon layer of thick white paint that its original panelling had been all but smoothed away. The locks and hinges were new though, bright steel fixtures clamped around the aged wood and docked into similarly sturdy hardware in the wall.

Elias noticed the Doctor staring at the security locks and patted him on the back.

'Don't worry, Doctor, he hasn't really shown any violent tendencies to anyone but himself. It's all just a precaution. The orderlies and I will be watching in any case, so if he tries anything there'll be plenty of people to back you up.'

'I'm not worried,' the Doctor said.

'Good. He remains pretty calm so long as he's with his paintings these days anyway.'

The Doctor nodded at one of the orderlies and gripped the handle of the door. The orderly tapped a few keys on a computer in the adjoining room and the Doctor felt the thud as heavy metal parts slid around inside the lock. He twisted the handle and the door opened smoothly. With a final brief glance back at Elias, sparing him an ambiguous look, he entered the room.

The cell was a spacious room lit both by a set of windows along the far wall and a wide skylight set into the ceiling. Closely spaced wire and steel grids had been bolted over the glass and now cast a complex moiré of shadows across the spartan furniture and thinly carpeted floor.

Most noticeable of all were the paintings that lined the walls. Ten unframed canvasses hung awkwardly by their wooden frames from ancient hooks. No single painting hung square; each was tilted a fraction to one side or the other without pattern as if they had been slapped into place without care for presentation, just an urgent desire that they be seen.

All of the paintings, without exception, depicted a single subject: Jeremiah Maru-Stahl. A few were almost familiar to the Doctor, looking like the idealised propaganda pictures of the dictator during his reign. Others were less ordinary. One depicted him wearing bloodied armour and wielding a sword that also dripped with red, his face upturned in exaltation. Another was an almost demonic representation of the man, dark, snarling in rage with his hands outstretched like claws, muscles bunching powerfully in his bare arms. None of them presented a comforting image, seeming to delight in dwelling on the bestial or terrifying.

Halfway along the length of the room, overshadowed by one of the larger canvasses, a couple of light, moulded plastic chairs stood facing each other. Close to it was a tall wooden easel, surrounded on all sides by a rainbow of paint marks and stains on the wall and floor. Beyond this was a man curled almost foetally against the bars across the window, and staring through it into space. He sat on a plain mattress set on the floor and covered with light blankets.

He was dressed in a simple thin white boiler suit, matching tabi socks on his feet.

In the corner opposite him was a steel toilet and washbowl with a few simple possessions arranged around it: toothbrush, soap, electric razor. The mirror was polished metal, smudged and subtly bent to throw curious highlights across the wall.

The door closed behind the Doctor with a soft thump and locked itself audibly. The man at the far end of the room did not react in any way.

The Doctor walked softly across the room and sat in one of the chairs, facing down the room towards Maru-Stahl's huddled form. He cleared his throat, but this still elicited no reaction.

'Jeremiah,' he called out finally.

Slowly the man at the far end of the room uncurled himself and got to his feet. He had probably once stood over six feet tall, but his posture was now slumped and drawn-in, making him appear smaller than he really was. It did not disguise the fact that he was now running to fat, and slack jowls of flesh covered his chin. Long dark hair fell down either side of his head, partially covering his face. It was unkempt and greasy, beginning to thin at the crown and recede at the temples. The bright white boiler suit looked odd against his sallow skin, contrasting too strongly.

'Yes,' Maru-Stahl said in a hesitant voice. 'What is it?' He sounded tired and weak.

'I'd like to talk with you for a while,' the Doctor said in a friendly voice. He smiled, and indicated the other chair with a wave of his hand.

Maru-Stahl shrugged resignedly and began shuffling closer, then paused and looked at the Doctor more carefully, his head tilted to one side. 'I know you,' he said slowly.

The Doctor acknowledged the statement with a curt nod. 'You may well do.'

The fallen dictator continued to regard the Doctor thoughtfully for a few more moments, then said, 'Yes, I remember. The Doctor. You were one of the leaders from Nova Croix.'

The Doctor shook his head. 'I led nothing. I was just trying to help the wounded.'

Maru-Stahl shrugged. 'I believe at the time both sides saw you as a leader. The DG Service, I remember, blamed you for an awful lot of things after that. I heard they intend to make you a Hero of the Hundred Days.'

'They held the ceremony yesterday,' the Doctor said.

Maru-Stahl nodded and sat down in the other chair, wrapping his arms around himself defensively. 'I'm sorry; they only let me have newspapers once a week. Congratulations,' he said without rancour, then sighed. 'A silly conceit anyway. It was more like a hundred and twelve days.'

'I believe they count it from the time the DGSI troops opened fire on the protesters after the local militias refused to do so,' the Doctor said, a slight edge entering his voice.

'Contrary to popular belief, I ordered non-lethal methods to be used,' Maru-Stahl said quietly.

'The troops don't seem to have shared that impression.'

Maru-Stahl shrugged and looked away. 'Take that as you will.'

The Doctor followed the man's gaze and saw he was looking at one of the pictures of himself. It was a pretty generic show-of-power piece, strongly reminiscent of old propaganda posters; Maru-Stahl dressed in the uniform of an army general, frowning over the sights of a chunky assault rifle.

'I need to replace that one,' Maru-Stahl said after a few moments of silence. He turned back to the Doctor. 'What do you want with me?'

'I'm here to try to help you.'

Maru-Stahl chuckled wheezily. 'I don't believe that for a moment. A Hero of the Hundred Days helping me?' He shook his head and levered himself out of his chair. He shuffled away across the room and stood beneath the dark, snarling self-portrait. 'Aren't we supposed to be honest with each other, Doctor? Nobody is here to help *me*.'

'Perhaps I am.'

'No, no.' Maru-Stahl chuckled. 'You're just like the rest. You all just want me nice and presentable for an impressive show trial and execution.'

The Doctor remained silent. As he watched, Maru-Stahl slowly placed his palms flat on the surface of the painting and lowered his head until it rested on the canvas. He remained there, immobile for a long few minutes, then straightened up again.

'Why should I co-operate with you?' he asked disdainfully. 'I'm not an infant they can manipulate.'

The Doctor held up his hands in a placatory gesture. 'Please, Jeremiah. Sit down. I'm not trying to trick you into anything.'

'They think they can hurt me,' Maru-Stahl said in a low voice, shaking his head. 'They have no idea.'

The Doctor raised his eyebrows slightly and said nothing. Maru-Stahl met his gaze evenly for a few moments before turning away. He walked delicately across the floor until he touched another of the pictures.

'They're very good,' the Doctor said conversationally. Maru-Stahl seemed to jump slightly at the sound of his voice.

'I can't say I care for them,' he replied.

'No?'

'No,' the dictator replied, carefully stressing the word.

'Doctor Greenwood told me you reacted badly when they tried to take them away.'

Maru-Stahl's head snapped round. 'You're not going to try to take them again?'

'No.'

'I don't believe you. All the new doctors try it. They don't understand.' Maru-Stahl's breathing hitched and he began to pant slightly. One hand was gripping the edge of the closest canvas protectively; the other was clenched in a tight fist, skin white over the knuckles.

The Doctor shook his head emphatically. 'I'm not going to take them away, Jeremiah.'

'Please,' Maru-Stahl said, his shoulders beginning to shake. 'Please don't take them away.' He pressed himself against the wall, reaching around the picture to hug it protectively.

The Doctor rose slowly, hands held low in a non-threatening pose. 'I won't, Jeremiah, I won't.'

'Stay away!' the dictator screamed, lurching backwards, dragging the picture off the wall with him. He stumbled and fell, his body slamming hard into the floor as he made no effort to save himself, only to hang on to the canvas. The Doctor instinctively rushed forward to help the man, but he only screamed and frantically scrabbled into the corner of the room, holding the portrait over himself like a shield. 'Stay away!' he cried again, his voice breaking.

The Doctor stopped short as he heard the security door behind him crash open and men run into the room. Two large orderlies shouldered their way past him and grabbed the prone figure of Maru-Stahl.

'I am Jeremiah!' he was screaming in a hoarse, desperate voice. 'Maru-Stahl!'

One of the orderlies tore the picture from Jeremiah's clenched hands and jammed a short stun gun into his neck. There was an electric snap and the cries were cut off.

Greenwood placed the tray down on the coffee table. This time instead of tea there was a decanter of whiskey and two plain crystal tumblers. He poured a generous measure for the Doctor and handed it over.

'I'm sorry,' Elias said. 'He does get excited sometimes. We thought it was better to err on the side of caution this time.'

The Doctor nodded. 'Thank you,' he said. He took a small sip of the whiskey and nodded appreciatively. 'Do you believe he would have hurt me?'

Greenwood shrugged. 'Probably not. But when he gets so agitated like that, it's sometimes difficult to make the call. He hasn't ever hurt anyone while he's been here, but the orderlies have had to restrain him on quite a few occasions.'

The Doctor sighed. 'It sounds like I'm just making him worse.'

Elias shook his head. 'He's shown little real improvement over the years he's been here. There comes a time when you have to risk making someone worse in order to help them in the long run.'

'You want me to continue?'

'Absolutely, Doctor. I've gone as far with him as I think I can. All we do now is re-tread old ground.'

The Doctor nodded and sipped more of the whiskey. 'Those paintings are interesting,' he said. 'Horrific, but interesting.'

'Yes,' Elias agreed. 'We originally thought they were an excellent therapy for him. Doctor Nguyen was so pleased. His first works weren't so… extreme.'

'He said the other doctors had tried to take them away from him.'

Elias nodded. 'You're not the first person I've consulted about this case. Most of the others who've seen him in the last two years thought the pictures were an unhealthy obsession and believed it better to wean him off them.'

'It never worked?'

'No. Every time he became frenzied and had to be sedated. Today's little performance was just an overture.'

The Doctor considered this over several slow sips of his drink. 'His time in the military prison wasn't in the notes. Can you tell me anything more about what happened there?' he asked.

Elias shrugged. 'Not an awful lot. We believe some of the guards had been beating him out of sight of the civilian workers, so they're not really all that keen to talk about it. They were all militiamen who'd seen action against the DGSI in Orléans or here in Encardia, so they had more cause than most to dislike the man. The suicide attempts are documented, of course, no way they could be covered up with the medical attention he needed. He managed to slash his wrists on a sharp piece of wire he got from his bed. He was hospitalised for almost two months while they stitched his arms back together.'

'Not just a cry for help then.'

'I don't think so. Certainly on the second occasion he barely survived.'

'And then he came here?'

'Yes. We had him on permanent suicide watch for nearly a year and he had to be sedated for a lot of the time. Eventually he stabilised enough to begin some therapy, which is when he began the paintings, but since then he relapses to a psychotic state every time he leaves them.'

The Doctor swirled his drink thoughtfully. 'But most of the time he's fairly lucid.'

'Oh yes. He's depressed and prone to emotional outbursts, but stable enough that we don't have to sedate him.'

'How soon do you think I'll be able to talk with him again?'

'Tomorrow should be fine. He'll sleep for most of the rest of the day after that jolt he was given, but he should be fit again by morning.'

The Doctor raised his glass and inclined it slightly towards Elias. 'To tomorrow then,' he said.

The cell door thudded closed behind the Doctor. Maru-Stahl was standing this time but was again immobile, staring out of the window. He ignored the Doctor.

The Doctor stood by the chairs for a moment, then walked to the far end of the room and stood next to Maru-Stahl and matched his gaze through the barred glass. The cell offered a different view from Greenwood's office. This room looked out directly over the city and little greenery could be seen, only a serried array of rooftops.

They stood side by side in silence for a few minutes, watching the immobile scene.

'I'm sorry for my outburst yesterday,' Maru-Stahl said eventually, sounding slightly embarrassed.

'Don't mention it,' the Doctor said. 'I've asked them to be a little less keen with the stunner today.' Maru-Stahl half smiled and rubbed a pale red patch on the side of his neck.

'I'd like to talk some more,' the Doctor said. Maru-Stahl sighed and nodded. He turned and walked over to the chairs. The Doctor followed a moment later and sat facing him.

'And what would you like to talk about today?' Maru-Stahl asked.

The Doctor steepled his hands and looked at the patient over the tips of his fingers thoughtfully. 'Why do you think you're here?' he asked.

'Here in this room, or in the more metaphysical sense?'

'Here, in this room, at this hospital.'

Maru-Stahl hesitated and rubbed his brow. 'Because I'm ill,' he said quietly.

'And why is that?' the Doctor asked, keeping his tone even.

Jeremiah grimaced and looked away. 'You're the doctor,' he said almost sulkily.

The Doctor nodded and watched as Maru-Stahl's gaze wandered around the room from picture to picture. He noticed the man was stroking the inside of one forearm with his fingers. The skin there had a shiny, uneven texture where the grafts had been hurriedly applied; deeply scarred.

'Tell me,' the Doctor asked quietly, 'why did you try to kill yourself?'

Maru-Stahl froze, his fingers stilled, and his brow furrowed. 'To...' he said hoarsely, then shook his head.

'To what?' the Doctor insisted.

'Escape,' the man muttered, then stood abruptly and turned away. 'I don't want to talk about it.'

The Doctor steepled his hands again and pressed the tips of his index fingers against his lips. Unconsciously one thumb gently stroked the line of scar tissue along his jaw.

Maru-Stahl kept his back turned for a short time, breathing deeply, one hand covering his mouth. Finally he cleared his throat and resumed his seat facing the Doctor.

The Doctor nodded and forced a smile. 'I'm sorry, Jeremiah. I didn't mean to upset you.' Maru-Stahl waved the apology away, not meeting the Doctor's eye.

'Perhaps we could talk a little about your time as president?'

'I'm not sure there's anything new I can tell you about that,' Maru-Stahl said, shuffling uncomfortably in his chair.

'I'm not really interested in the historical fact. I want to hear about your perspective, your impressions of the time.'

'What do you want me to say, Doctor?' Maru-Stahl snapped. 'Would you like me to spell out what a monster I was for you? Am I to practise my speeches for my trial?'

The Doctor shook his head. 'No, no, Jeremiah, please. I just want to hear your side of the story.'

'You think I was... unwell back then? I'm sure it would comfort many people to think so.'

'I don't think you were ill back then, but understanding those times may help me to help you now. I'm not looking for any answers in particular, I have no agenda here.'

Maru-Stahl chuckled joylessly. 'Everyone has an agenda, Doctor. Now more than ever. I'm sure you read the papers.'

'I'm just a visitor, Jeremiah. I'm only here because I thought I might be able to help you.'

Maru-Stahl sighed, then shrugged extravagantly. 'Ask away then. It makes no difference to me what we talk about.'

The Doctor smiled, more genuinely this time. 'Good. Could you tell me a little about the Bihaç uprising?'

Maru-Stahl canted his head slightly and stared at the Doctor for a long moment. He nodded resignedly and looked away again to stare at another of his paintings. 'Nowy Bihaç was an industrial town,' he said slowly. 'Steel, mainly; some manufacturing, but mainly steel.'

'Go on,' the Doctor said, sensing the man's reluctance. 'I understand you were a steelworker.'

Maru-Stahl shook his head. 'Not really. I was an engineer on the production systems. I never really worked on the floor.'

'Nevertheless, most of the workers followed you when you formed a union.'

'Yes,' Maru-Stahl said curiously and turned to stare out of the skylight. 'Yes they did.'

'You were surprised?'

He nodded silently. 'I was amazed,' he said, after a pause. 'Unions were still illegal then. I half-expected to be arrested on the spot. I think they saw me as a joke at first, not worth bothering with.'

'But you showed them.'

Maru-Stahl closed his eyes and grimaced. 'Yes, yes, I did it all out of a sense of injured pride,' he said sarcastically, fixing the Doctor with a contemptuous stare. 'I'm not a child, Doctor. I led those thousand steelworkers and the others that joined us and destroyed an Imperial Army Battalion sent to put us in our place. That takes... ah!' he threw up his hands angrily. 'Who cares?'

'Takes what, Jeremiah?' the Doctor pressed.

Maru-Stahl glared back at him. 'You tell me, Doctor. You led the column from Nova Croix. You killed nearly five hundred DGSI troops there alone.'

'What did it take you, Jeremiah?'

'Six hundred more ambushed and killed at Orléans. Regular army this time, I think. I seem to remember something about the officers being executed,' Maru-Stahl said with a ghastly smile. 'What did that take *you*, Doctor?'

'I tried to stop them,' the Doctor snapped, bunching his fists.

'And failed?'

The Doctor stopped and stared across at Maru-Stahl, his hands slowly relaxing. He turned away and looked up through the skylight at the clouds. He remained still for a long time, then turned back to face the dictator.

'Violence is not an answer,' he said.

'When your back's against the wall and the multitude you just led into some horrendous mess are all looking to you for a way out, sometimes it's good enough.'

The Doctor shook his head. 'There's always another way,' he said.

Maru-Stahl leaned forward in his chair. 'Do you believe that?' he asked earnestly.

The Doctor nodded. 'Absolutely,' he said with conviction.

Maru-Stahl shook his head and looked down at the floor, pursing his lips. 'I think I did too, once.' He sighed deeply and slumped back bonelessly in his chair.

'What happened?' the Doctor asked, gently resuming his own seat.

Maru-Stahl shrugged limply. 'We'd won the war, but I'd barely even planned that far. All of a sudden thirty million people turned to me all around the planet and asked me to build them a new world. The Imperial family was dead, but there were God knows how many nobles all with their little private armies and networks of influence. They weren't going to just lie down and give up.'

'And the DGSI was your answer?'

Maru-Stahl gave a mordant laugh. 'You think I had a choice?'

'You know I believe there's always another way, Jeremiah.'

'Do you think I had some grand plan for a peaceful resolution and just ignored it?' Maru-Stahl snapped abruptly. 'Is that what you want me to say?'

The Doctor inclined forward and looked into the dictator's eyes. 'I want the truth,' he demanded through clenched teeth.

Maru-Stahl held his gaze steadily for a minute or more then, gradually, it faltered until he blinked and looked down. 'The truth,' he said in an empty voice. He looked back at the Doctor and, as tears began to flow from his eyes, said, 'I searched for another way, Doctor but, God help me, I couldn't find it.'

Slowly Maru-Stahl hugged himself, slid into a sad huddle on the floor and wept like a child.

'How are you feeling today, Jeremiah?' the Doctor asked as the door thudded closed behind him.

Maru-Stahl looked up slowly from his position by the window. 'Better,' he said, his voice slightly slurred.

'You sound worse,' the Doctor said.

'I'm just tired. I haven't been sleeping well the last few nights.'

The Doctor nodded, then turned to the easel behind him. 'I see you've begun another painting.'

Maru-Stahl stood slowly and walked to the washbasin. He ran the cold tap and splashed the water onto his face. He turned back to the Doctor, wiping the dampness away with one hand and nodded. 'I felt the need.'

'I'm glad,' the Doctor said, glancing at the small canvas that was, so far, only covered by a dark but carefully shaded blue field.

The Doctor motioned towards the two chairs. Maru-Stahl sat down facing away from the window.

The Doctor remained standing. He walked over to one of the pictures, the one depicting the bestial, snarling Maru-Stahl. He tapped the thickly painted canvas with a fingernail. It responded with a soft drum-like resonance. 'People have called you a monster,' he said. Behind him Jeremiah nodded.

'I expected they would,' he said in a resigned voice.

The Doctor turned to look at the seated man. 'In my experience most men called monsters by others believe wholeheartedly in their own righteousness.'

'Have you met many?' Maru-Stahl asked.

'A few,' the Doctor said, favouring him a humourless smile. 'Some worse than you. Some less so. I find helping people so often pits me in opposition to them.'

'You think I'm a monster too, then?'

'Oh yes,' the Doctor said quietly, turning his attention back to the picture. 'The question is,' he mused, eyes fixed on the canvas, 'why?' Behind him he heard Maru-Stahl sigh deeply.

'You were a figurehead for freedom twenty years ago, Jeremiah. What happened to you?'

'Nobody wants to know that answer, Doctor,' Maru-Stahl said evenly. 'People want to fight monsters, not other people.'

The Doctor turned back to Maru-Stahl and took the seat facing him, leaning forward earnestly. 'I want to know.'

'I can't give you any comforting answers, Doctor.'

'I'm not looking for comfort, Jeremiah. I'm looking for the reason behind all this.'

Maru-Stahl looked away uncomfortably. 'I am a monster,' he said softly. He sighed again, his breath just slightly hesitant. 'Not because I was mad, or evil, but because I *chose* to be.'

The Doctor leaned back in his chair slowly. 'Go on,' he said, unable despite himself to prevent a trace of coldness in his voice.

Maru-Stahl's eyes flickered briefly towards the Doctor, then away again, downwards, as if ashamed.

'I faced a vast enemy,' he said almost too softly to be heard. 'One that wouldn't listen to reason, or compromise. There was just no way, Doctor, please believe me.' Maru-Stahl glanced up again, looking for some kind of support. The Doctor said nothing, moved not even a muscle.

Maru-Stahl exhaled slowly and closed his eyes. 'I became a monster to fight monsters.'

The Doctor leaned forward in a sharp rush of motion, bringing his face to within inches of Maru-Stahl's. The man recoiled slightly from the movement.

'You killed half a million *people*,' the Doctor snarled. 'Not monsters, not even enemies most of them. People!' he shouted.

Maru-Stahl turned away from the onslaught and stumbled from his chair. 'I know,' he choked. Without looking back he lunged across the room, almost falling as his legs tangled clumsily, and grabbed one of the portraits from the wall.

The Doctor stood but made no move to follow, trying not to make any threatening movements.

'I can hear them,' Maru-Stahl whispered, 'all around me.' He held the picture up with both hands like a shield, swinging it back and forth as if expecting an attack.

'Jeremiah,' the Doctor said in a calm voice, holding one hand out.

'Waiting for me,' Maru-Stahl said, ignoring him, his eyes searching the room.

'There's nothing to be afraid of,' the Doctor said placatingly. 'Please try to calm down, Jeremiah.'

Maru-Stahl's eyes fixed on the Doctor's and he grinned insanely. 'They still fear me!' he cried. He held the canvas up, turning circles in the middle of the room. 'I am Jeremiah!' he screamed. 'Maru-Stahl!'

'I can't help him, Elias,' the Doctor said.

Greenwood looked surprised. 'But you've made such progress with him, Doctor.'

The Doctor frowned and shook his head. 'He has too much blood on his hands. What could we make of him that could live with itself? Keep him locked away and move on.'

'What about the trial? He's still effectively under sentence of death.'

The Doctor placed his hands on the edge of Greenwood's desk and leaned over it. 'I'm not so vain to think I could make so much progress so quickly after years of others trying, doctor. You barely lifted a finger to help that man.'

'That's not true,' Elias protested, getting up from his chair. The Doctor straightened up and looked straight into his eyes.

'Don't lie to me, Elias. This office, this hospital; a cushy job if ever I saw one. Tell your friends in the government they'll have to fight the election without their show trial to remind the people of what they did in the Hundred Days.'

'That's... that's...' Greenwood blustered.

'It's the only way,' the Doctor insisted. 'The soldiers of the revolution are just that: soldiers, not rulers. Let them go into obscurity for the sake of never needing them again.'

Greenwood sighed and turned to look out of the window. 'I wanted to help him,' he said sadly. 'I wanted to rise above my hate, prove myself a better man. I couldn't do it. I suppose that makes me weak.'

'It can't have been easy to go even as far as you have.'

'You should know, Doctor. You've as much reason as I have to hate the man.'

The Doctor paused in silence for a moment, then turned to go. 'I don't hate him,' he said, his back turned.

'Not even a little?' Elias asked sceptically.

The Doctor shook his head, partly to himself. 'Not even a little,' he said.

Also Available

DOCTOR WHO™

SHORT TRIPS 1: ZODIAC

A short-story collection edited by JACQUELINE RAYNER

ISBN 1-84435-006-1

Take a TARDIS trip through the constellations, as the Doctor travels to twelve thrilling tales inspired by the mystical zodiac.

Telepathic fish, miniature lions and twin planets are the least of his problems, as the Doctor - all eight of him - faces the Capricorn Killer, endures a mindswap with the Machiavellian Master and dances with Death herself.

And that's not the half of it - as the two K9s can attest...

Featuring stories by Paul Magrs, Mark Michalowski, Paul Leonard, Simon A Forward, Joe Lidster and many more!

Also Available

DOCTOR WHO™

SHORT TRIPS 2: COMPANIONS

A short-story collection edited by JACQUELINE RAYNER

ISBN 1-84435-007-X

Adventures in time and space are no fun if there's no one to share them. The Doctor has taken along many people on his travels – humans, aliens and robots. Did he really care for any of them? What in their previous life fitted them for the role of companion – and how did they cope after they left the TARDIS?

These seventeen stories look at the Doctor's trusty companions, before, during and after their travels with the eccentric Time Lord. Discover the truth about Romana's regeneration, find out what happened when Zoe encountered the Doctor again and learn which of his companions the Doctor cared for the most...

Featuring stories by Peter Anghelides, Justin Richards, Steve Lyons, Gary Russell, Tara Samms and many more!

Coming Soon

DOCTOR WHO™

SHORT TRIPS 4: THE MUSES

A short-story collection edited by JACQUELINE RAYNER

ISBN 1–84435-009-6

Tell me, O Muse, of that many-aspected hero who fled his home world to travel every corner of time and space. Tell me, daughter of Jove, of his battles and his tragedies, of the strangers he encountered and the evil plots he foiled. Speak with laughter, with tears, through songs and visions of the Doctor, the hero and champion of this world and many more.

The nine Muses have since ancient times brought inspiration to those willing to receive it. Nine authors have received the inspiration of the Muses, to speak of the mysterious Time Lord known only as 'the Doctor'. They will tell tales of History, of Dancing, of Comedy and Tragedy, of Sacred Poetry, Epic Poetry and Love Poetry, of Music and Astronomy. May they speak to your hearts.

Featuring stories by Gareth Roberts, Robert Shearman, Justin Richards, Simon A Forward, Paul Magrs and many more!